Palma Harcourt was born in Jersey, where she now lives, and educated at St Anne's College, Oxford. Later she worked in various branches of British Intelligence, travelling widely and living in various capitals around the world. Her experiences have provided her with background material for her thrillers with diplomatic settings.

Also by Palma Harcourt:

PALMA HARCOURT

Agents of Influence

Futura

A *Futura* Book

First published in Great Britain in 1978
by William Collins Sons & Co Ltd

This edition published in 1985
by Futura Publications, a Division of
Macdonald & Co (Publishers) Ltd
London & Sydney

ISBN 0 7088 2640 7

Reproduced, printed and bound in Great Britain by
Hazell Watson & Viney Limited,
Member of the BPCC Group,
Aylesbury, Bucks

Futura Publications
A Division of
Macdonald & Co (Publishers) Ltd
Maxwell House
74 Worship Street
London EC2A 2EN
A BPCC plc Company

For Gina and Murray

London

Prelude

The stridency of the telephone, though not unexpected, jarred me from a mediocre daydream. I made a long arm, turned down the Brahms which had been serving as background music, lifted the receiver and said: 'Hallo.'

'Hallo, Keith. This is Charles Crowne. Sorry to disturb you on a Saturday night, but there's something I'd like you to do for me. Not interrupting a heavy date, am I?'

'Far from it, sir.'

It always pleased Brigadier Charles Crowne, DSO, retired, to go through the motions of politeness. But after five years of working for him I had learned – the hard way – not to have any sort of date when I was officially on duty.

'Keith, you remember Peter Krail? Nice chap. Has an endless fund of good stories. He's just back from the Far East. Flew in today and wants to see me, but evidently there are complications. So I thought it might be an idea if you were to meet him instead. He'll tell you what he wants and give you the essentials.'

'Yes, sir. I understand.'

'Fine. He's going to a party in Montagu Square tonight. A large affair, I gather, given by someone called Dolly. I got the impression she won't mind an extra guest. Probably won't even notice you. It's that kind of party.'

'It sounds smashing.'

'Hope you enjoy yourself. Let me know how you get on.'

'Yes, of course, but –' I had sensed the finality of his remark and wanted to hold him. 'Is – is that all?'

'Yes. I'd go along soon after nine, if I were you. And don't bother about Peter. He'll contact you. Okay?'

I knew better than to argue. 'Yes, sir.'

'Goodbye, Keith.'

In one movement I put down the receiver and looked at my watch. It was now twenty minutes to eight. My flat, in one of the less fashionable parts of Marylebone, was only a short distance from Montagu Square but I decided not to walk; the car might be useful later. That meant I had to find a parking place as well as locate this party that Dolly someone was giving. Both things could be time-consuming and Charles Crowne had advised me to arrive soon after nine. I did some rapid mental arithmetic; I had an hour in which to bath, shave, dress – and possibly eat.

I poured myself a pink gin and took it into the bathroom. While I waited for the bath to fill I ran an electric razor over my face. Luckily my beard is light and matches my fair hair – it's the dark brows and brown eyes that are a surprise – and shaving wasn't a problem. In no time I was lying in the water, sipping my gin and thinking of the evening ahead. Charles Crowne had made it sound like an easy assignment, but I had been caught before and I didn't like the vagueness of his instructions. Still, there was no use worrying; all I had to do was play along. It was Peter Krail's show and though Peter was a casual sort of character he was tops at his work.

Crowne had been colouring our telephone conversation when he asked me if I remembered Peter Krail. Peter was someone I was most unlikely to forget. It was he who had interviewed me for my present job. At that point in my life I had been a reject of Her Majesty's Diplomatic Service, and a pretty bitter reject. I couldn't understand why they didn't want me. I had a First Class Honours degree in oriental languages from London University, for which I had sweated blood. I had excellent sponsors and references, obtained by some boot-licking for which I despised myself. And, if my background was what is euphemistically known as modest, I dressed and spoke acceptably and didn't eat peas with my knife; anyway, the year before they had taken a friend of mine whose circumstances were much the same and who hadn't got such a good degree, so it wasn't that. Nevertheless, for some reason which no one bothered to explain, they had turned me down. I had to face up to the fact I had failed. I was not going to have the career on which I had set my heart.

Feeling bloody-minded, I had damn near not gone to that interview with Peter. The letter had said there was a vacancy in a 'Research Department' of the Foreign and Commonwealth Office for which I would seem to be qualified; if I was interested, would I . . . I was not interested! There was only one thing that interested me. But I went to be interviewed. I couldn't spend the rest of my life swelling the unemployed and cadging off my dad. I had to get a job. I had to earn some money.

A week later I was working for the Secret Intelligence Service. Peter Krail was the head of the Far East Section of the so-called 'Analysis' Division of the SIS, and Brigadier Charles Crowne was the Division's Director. It was not what I had wanted but there were compensations. The pay was much better than in the Foreign Office proper, the perks compared favourably, the work was more varied – there was little chance of being stuck in some absolutely appalling post for three or four years – and, contrary to expectation, most people lived to enjoy a good pension. Inevitably my bitterness dissipated itself and a couple of years later, when Peter told me that Crowne had pinched me from the Diplomatic Service who had in fact been keen to have me, I didn't blow my top.

Suppressing a shiver, I realized I had let the bath water get cold. Hurriedly I climbed out, dried myself, dressed and went into the kitchen. My repertoire is fairly wide, but for now, since there was no knowing what my hostess-to-be might provide, I decided to be content with scrambled eggs, fruit and coffee. While I ate I read. I didn't think much about the evening ahead.

At nine o'clock I was slowly circling Montagu Square for the third time. There was nowhere to park and, as far as I could make out, I had a choice of two or three parties. It was a beautiful summer's evening. Windows were open and curtains undrawn. Sounds of voices, laughter, music, drifted into the square. I wondered how many doorbells I would have to ring, asking for Dolly.

Five minutes later a Jaguar, in which two middle-aged women had been having a protracted argument, suddenly turned on its lights and shot into the road ahead of me. It left me a perfect place to park, on the east side of the square, about fifty yards from the house I had decided was my best bet.

The party here was on the first floor and was clearly a going concern. The music was loud, the laughter bright, the general noise level high, and guests continued to arrive. I waited until a taxi drew up and disgorged a couple who looked ideal for my purpose. He was wearing dark trousers, a light jacket and a frilled shirt; she had on a long flowered skirt and an off-the-shoulders blouse – nothing exotic. I would blend with them nicely.

Getting out of my Ford, I locked it and walked briskly along the road. The man was raking through his change for a suitable tip. I joined the woman on the doorstep and gave her the tentative smile of a fellow-guest who hasn't been introduced.

'Good evening. I'm Keith Sterling. I assume we're both friends of Dolly's.'

'Yes, indeed. I'm a very old friend. I've known her for ages.' She returned my smile. 'Dolly's a super person, isn't she?' And then, disconcerted perhaps by the approach of a husband who didn't share her enthusiasm, she watered her praise. 'Dolly's quite mad, of course, quite mad. Incidentally, we're the Cunninghams – John and Helen. Sweetie, this is Keith Sterling.'

I shook hands with John Cunningham and his wife. They were older than I had originally thought, in their late thirties, but they were pleasant enough and, with luck, would provide me with an excellent means of introducing myself to Dolly. I followed them into the house.

A uniformed maid, obviously hired for the occasion, directed us up the stairs. On the landing I paused, pretending to adjust my shoe, and let the Cunninghams go ahead of me. My caution was rewarded. There were loud greeting noises from immediately inside the drawing-room. Dolly was welcoming her guests on the threshold in the traditional manner.

'But where's Keith Sterling?' I heard Helen's high voice. 'He was with us a moment ago.'

'Keith?' Dolly was a contralto.

A Chinese gentleman in a Mao jacket and trousers of heavy grey silk walked around me as if I had been a stain on the carpet. Music unexpectedly blared and then subsided. I counted slowly to nine, which is my lucky number, and went into the drawing-room. Dolly turned from bowing respectfully to the Chinese gentleman. She looked at me blankly.

'Hallo. I'm Keith Sterling.' I held out my hand. 'I came with the Cunninghams. I hope you don't mind.'

12

'Why, no. You're welcome.'

By her accent Dolly was a Canadian. She was a big, blowzy blonde in a boudoir-pink caftan which moved on her body as if there were nothing between it and her skin. But she didn't come cheap. Her fingers were heavy with rings, she had a wide diamond bracelet on one wrist, and she smelled as if she had bathed in Guerlain. Her eyes were shrewd. Charles Crowne's idea that she was a casual hostess who wouldn't mind a gate-crasher or two was, I was sure, wide of the mark.

However, she accepted me. Some more guests arrived. I sighted Helen Cunningham in a far corner and waved frantically. To my relief she waved in return and, giving Dolly my best smile, I made my way towards her, pausing only to pick up a gin and tonic from a tray held by another hired help.

I stood and chatted. This was a good vantage point from which to view the scene. The room, which extended the width of the house and stretched back to form a wide dining 'L', contained about forty people. They were a mixed bunch. A moderately-successful actress, draped on the arm of a left-wing MP, was flirting with a BBC announcer. An Indian in a beautiful sari giggled as she popped titbits into the mouth of a man who, I happened to know, worked in the Cabinet Office. There were a couple of queers, some arty types, the Chinese gentleman, two chaps who turned out to be First Secretaries at Australia House and Canada House respectively, and a woman so dowdy and lost-looking that she had to have some claim to fame.

Everyone was drinking – even if only bitter lemon – and eating and talking; they seemed to be enjoying themselves. The hi-fi system continued to produce a variety of sounds, progressive jazz, the latest French *chanteuse*, light classical stuff – something for everyone's taste. And as I moved to have a closer look at a vivid modern painting hanging beside a wall scroll, I caught the sickly-sweet smell of cannabis; it was so strong I was surprised I hadn't noticed it before. I wished that Peter would come.

At quarter past ten, when he still hadn't arrived, I became restless. Some of the guests had gone and I was afraid the party might be breaking up. My fear abated, however, as a cloth was spread over the dining-room table and the help began to arrange a buffet supper. But more people were leaving and I had an anxious moment when I saw Cunningham making signals to his wife. I wasn't sure what I would do if they departed without so much as a backward glance in my direction. Dolly, who was hovering in the doorway as though, like me, she was waiting for someone, would be bound to ask questions.

Luckily that too turned out to be a false alarm. After whispering together the Cunninghams decided to stay and, to celebrate, I got myself another gin. I went and stood by one of the big windows. It was cooler here and I could look down into Montagu Square, across the trees of the private garden – shadowy in the reflection of the street lamps – to the lights from the houses on the far side. I watched an approaching taxi idly, then with sharpened interest as it drew up in front of Dolly's house, directly beneath me. I heard a girl laugh and caught a glimpse of long, pale hair. More guests were arriving. My pulse quickened. Peter had to be among them.

My attention was distracted. A Ford – the twin of mine – came very fast around the square, braked sharply and parked in the shadow of some trees, beside the garden, where parking was forbidden. Nobody got out. It crossed my mind that the driver had been following the taxi and had been taken by surprise when it stopped, but I didn't give this much credence; excess of suspicion is an occupational disease in my job. Besides, the driver was getting out and . . .

'My dear, I'm so sorry. Peter and I are dreadfully late.'

I turned slowly away from the window and regarded the newcomers with a mild interest, or rather that was what I intended to do. My eyes passed easily over Peter, who leaned against the door jamb, a grin tilted across his nondescript face, but they couldn't give the girl such casual treatment. As she unfolded herself from the embrace of Dolly's pink caftan and turned to introduce Peter, I stared. So did half the males in the room and many of the females.

The girl wasn't beautiful in a conventional sense; her cheekbones were too broad, her nose too short, her wide grey eyes too large. But none of these things were faults – at least to me. Her skin was golden from the sun. In contrast her hair, cut in a fringe across the width of her forehead and falling to her waist, was straight and pale. Her figure, under a lemon-coloured *cheongsam,* moved with a grace unusual in a Western woman. And there was something about her, something indefinable, which exacted homage. It was lucky I didn't believe in love at first sight.

I looked again at Peter. He was making himself charming to Dolly, and he could be very charming. In return she was gracious, welcoming and, unless I was mistaken, somewhat strained. The girl was watching Peter, not Dolly. I felt a most uncalled-for twinge of envy.

Then another man, tall, lean, hollow-chested, with a dark, intelligent face, appeared in the doorway. At the same time there was a lull in the general conversation and the taped music came to an end. I was able to hear as well as see what was happening.

Dolly swung around. 'Who the hell are you?'

The newcomer blithely ignored her and held out both hands to the girl. 'Monica, honey! I've followed you here from half across London.' His accent was pure Boston. 'Your cab stopped right beside me at some traffic lights in Knightsbridge. I bruised my hand banging on the window but you wouldn't pay me any heed. What else could I do?'

Pretending indifference, I watched them closely. I hadn't been mistaken about Dolly; she was uptight. So was the girl called Monica, though she was hiding it better. She kissed the tall man on both cheeks as he bent towards her, fondly but without enthusiasm; her face was expressionless. And Peter, whom I knew and could read more easily, widened a vacuous grin; he too was tense. The advent of the American had shattered the composure of all three of them. I was fascinated.

'Jake, you are a surprise. I'd no idea you were in England.' Monica had reacted quickly; she even sounded pleased. 'Why didn't you tell me you were coming?'

'My trip was unexpected, honey.'

'Just like happening to stop beside Monica's taxi at some traffic lights?' Peter didn't bother to hide his incredulity.

'Hi, Pete! And what are you doing in London Town?' Jake mocked him. 'Business or pleasure?'

'Some of each. What about you?'

'The same.'

They grinned at each other as if they shared a secret and as if this somehow compensated for a latent antagonism. But

15

Dolly coughed to remind them that she was there, that after all she was their hostess, and Monica turned to introduce Jake. Meanwhile a new tape must have been put into the system because the music began again. And the party resumed. The whole episode hadn't taken more than a couple of minutes.

People were drifting towards the buffet. The women went first, helped themselves with lots of flattering comments about the food, and then decided where to sit; extra chairs were being brought in and cushions thrown on the floor. The men, waiting their turn, made conversation together. I found myself discussing ink painting with the elderly Chinese gentleman and the left-wing MP, who appeared to be an enthusiast. Of course, what I would have liked to do was go and chat up Monica. But that was impossible because of Peter.

Besides, Dolly was organizing her guests. She had directed an overspill of females to a bay on the landing at the top of the stairs, and was looking around for suitable males to send after them. I hurriedly avoided her eye; I didn't want to be segregated. It wasn't going to be easy for Peter and me to have any sort of private talk at this party and when he could make an opportunity I had to be ready to grab it. Which meant keeping myself as available as possible. Dolly, however, was not to be thwarted.

'Come along with me, Keith.' Purposefully, she slipped her hand through my arm and gave me an overbright smile. 'There isn't an inch of space left in here, and there are some pretty girls on the landing – including Helen.'

Busy trying to think of a valid excuse not to go with Dolly, I just stopped myself from asking her who Helen was. That would indeed have been a bad blunder; if I didn't know Helen Cunningham, what was I doing there? Shaken by this near miss I followed Dolly meekly and allowed myself to be ensconced in the bay with the unfortunate Helen, who must have been bored with me by now, the extremely dowdy woman, the actress and the BBC announcer, who could scarcely wait to get into bed together, and the two queers. And on her way Dolly had picked up a cushion for me. It had been lying almost at Monica's feet! Silently I cursed the big, blowzy blonde.

I ate the food – it was Chinese and to my surprise as good as any I had eaten outside Asia – drank the plonk and made desultory conversation. I had purposely given myself very little and, though I had started last, it was easy to finish among the first. I collected some empty plates and went back to the buffet, meeting Jake en route. He was bearing a bottle of wine to my little group and it interested me that he too was being helpful and mobile; in spite of his effort to catch up with her, he wasn't staying close to Monica. Nor was Peter. As I selected an egg roll for Helen Cunningham, I found him at my elbow.

'Think I may have panicked, chum,' he murmured. 'Expect to be in the office Monday latest. But better sure than sorry.' He grinned at me as we got in each other's way and mutually apologized. 'Stand by to follow when we go – Monica and me. You've a car?'

'Yes. Fifty yards down the road.'

'Good. Overtake and offer us a lift to South Ken. After that play it by ear.' For a moment he mused. Then he added: 'We'll need to shake Jake. He's a complication I could have done without.'

Nodding pleasantly, Peter moved away. I collected some more food and bore it off to the bay, where no one seemed to want it. So I did the simplest thing, stacked one plate on top of another and hid the lot under the window-seat. It would be too bad when Dolly counted the forks.

I sat and sipped the wine Jake had provided. I let the poofs take orders for the next course. Cut off here from the main party, I had no means of knowing when Peter was about to leave. On the other hand, I didn't want to draw myself to Dolly's notice by always being in the drawing-room. It seemed reasonable, however, to volunteer to fetch the coffee, and my luck was in. Peter, ostentatiously moving a chair out of the path of my laden tray, said:

'We're off. Monica has a headache. She's saying goodbye now.'

Half turning in the doorway, I saw Monica talking to Dolly. I had to be quick. I hurried back to the bay, distributed the coffee and murmured something about going to the washroom. Helen Cunningham gave me a tired smile. No one else paid any attention. I went downstairs. Quietly I eased myself out of the front door and, keeping well to the inside of the pavement lest Dolly or even Jake looked out of the window, made for my Ford.

As I slid behind the wheel I glanced at my watch. The time was twenty-six minutes past eleven. I started the engine and let it tick over. The square was quiet except for the muted sounds of Dolly's party and the distant hum of traffic. I felt my excitement mounting. I thought of Monica.

At eleven-thirty the front door of Dolly's house opened to allow a wide band of light to stream across the pavement. Monica and Peter came out. Peter shut the door, cutting off the light, but there were plenty of street-lamps and I could see clearly. They started to cross the road, then appeared to change their minds. They stood as if arguing about which way to go, and I willed them to hurry before Jake appeared. I saw Peter shrug. He slid his arm around Monica's waist and they began to walk towards me. I was pleased when she pushed his arm aside.

I would have preferred to overtake them because that way my offer of a lift would have looked more natural. As it was I decided to wait until they were passing and call to them. But they never reached me.

Suddenly I heard the roar of a powerful car coming up very fast behind me. In my driving mirror it was a dark heavy shape, and I had no sooner registered that the fool driver had forgotten to turn on his lights than two searching beams transfixed Peter and Monica.

There was still no need for an accident. The driver must have seen them long before he put on his headlights. He could have braked. He could have swerved. He could have made some effort to avoid them.

What he did, however, was press the accelerator to the floor of his Volvo. He deliberately mowed them down and, scarcely losing speed, hurtled out of Montagu Square, his tyres squealing on the corner. I had an instant picture of Peter spread-eagled on his back, of Monica lying crumpled in the gutter where he had pushed her, of Jake framed in the doorway of Dolly's house.

Almost at once Monica was picking herself up and running as fast as a high-slit *cheongsam* would let her, not to Peter, not back to the party to get help – but just away. Jake went straight to Peter; he was much nearer than I. While I stumbled on to the pavement and began to run towards them, he was making a hurried search of Peter's clothing. Then he hared for his car and took off after Monica. I shouted but he didn't even turn his head. And, as I ran, I cursed him.

Peter was dead. Once the Volvo had caught him he hadn't had a chance. Not that that was any excuse for Jake – or Monica. I knelt beside him. I had been right about Jake searching the body. Peter's wallet, still fat with money, was half sliding from his jacket. I put out my hand to it and drew back. The wallet was sticky with blood. There was blood on my fingers, Peter Krail's blood. I had been fond of Peter.

The next moment I was staggering to my feet, leaning against a parked car, vomiting into the road. Peter, I thought, would have been bitterly ashamed of me.

Somewhere a dog was barking. Slippers slapped along the road. In a dim recess of my mind I registered these things. I pushed myself off the car, wiped my mouth with a handkerchief and turned to face the newcomer. I could see nothing; he was blinding me with a handlamp. Involuntarily I jerked to one side and, apologizing, he turned the beam away. For a moment he bent over Peter's body. Then he straightened and shook his head.

'I watched it all,' he said, 'the whole thing – from my bedroom window. Nobody can sleep when that damned woman gives a party, and I was just standing there, wondering whether to ring the police again, when it happened.'

He was a small, military man, grey hair, grey moustache, a Paisley dressing-gown. If it ever came to a trial, which I very much doubted, he would make a good witness.

'You all right?' he said.

'Yes. I'm fine. You called the police, you say?'

'Earlier. About the noise of that party. Not about him, poor devil. I came straight down in case there was anything I could do to help. I can't imagine what that chap in the Ford thought he was doing – him or the girl – to dash off like that after an accident. People don't have any sense of duty these days.'

'Did you – did you get the number by any chance?'

'Of the Ford? Yes. What's more I noticed it, parked where it shouldn't have been, when I was walking my dog. It had an Avis rent-a-car sticker, so it should be easy to trace.'

My heart warmed towards the little man. But he was eyeing me with a benevolent interest, and I didn't want him focusing his curiosity on me. I wanted to be rid of him quickly, before another vehicle decided to drive by or more of Dolly's guests emerged or some other neighbour appeared on the scene.

'That's splendid, sir,' I said, thinking he would like the 'sir'.

'It'd have been better if I'd got the number of the car that killed him. The driver must have been drunk not to stop.' He shook his head again, this time in wonderment at such manic behaviour; he had no conception of the truth. 'I could only get a blurred impression. I suppose you didn't – '

'No. I'm afraid not.' I didn't add that it was unimportant. The Volvo would have been stolen anyway. 'Sir, hadn't you better go and telephone the police?'

'I'm on my way. Not that a minute or two will make a pennyworth of difference. Incidentally, my name's Minton, Major Minton, RAMC, retired.' He paused, but I failed to introduce myself and he wasn't prepared to ask directly. He held out the handlamp. 'Here, you take this. You can signal any car that comes along. The boys in blue won't like it if the evidence gets messed up.'

I took the lamp and thanked him for it. I waited while his slippers flapped along the pavement, his front door opened – and shut. Then, placing the lamp so that its beam was directed at 'the scene of the accident', I took one last look at Peter and bolted. I was safe in my Ford and busy making a U-turn when a group of Dolly's guests crowded out of her house. I caught just a glimpse of them, but I thought I recognized the unlucky Cunninghams. Somebody screamed.

I headed south, into the heart of Mayfair. Charles Crowne would be expecting me; but he wouldn't be expecting what I had to tell him. Or would he? One couldn't ever be sure with Crowne. As for me, this could be the end of the matter.

'I want you to take over from Peter,' Crowne said.

My jaw must have dropped because he smiled thinly. The smile didn't reach his eyes. Peter's death had been a blow to him on both business and personal levels, and someone was going to pay for it. I had been elected to exact the payment. It would be the first time I had been in charge of an operation.

'You'll answer directly to me, Keith, but it'll be your show. And God help you if you make a mess of it.'

Crowne stretched his long legs and regarded his highly-polished brown shoes; he had taken his batman with him when he left the army. His craggy face was immobile. I wished I knew what he was thinking. His next words didn't give me any clue.

'I'm going to do some phoning, get our friends at Special Branch on to these characters you met this evening. Then I'll put you in the picture. Help yourself to a drink while you're waiting.'

'Thank you, sir. But could I use your bathroom?'

Already dialling the number he wanted, Crowne nodded and gestured to the right. I went along the corridor, blundered into an austere bedroom and found the bathroom. I had a pee, washed my face and hands, and swilled my mouth. I could still taste the vomit at the back of my throat but I felt better.

I went back to the living-room. Crowne was listening hard and saying 'm-mm, m-mm, m-mm' at such steady intervals that he sounded like a contented bee. I poured myself a gin and added three drops of bitters. The first sip was wonderful.

I had never been in Charles Crowne's private domain before and I surveyed the room with interest. It was well-proportioned, but otherwise not to my taste; I don't like Victorian furniture and Axminster rugs. But I approved of the books, the rack of LPs and the picture of a glowing horse that must have been a Stubbs. These, I was sure, were Crowne's personal property. I didn't know about the rest. The flat – it was really a maisonette, with direct access to the office but a separate entrance on to a mews – went with the job. If one could stand the strain, it was quite a job. Crowne had had it for seven years.

He was putting down the receiver after a particularly long 'm-mm'. 'Feeling better, Keith?'

'Thank you, sir – yes.' His remark hadn't pleased me; I thought I had hidden my feelings pretty well. 'Anything interesting from Special Branch?'

'They know your hostess of this evening. She calls herself Dolly Bell-Pauson. She was born in Canada, forty-two years ago, of British parents – a Miss Bell and a Mr Pauson. She became a nurse, married an elderly patient and inherited his money. Her second husband appeared a more suitable match but the marriage didn't work and they got a divorce. Dolly came to London, bought the lease of her present house – it must have cost a tidy sum – and settled down to giving parties, going to first nights and art exhibitions and, through her contacts in Canada House, generally hovering on the edges of the diplomatic scene. She'd been in London before, with her ex-husband – and immediately before their break-up she'd spent three years with him in Hong Kong. He was the Canadian Trade Commissioner there.'

Crowne paused as if he expected me to comment, but what he had told me had made me feel rather sorry for Dolly, and it was only background. I kept my mouth shut. Crowne gave me a quizzical glance.

'The reference to Hong Kong means nothing to you?'

I remembered the wall-scrolls, the Chinese gentleman in the grey silk suit, the excellent Chinese food. And Peter had flown in from the Far East. But I wasn't going to make guesses. I shook my head.

'It will,' Crowne said.

There was a silence. He seemed to be waiting for something – a knock on the door. His batman came in carrying a tray with coffee, sandwiches and a bowl of consommé. Suddenly I was overwhelmed by hunger, and by Charles Crowne's foresight; he was a kind man after his fashion.

The batman arranged a table beside me. The soup and sandwiches were all for me. The coffee was for both of us, black. Crowne and I were going to have a long session.

When the batman had gone Crowne said: 'You eat while I talk, Keith. Ask your questions afterwards.'

I did as I was told. Crowne brought his coffee from his desk where he had been sitting, and took the armchair opposite me. He looked totally relaxed, and that in spite of the Gieves suit, striped shirt, white collar, Guards' tie – correct wear for retired officers up from the country to attend a board meeting. But Crowne was never out of countenance. I envied him.

'I sent Peter Krail out to Hong Kong two months ago,' Crowne said. 'The chap who was our Co-ordinator of Intelligence there wanted to come home for family reasons, and Peter was tired of being what he called a "London office boy". It seemed a reasonable swap. It worked well. As you know, there's always something going on in that part of the world and Peter enjoyed himself. His cover was trade – officially he was seconded to the UK Trade Commission – and he travelled a lot.'

Crowne paused to offer me coffee and to pour himself another cup. For a moment he sat silent, stirring the brown sugar; his thoughts were half way round the world. Eventually he continued.

'When Peter was in Singapore he heard a rumour that the Chinese had been mounting some sort of special operations against high-powered visitors to Hong Kong. By itself that means damn all, of course. But then he heard the same rumour from a different source and was intrigued. He decided to follow it up. Presumably he did but, if so, he didn't tell me about it.' Crowne sighed. 'That was Peter's weakness, you know. He liked to produce rabbits out of his hat without explaining how he'd come by them in the first place. And it doesn't pay in this game. Now that he's dead his information's lost and we've got to start again. Because he was undoubtedly on to something, something big, though whether or not it was connected with this rumour I've not the faintest idea.

'The next I heard he was holding a hot potato, and was coming home. He arrived yesterday according to schedule. We sent a car to Heathrow to meet him, but he ignored the driver and went off with a girl about five foot six, slim, sunburnt, long pale hair.'

'Monica?' I bit my tongue but too late; against my will the name had escaped me.

'I shouldn't be surprised. The description fits. Anyway, she and Peter got into a Rolls and were driven away by a Chinese chauffeur. At which point our man not only failed to follow them, but he didn't even get the number of the Rolls.' Crowne sounded disgusted. 'Still, Peter obviously hadn't gone off with her under duress, so I waited to hear from him. This evening we did.'

Crowne got up from his armchair and went back to the desk. There was a click as he turned on the recorder; the tape was already in its slot. I drained the last of my coffee and put the cup down quietly. This could be vital.

I heard the buzz of the telephone followed by the click of a lifted receiver. A cool, non-committal voice said: 'Hallo.' Peter, I guessed, had rung one of the SIS emergency numbers which gave warning that he was in trouble, and possibly overheard. For his part he would know that, however odd his remarks might sound, he would be given every support, his call would be monitored, recorded, analysed and, if necessary, practical help would be available. The numbers were not used lightly.

'Hallo, Susan darling. This is Peter, safely back from Hong Kong. How are you all?'

'Peter! How lovely. We're fine. What about you? Where are you?'

'I'm all right. I'm in London. About to have dinner. Then I'm going to a party. Which, my dear sister, is why I phoned. I'm terribly sorry. I know you'll be disappointed, but I shan't be able to make it out to Wimbledon tonight.'

'Yes – I am a bit disappointed. You couldn't come after this party?'

'Not a hope. We shan't get there till nine and it's a long way from Montagu Square to Wimbledon. Besides – ' Peter laughed – 'I gather Dolly – she's a friend of the very special girl I'm with – gives pretty good parties. I wouldn't want to miss anything.'

'Of course not. I understand. When can we hope to see you?'

'Tomorrow, if I don't have too big a hangover. Meanwhile, my love to Charles and the kids and blessings on yourself. Goodbye for now, Susan.'

'Goodbye, Peter dear.'

That was all. Crowne switched off the machine. And I hated myself. The sole object of Peter's call had been to enable me to meet him at Dolly's party. But I had blown it. I hadn't been the slightest use to him. I had learnt nothing new about Monica, precious little about Jake. On the whole, Major Minton had produced better results than I had.

'Well, Keith, what questions?'

There were plenty of questions, but I didn't think that Crowne could answer them, not the important ones. Monica had taken Peter – a somewhat reassured Peter, who had admitted to me that he might have panicked – to Dolly's party. Why? Monica had decided when they should leave. Monica had fled. Why? How much was she implicated?

'Lots,' I said, 'but it's too early to start guessing, isn't it?

Perhaps the Special Branch will get some hard info from Dolly. Incidentally, why were they interested in her before this?'

'Heroin. Eight months ago a fairly senior civil servant, who turned out to be a boy-friend of Dolly's, died of an overdose. They never found a connection between her and a source – apart from the fact that she'd lived in Hong Kong, which isn't exactly a crime – but they kept an eye on Mrs Bell-Pauson.'

'Is there a possibility that Peter's "hot potato" has to do with narcotics, then?'

Crowne shrugged. 'A possibility, yes. But I don't believe it. Why should Peter get excited about drugs? They're not our pigeon. If he'd got hold of something in that line, he'd have just passed it to the right people. So let's not forget them, but let's not concentrate on them either. Or on Dolly Bell-Pauson. I've a hunch the girl Monica will prove better value – if we can find her.'

'And Jake, sir?'

'Jake too. Presumably he fits in somewhere. However, as you said, it's too early to start guessing.'

With anyone else this would have been a signal to mull the whole thing over for another couple of hours, but not with Charles Crowne. Fifteen minutes later he must have pressed a bell because the batman appeared.

Crowne got to his feet. 'I suggest you go home and get some sleep, Keith. I'll telephone you mid-day. There should be some news by then. All right?'

'Yes, sir. Thank you. Good night.'

'Good night.'

At noon precisely my telephone rang; Crowne was as dependable as death, and often as unwelcome. Today I was counting the minutes, my curiosity about Monica sharper than ever. But I was to be disappointed.

Dolly had been unco-operative. She was sorry about Peter Krail but she had never seen him before that evening. He had been brought to her house by a girl called Monica, whose last name she couldn't remember – Cane, Combe, something like that. She had met Monica when she was having coffee at Harrods. They had shared a table and had gossiped together. On the spur of the moment she had invited her to the party

25

and suggested she bring a friend. The gossip? This and that. Clothes, the price of hair-dos, holidays abroad — whatever women chat about. She had no idea where Monica lived. Jake might know. Jake was an American. He hadn't been invited to the party; he had followed Monica. Unfortunately Dolly had never seen him before either and knew nothing about him. Anyway, she couldn't be held responsible for what her guests did once they left her house. She was a Canadian citizen and if the British police intended to victimize her she'd appeal to Canada House.

'And that is bloody all,' Crowne said, 'if we discount an excellent description of a gate-crasher who said his name was Keith Sterling. Of course Dolly's lying through her teeth. She's given us a mixture of truths, half-truths and downright whoppers. But the Special Branch aren't eager to lean on her too heavily, not yet. They're having the house watched and they've put a tail on her. Something may come of it. Personally I'm not hopeful.'

Nor was I, though my concern was not exactly the same as Crowne's. Sure I wanted to catch the swine who had killed Peter and the man who had given the order, and I wanted to solve the problem Peter had bequeathed us — it was my job. Common sense prompted me to be satisfied with that, if it could be achieved; the gods didn't favour those who were greedy. Nevertheless, had I posted a prayer it would have been a request to meet Monica again. Again? I hadn't even spoken to her at Dolly's party. She didn't know I existed.

'Keith!'

'Sorry, sir. Thought I heard someone at the door,' I lied glibly. 'You were saying?'

'We're temporarily stymied over Jake's car too, because today's Sunday. Since you suggested he might have flown in we tried the Avis people at Heathrow, but the shift on duty knew nothing and records had gone to the London office. We'll have to wait till tomorrow now. Once we've got something on him the US Embassy may be able to help trace him. Otherwise we're at a complete dead-end.'

'Should I come in to the office, sir?'

'No. Take the time to make any personal arrangements necessary, but be in bright and early in the morning. You'll be flying out Wednesday.'

He didn't tell me, and I didn't ask him my destination. It was self-evident. My adrenalin flowed faster as I thought of Hong Kong. This wouldn't be my first visit, but the other occasions hadn't been more than stop-overs. I didn't kid myself. Crowne wasn't posting me to Hong Kong to replace Peter as Co-ordinator of Far East Intelligence. I didn't have the experience. I was being sent there for a specific job but, with luck, it might be possible to string it out for several months. The prospect filled me with joy. I even forgot about Monica, temporarily.

Nor did I have much time to think of her in the next two days. I was on a crammer course which entailed work, work and more work. My briefing on Hong Kong was detailed and all-inclusive. I became an expert on the constitution and administration of the Crown Colony, its history and geography, its industry and trade, its roads, its police, its universities, television, radio, press, social services – its night life. I was far better briefed than most First Secretaries whom Her Majesty sends out to foreign posts.

Ironically that was to be my cover. In theory I was to be seconded from the Diplomatic Service for a tour of duty in the Colonial Secretariat, which co-ordinates and supervises the work of all Hong Kong government departments. I was to be Personal Assistant to the Deputy Colonial Secretary, at the present time a man called Howard Farthingale. I read with interest the information the office had provided; he sounded a pleasant guy. However, neither he nor the Colonial Secretary was to know my real job. Only the Governor, Sir David Milment, KCMG, was to be informed that I was SIS. To facilitate meetings with His Excellency I was to pose as a friend of his son John who was, in fact, in the Foreign Office. The lunch John Milment gave me at his club was at least a cheerful interlude, if not a rest from work.

And duly on Wednesday, full of half-digested information, I took off from Heathrow for Rome, New Delhi – and Hong Kong.

Hong Kong

About twenty hours and eight time-zones later I was flying over the South China Sea. Below me lay a scattering of humped green islands which, with Kowloon on the mainland, form the British Crown Colony of Hong Kong. The water, dotted with sampans and junks, was flat and very blue and the bright sun gave it a golden sheen. In the clear light all the colours were intensified.

As the pilot made his final approach over the island of Hong Kong which gives its name to the colony, I looked down on white Manhattan-type skyscrapers clinging to almost perpendicular hillsides, Government House with its Union Jack motionless in the still heat and – I suppressed a grin – immaculately-clad figures playing cricket on an immaculately-kept pitch. Then we were over Victoria Harbour, which separates Hong Kong island from Kowloon where the airport is. And I caught a glimpse of destroyers belonging to the United States Seventh Fleet, a British submarine, a hydrofoil probably in from Macao and some junks flying the yellow-starred red flag of the People's Republic of China. It was a fascinating edge of the world.

We were coming in to land now. Convulsively I gripped the armrests and, as we touched down and the reverse thrust pushed me into the back of my seat, I prayed hard. I'm not usually a nervous flyer but the last time I had flown into Kai Tak, at the tail-end of a typhoon, we had used up all but a yard of the runway before we managed to stop. The previous plane hadn't been so lucky and, since the runway juts into the sea, it had gone straight into the water. Remembering, I shivered. Although I'm a fair swimmer I have a thing about drowning.

'Mr Keith Sterling. Mr Keith Sterling.'

It took the steward a minute to locate me. He hadn't expected to find me in the economy class, and I hadn't expected any special attention. I had received a telegram to say I would be met at the airport but the possibility of VIP treatment hadn't occurred to me. I should have realized that a chum of a member of the Governor's family would rate high.

The steward got my raincoat down from the rack, picked up my briefcase and led the way through the first-class compartment. Several of the fat expense accounts glared at me – they didn't like being made to wait – and some of the other rich regarded me with a rude curiosity. I ignored them. Collecting my raincoat and briefcase from the steward, I nodded my thanks and walked down the steps of the aircraft to the waiting car as if this were my usual life-style.

For one awful moment nothing happened and I thought there had been a mistake, the car had been sent for someone else. I prepared to die of ignominy. Then the chauffeur leapt out of his seat and opened the rear door to allow an excessively tall, thin man to get out. He came forward, hand outstretched.

'Keith Sterling? Hallo. I'm Ian Hackard, PA to the Colonial Secretary.'

'Good of you to meet me.'

'Not a bit. The Old Man's ADC couldn't get away but he laid on the car for us. Shall we get in? It's air-conditioned and you must be feeling the heat in that suit.'

He ran his eye over me, and clearly envied me my tailor. I thought how surprised he would have been if he saw the variety of clothes I possessed or knew that Her Majesty's Government gave me an allowance for them. Peter always said it made him feel like a kept woman. Peter!

There were a lot of things that would have surprised Hackard, Personal Assistant to the Colonial Secretary, not least how much I knew about him. I knew how old he was and where he had been at school and the name of his wife and the fact that she was expecting a child and – what he didn't know himself – that she had made a cuckold out of him; the child had been fathered by a chap from the American Consulate, now back in the States. I sighed. The interest I was compelled to take in other people's private lives was one thing I did not like about my job.

Hackard smiled at me sympathetically. 'You must be tired. At best it's a frightful journey. Which way did you come?'

'Rome–New Delhi. It was fine as far as Delhi. I don't know

why it is, but whenever I get on a plane in the Far East some Asian kid blocks up all the lavatories.'

Hackard didn't laugh. 'You know this part of the world then?'

I took a deep breath of the car's conditioned air. God, I was being careless! My brain wasn't functioning. I could have blown my entire cover by one such stupid, ill-considered remark. As Hackard had said, I was tired.

'My last overseas post was Canberra.'

'Ah. I've never got as far as Australia myself.' To my relief he dismissed the entire continent in this one sentence. He became practical. 'Let me have your passport and baggage slips, will you? Shan't keep you long.'

The chauffeur, considering his car rather than his passengers, had found a patch of shade in which to park. He went in search of my luggage while Hackard dealt with passport formalities. As good as his promise Hackard returned almost at once with my passport duly stamped. To locate my bags took a little longer, but not much. Then we were driving through the busy four-lane tunnel that links Kowloon with Hong Kong island. I had arrived.

'Are we going straight to the Secretariat?' I asked.

'Heavens, no,' Hackard said. 'There's absolutely no need. The Old Man wants to see you later today, but Howard doesn't expect you until tomorrow morning, and then not too early. Howard – Howard Farthingale, the Assistant Colonial Secretary – is to be your boss, as they may have told you in London. You'll like him, I'm sure. Everyone does. Incidentally, he's a terrific authority on Hong Kong.'

My mind sifted through the information it had on Howard Farthingale. Born in Shanghai, forty-two years old. Unmarried. Only son of John and Margaret Farthingale, who had devoted their lives to furthering the cause of the Methodist Church in China. Twin sister deceased. Apart from schooling and short periods in England, has always lived in Far East. Owns a converted Chinese barge.

It was the last item that had caught my imagination when I was studying the info on Farthingale; given the right engines a barge can cover a great many nautical miles in the China Sea. The Hong Kong Special Branch, however, keeps a pretty close watch on any potential smuggler, and there had never been a breath of suspicion against Farthingale. Nor was smuggling my business. I had no reason to be curious. I concentrated on Ian Hackard which, considering what he was saying, wasn't difficult.

'We've arranged for you to stay in Peter Krail's apartment. Housing's always a problem in Hong Kong, and Howard thought you'd prefer the flat to a hotel. If you decide you like it you can take over the lease.'

'But what about this Peter – Crane? Doesn't he want it?'

'Krail,' Hackard corrected me automatically. 'He'll not be using it again. The poor devil got himself killed while he was home on leave – in a car accident after some party, I gather.'

He didn't sound particularly regretful and I wondered if his wife had cast a wandering eye in Peter's direction. Which reminded me of the fair girl called Monica. I doubted if I would ever see her again, but that didn't stop me from having nice Walter Mittyish fantasies about her.

'Here we are,' Hackard said as the car drew up in front of an apartment block of dazzling whiteness. 'This part of the island's called Mid-Levels. It's between Victoria Peak, which is the best residential district, and the business area. You'll find it very convenient.'

After that condescending remark I didn't need to ask him where he lived. Nowhere but The Peak for the Hackards, I guessed, and thought of his large overdraft at the bank. I was beginning to dislike long Ian.

We left the chauffeur to deal with the baggage – in order to create the illusion of a posting I had brought far more than I was likely to need – and went up to the apartment. Hackard rang the bell and we waited. When nobody came he rang again.

'Damn the woman. Where is she? She knew you were coming today. I telephoned myself first thing this morning.'

'What woman?'

'The maid. Her name's Ling. She goes with the apartment, though I dare say you don't have to have her if you can't afford it.'

The door opened three inches. Hackard pushed it wide. A very small, wizened Chinese woman, wearing the conventional jacket and trousers of Mao's China, stood aside and bowed to us. From somewhere in the apartment an unseen listener turned off the radio, and the relentless Chinese opera, that a moment ago had been blaring forth, suddenly ceased. In the silence Hackard's voice sounded unnaturally loud.

'Ling, this is Mr Sterling. He's come to take Mr Krail's place. You understand?'

I winced at Hackard's introduction, and wished he had worded it differently. There was nothing unusual in accommodation being passed on from one foreign serving officer to the next. At this stage, however, I would have preferred not to be associated too closely – in anyone's mind – with the late Peter Krail of the UK Trade Commission.

The woman bowed again but didn't speak. Her simple gesture made Hackard appear both gauche and domineering. In my turn, without speaking, I bowed to her and, as I raised my head, our eyes met. Her eyes were old, intelligent – and afraid.

'Would you like some refreshment after your journey, sir?'

'Yes, please, Ling. I should like some tea.'

'Not for me,' Hackard said at once. 'I must be off, as soon as you've got your luggage.'

'All right.' I wasn't going to press him to stay. 'I'll see you tomorrow then. Many thanks for your help.'

'My pleasure. I'd offer you a lift in the morning, but you'll come in when it suits you. What it is to know the right people!' He gave a forced laugh. 'Incidentally, I told you the Old Man wanted to see you later. Government House will send a car at six-thirty. That'll give you time for your tea and a bit of a rest. It's just drinks with the family, I gather – they've got some official dinner afterwards – so there's no need for you to dress.'

'Good. That's perfect. I could do with an early night, but I've a letter from John for Lady Milment that I'd like to deliver promptly, and a small parcel for Sally.'

'Another wedding present, I suppose?'

'Yes, from John's five-year-old.' I grinned at him.

In response his mouth hesitated between a smile and a sneer. Hackard envied me my connection with the Governor and his family, but he despised me for boasting of it. In fact I was merely reproducing my cover story, not for him since he had already been impressed with it, but for whoever was in Ling's kitchen.

Luckily at this point the chauffeur arrived with the rest of my luggage and Hackard was able to say goodbye. Reiterating my thanks I shut the front door behind him. Then, without any pretence, I began a casual inspection of the apartment. Keeping an eye on the passage to the front door I looked into the living-room, the dining-room, a bedroom, a bathroom, another bedroom. This was a nice place, even if it wasn't on The Peak. Peter had done himself well.

And now I was getting warm. I could hear sounds of tea-making in the kitchen. I coughed loudly to show that my tour of inspection was innocent. I opened a door and found myself looking at a third bedroom. It was a narrow slit of a room containing a single bed, a chair, a chest of drawers and a tin trunk. In one corner was a small godshelf altar with joss sticks smoking fiercely. I was not pleased. With Ling living on the premises the apartment was in no sense a private place.

I shut the bedroom door and went into the kitchen. My tea was ready; Ling had been about to pick up the tray. As she steadied it on one arm the cup and saucer rattled together. Keeping her eyes downcast and speaking very rapidly, as if repeating a lesson she'd been taught but didn't understand, she said:

'Sir, this is my grandson, Teng. I am an old woman, and sometimes he comes to help me with work that I find heavy. He is a good boy.'

The 'good boy' stood up and bowed his head. He was tall for a Chinese, with a slim, powerful body. I put his age at twenty but he could have been five years older. From his clothes – black slacks and red shirt, far too smart for house-work – his well-kept hands and his overlong hair, he looked something of a dandy, but I didn't underrate him. There was an arrogance about him that didn't go with his subservient attitude. And, grandson or not, Ling was afraid of him.

'You don't mind my coming here, Mr Sterling?'

'Not a bit, Teng. But if you're to help your grandmother,' I said deliberately, 'make sure she gives you an occasional meal in return.'

It was the sort of patronizing remark that a foreign devil, rather stupid and new to Hong Kong, might have made, and Teng should have disregarded it. But he didn't. He resented it bitterly, deeply, and he failed to hide his feelings. I was in no doubt now that he was an enemy. Nodding pleasantly – I hoped he would take me for a fool – I wandered out of the kitchen.

Ling followed me into the drawing-room. She said nothing, but her anxious, tinkling tray spoke for her. She poured my tea and I stood by the window, looking out over the teeming roofs of Hong Kong. But what I saw lay beyond, the Mountains of Nine Dragons, the New Territories, the Shamchun River – and the red shadow of the People's Republic of China.

The car from Government House arrived on the dot of six-thirty and since I was alone I sat beside the driver. He was the same man as had met me earlier at Kai Tak. Born in Hong Kong, the product of a Scottish soldier and a Chinese bar girl, he was a small compact person with his mother's features and his father's sandy colouring. His name was Macfar.

In the presence of Ian Hackard he had been monosyllabic to the point of taciturnity but with me, after a little prompting, he let himself go. He seemed to have two passions. One was the British Raj, as personified by whatever family happened to be in residence at Government House; the Milments were the third Excellencies he had served. The other was automobiles.

'It's a bit of luck you getting posted here in time for the wedding, isn't it, sir? Miss Sally was telling me a lot of her friends and Mr Bill's would find it too far and too expensive to come to Hong Kong.'

'I'll say. I'd never have made it otherwise.'

'There you are then. You know, between you and me, Mr Sterling, if Miss Sally had had her way, I think she'd have liked a London wedding, just for the family and close friends. Sir David would have preferred it too. He told me so himself. He's a very sensible gentleman. But Lady Milment wouldn't hear of it and the odd thing is Mr Bill supported her.'

'So it's to be Government House, Hong Kong – and a bang-up affair.'

'That's right, Mr Sterling. Sir David says it's going to be a three-ring circus. Not that anyone here's complaining. It'll be the biggest social event of the year.' He sounded as proud as if Sally Milment were his own daughter. 'Have you met Mr Bill, sir?'

'No, not yet.'

'He's a nice young man and devoted to Miss Sally, but a bit of a surprise like.'

'What sort of surprise?'

'Well, he's a quiet unassuming type, not what you'd expect of the son of a self-made tycoon, which I gather is what Lord Reddington is. Nor what you'd expect Miss Sally to choose neither, seeing as how she's such a bright attractive young lady and could have married anybody. I thought at one time it was that poor Mr Peter Krail she fancied. Great friends they were – and continued to be, even after she got engaged.'

Luckily Macfar's slanting eyes were on the road and he couldn't see my expression, because at this point my jaw must have dropped. I had assumed that Peter had known the Milments – it would have been strange if he hadn't – but I had no idea he had been one of Sally's boy-friends. It made me curious to meet her.

We were driving up Garden Road now and Macfar had fallen silent. I thought that perhaps the proximity of the Governor's Residence had dammed his flow of gossip, but it seemed he had a problem. As we turned through the big gates and the Gurkha sentry saluted, his words flooded out.

'Mr Sterling, I hope you don't mind my asking but it's about Mr Krail's car – his Mini. Seeing as how you're taking his place, I – '

'His apartment, you mean?'

I had picked him up too quickly, too sharply, and he retreated at once. In polite neutral tones, he said: 'Yes, of course, sir. His apartment, his flat. What else would I have meant, sir?'

Though one or two alternatives occurred to me, I didn't answer his question. His previous remark was the important point. I kicked myself for forgetting that Peter would have had a car and, maybe, a boat. Making the enquiry casual and friendly, I asked Macfar why he was interested in the Mini.

'It's almost new, sir, and if the price isn't too high I'd like to buy it – unless you want it yourself, that is.'

'I'll have to look at it first before I decide. Where did Mr Krail keep it?'

'In the garage under where he lived. It's a white Mini. The porter would show you. It's only done –'

The doors of Government House were open and the ADC, resplendent in full mess kit, was waiting to greet me. I couldn't linger in the car chatting to the chauffeur.

'Okay. I doubt I'll want it but I'll let you know,' I said hurriedly. 'And I'll find out who's dealing with Mr Krail's affairs. He didn't have a boat, did he?'

'No, Mr Sterling. He used to borrow Miss Sally's sometimes.'

'Thanks.'

'My pleasure, Mr Sterling, sir.'

I got out of the car and Macfar – an excellent source of information if one pressed the right button – saluted smartly. I jogged up the wide, shallow steps. The ADC came forward and introduced himself. We shook hands.

'Come along,' he said. 'Sign the Book, will you? Then we'll go straight in to H.E. He's looking forward to meeting you.'

Fifty minutes later I was once more in the car and heading home. It was the same car, but not the same driver. Mr Macfar was driving the Rolls, which was taking the Governor and Lady Milment, accompanied by the ADC, to dine with the Commander, British Forces. Sir David had apologized for the brevity of our meeting and the absence of his family; Lady Milment was dressing and Sally was at a tennis party. But he hadn't sounded exactly grief-stricken.

Sir David Milment was a small, pleasant man with a deceptively mild manner; his mouth was thin. From what I knew of him he was very capable, but his career in the Diplomatic Service had been undistinguished and honour had come to him only with this, his last posting. Very reasonably he didn't want me fouling his nest. And as soon as the ADC had made us all tall iced drinks – mine was gin but I suspect Sir David's was plain soda water – and we had finished with the pleasantries, he made his position clear.

He would co-operate because he must, but the less he had to do with me and any nefarious acts of mine, the better he would be pleased. He appreciated that it was not my fault. Nevertheless, he objected to his public position being used for intelligence purposes. He objected even more strongly to the involvement of his family – to the fact that they were asked to accept as a personal friend a – a –

He had come to a full stop there. I had supplied the phrase – a *persona* who was not really *grata*. It had brought a dull flush to his cheeks, but he had the grace not to contradict me. I could interpret the words as I wished.

Remembering Peter, whom the Milments had obviously accepted at his own value, I had permitted myself a half smile.

And Sir David, glancing at his watch, had risen. Still, even though the ADC had reappeared, he had seen me off himself, thanked me for the parcel and the letter I had brought from England, patted me on the shoulder, called me 'my boy' and said I must pay them a proper visit soon. I gave him full marks for that.

Suddenly I felt exhausted. The hours of lost sleep during the flight had caught up with me. After the third yawn I made myself as comfortable as possible – on the return journey I was sitting in the back of the car – closed my eyes and prepared to doze. My thoughts drifted from the Milments to Peter, to Macfar, to Peter's white Mini. I remembered the Mini and jolted awake.

There was no point in searching Peter's apartment. There had been every opportunity for anyone – Teng, say – to get ahead of me. But I thought I knew something about Peter's cars that others might not know.

When I got back to the apartment block I went immediately to the garage. The porter wasn't around but there was only one white Mini, dust-covered and locked. I peered through its windows. The inside was neat, neutral. All the ashtrays were open and seemingly empty. There were no maps on the shelf. Peter had never kept his car as tidy as that. I had been forestalled again.

It was a forlorn hope but once, on a crucial occasion, Peter had reached his car only to discover that it was locked and he had no keys. Since then he had always kept a spare set in a metal box taped under the nearside front wheel-well. Now my groping fingers sought and found that box. They shook as I pressed open the lid.

Except for the keys, the box was empty. My disgust was enormous. I nearly hurled the damn thing across the garage. But, because it was easier than sticking it back on the car, I put the box in my pocket. It wasn't until a couple of hours later, when I was undressing for bed, that I noticed the faint scratch marks on its underside.

With the help of a magnifying glass I managed to decipher them. There were five figures and some words. I thought of a telephone number, part of a car licence, the combination of a safe; there were other possibilities. The words that came after the numbers – 'ROUGE TO PLAY' – were open to still wider interpretations.

All in all my first day in Hong Kong hadn't been unprofitable. It was some time before I slept.

Two

It was Sunday mid-morning, the first day of September and my fourth day in Hong Kong. In pyjamas and dressing-gown I sat on my balcony enjoying the warm sunshine. Ling had just removed the breakfast tray and, with a last cup of coffee, I was savouring the sights and sounds around me.

Two women, hanging out their bright washing like flags on bamboo poles, called to each other from one apartment to the next. Their high, twittering Cantonese made me smile; they were complaining about their husbands' laziness. From a neighbouring balcony came the clatter of a mah-jong game. Farther away, against a continuous background of Chinese opera, cars hooted and children shouted as they played. I could feel the pressure of people all around me.

Inside the apartment the telephone rang. Ling answered it and spoke in English. I groaned, sure I was going to have to make excuses for refusing an invitation to sail or picnic with one of the couples I had met last night at the Hackards'. It had been kind of the Hackards to ask me but it had been a dreary party. The food had been Anglo-Saxon and poorly cooked. The guests had been uncongenial, especially a chap from the Australian Trade Commission who had made some snide remarks about Peter, and an Englishman who seemed to spend his time directing Chinese Westerns – a flourishing business in Hong Kong – and poncing for his acquaintances. In fact I hadn't liked any of them and I would have left early except that after dinner Joan Hackard glued us to bridge tables. In the end I won the princely sum of a hundred Hong Kong dollars – barely enough for a good steak at the Mandarin or the Hilton and not nearly enough to compensate for the hours of boredom.

Ling brought the telephone out to the balcony. I gestured to her to take it away; today was Sunday, my day off. But she paid no attention. Carefully she arranged the long cord and set the instrument on the table beside me.

With her hand over the mouthpiece she said: 'Government House wishes to speak to you, Mr Sterling. Lady Milment.'

I seized the receiver from her. 'Hallo. This is Keith Sterling.'

When I got to know Lady Milment better I realized she wasn't the kind of person to wait on the end of a telephone; others could do that. Now, when a voice said: 'One moment, please,' and the moment stretched to five, ten, fifteen, I began to wonder if someone was playing a silly joke – or if someone had a reason for making sure I was at home. But at last she spoke.

'Good morning, Mr Sterling. I think we said twelve-thirty for lunch today, but Sir David and I are just off to matins at the Cathedral and we may be a little late getting back. There are always so many people one has to talk to after the service.' She enunciated her words very distinctly. 'Would you mind coming between twelve forty-five and one instead? It would be more convenient for us.'

'I – I should be pleased to, Lady Milment. Thank you very much.'

'Good. That's splendid. We'll expect you then. Goodbye.'

There was a sharp click as she cut the connection and I found myself listening to the hum of an open line. Slowly I put down the receiver. In my mind I went through the brief conversation, word for word. It was very ordinary, except for one thing: this was the first I had heard of an invitation to lunch at Government House. Certainly Sir David hadn't mentioned it when I saw him on Thursday.

I stood up and stretched. The lovely lazy day I had planned was ruined. I could imagine the heavy lunch and the equally heavy talk in store for me. Lady Milment had given me no idea what other guests, if any, would be there, but I foresaw the worst. It would be last night all over again – unless perhaps Sally Milment was to be at home. Ah well, whichever way I looked at it, it was work.

Ling received the news that I was going out with stoic indifference. If she had already prepared food for me she didn't mention the fact. When I was gone she would burn another joss stick – she was still very frightened – or she would

43

telephone Teng to come and search my belongings. I was sure he had only delayed in order to give me time to settle in and feel at ease.

I went into the bathroom, showered, shaved, and afterwards dressed with what I hoped was careless elegance. While I attended to these practical details I was busy debating with myself whether or not to take this opportunity to send a signal to Charles Crowne. Finally I decided against it. Except for impressions of people I had almost nothing to report. The scratch marks on the tin box I had found under Peter's Mini could be totally irrelevant; at any rate I had made no sense of them. And it was stupid to chance annoying Sir David, who was my one secure link with London, by asking him to use his authority to send an unimportant message.

So it was with no ulterior motives that, in accordance with Lady Milment's autocratic request for my presence, I arrived at Government House at twelve fifty-three precisely. At worst the luncheon, which I could mention casually tomorrow, would be support for my cover-story. At best I would be able to give Sally Milment personally the wedding present I had bought for her, but HMG had paid for. And there was always the possibility of learning something of interest.

The butler opened the door to me. 'The family', he informed me, was on the terrace, but first His Excellency would like a word with me in private. He showed me into a small, book-lined room where Sir David was waiting. H.E. had changed since church. He was wearing slacks and a silk handkerchief knotted in the neck of his shirt. He made me feel over-dressed.

'Good morning, sir.'

'Good morning.' He didn't waste time. 'I have a signal for you, which is why I asked my wife to telephone.' He took a sealed envelope from his trouser-pocket, gave it to me and produced a beautiful little ivory paper-knife. 'Can you decipher it here, or what do you want to do?'

'I have no need, sir. It doesn't require immediate action.'

'How do you know?'

'If it did, you would have been so instructed, sir.'

He looked at me. He couldn't quite believe it was as simple as that. Suddenly he laughed, and the laugh was against himself. I grinned in sympathy.

'Come along, Keith. The others'll be on their second drink by now.'

I followed him out to the terrace which overlooked wide lawns. Here was quiet and peace. A bird that I couldn't name, its plumage bright, flew back and forth along a line of magnolia. Butterflies played in the grass. The air was fragrant with jasmine from the frangipani trees and, close to Lady Milment, the more sophisticated scent of Carven's *Ma Griffe*. The only sounds were lazy voices and the creak of protesting ice-cubes as gin was poured on them.

It was all a million miles from the canyons of the Chinese quarters with their teeming tenements, from the temples of Tin Hau and Kwun Yum, from the girlie bars of the Wan Chai area or the boat-dwellers at Aberdeen. It was a long way from the posh apartments on The Peak or the Yacht Club, even from the Hong Kong Club or the Mandarin Hotel, which is one of the best in the world. Apart from the heat and the exotica we could have been in one of England's privileged country houses.

'This is Keith Sterling, John's friend, who's been seconded to us for a while.'

Three pairs of eyes regarded me. Sir David waved a hand. 'My wife.' Lady Milment was blue-eyed, sharp-nosed, at least ten years younger than her husband and possibly ten times as intelligent. 'My daughter, Sally.' The eyes were not so blue, the nose almost snub; she was round, puppyish, charming – and nobody's fool, but never a girl-friend of Peter Krail's if I'd known anything about him.

'And Bill, her fiancé.' Bill had brown eyes in a dark, clever face, and an amused, self-deprecatory manner.

'Bill's in charge of drinks this morning, so give him your order, Keith.'

Everyone smiled. I shook hands, gave Sally her present, told Bill I would like a gin and tonic and sat down where Lady Milment indicated. Bill poured my drink while Sally opened her parcel and thanked me as if a set of apostle spoons was the one thing she needed. We talked about Hong Kong and England and they asked me polite, friendly questions. Had I known John long? Did I know his wife, and the children? Where was my last posting? Did I play tennis? Was I as good as John? I had to keep my wits about me but I was relaxed, enjoying my drink.

'And what about Albert?' Sally asked, suddenly serious.

'Albert?' I hadn't the faintest idea who Albert was, and it was obvious I should have known.

'Yes, how is poor Albert?' Lady Milment said, covering my hesitation. 'Personally I think John's a fool about that dog. He should have it put to sleep. Once a dachshund slips a disc there's really nothing you can do for it.'

'But it's a dreadfully hard decision to make, and if Albert's not in pain – ' I left the question open.

Lady Milment's very blue eyes met mine and she smiled approvingly. In three short sentences she had told me everything I needed to know about Albert, and I had picked up my cue. No one had noticed I had fluffed my lines a little. I was grateful to her. Nevertheless, I was not pleased that Sir David, contrary to all instructions, had seen fit to tell his wife about me. It made my position that much more untenable.

I endured the luncheon. I should have enjoyed it. Contrary to my expectations we had a cold green soup – I detected cress and Chinese spinach and cucumber – followed by grilled mullet with a beautiful subtle sauce, a mixed salad, fresh pineapple and coffee. My opinion of Lady Milment went up even more, but she made me nervous.

Conversation during the meal was casual, unimportant. Inevitably we talked about the wedding. Lady Milment insisted that as John's friend I must be an usher and, though I thought she was being mischievous, I let myself be persuaded. I asked about the honeymoon. But it seemed there was to be no honeymoon.

'We're having it now, in advance,' Sally said.

'Sally!' Her mother pretended to be shocked.

Bill grinned at me. 'The timing's been difficult. I have to be back at school on the nineteenth. The kids arrive at the weekend.' He noticed my expression. 'You didn't know? I'm a teacher. Or I'm about to be. This is my first term.'

'But one of these days we'll have our own school and it'll be the best prep school in the country,' Sally said with determination.

'We'll see. You're both very young. You may well change your minds.'

'Rose – '

'Mother –'

Father and daughter spoke together. Bill said nothing. Lady Milment laughed and looked at me for support. But I was having no part in worrying a family bone. If the son of Lord Reddington, with all his lovely filthy money, chose to be a schoolteacher, that was his affair. Good luck to him.

We finished coffee. Crowne's signal was beginning to burn a hole in my pocket and I wondered how soon I could make a decent departure. Once again Lady Milment came to my rescue, this time by saying she was going to have her afternoon rest. Sir David then pleaded documents to be read and, making a similar excuse, I refused an invitation to go water-skiing with Sally and Bill. However, since I had come in a taxi and had no transport, I begged a lift back to my apartment.

Sally drove. I sat beside her and Bill sat behind, leaning over the back of the seat between us. Something seemed to be amusing him.

'Are you sure you won't come water-skiing with us, Keith?'

'Thanks, no. I have to start work in earnest tomorrow and there's a lot of reading I should do.'

'You mean you've inherited Peter Krail's apartment but not his devotion to us? Well, that makes a pleasant change, anyway.'

'Bill!'

Sally protested, but they both laughed. I looked politely puzzled. I waited for them to explain the joke.

'It isn't really funny,' Sally said. 'Peter Krail was a dear. We were very fond of him and it's terrible he should have been killed like that. You didn't know him, did you?'

'No,' I lied, 'though someone told me he was an ex-boy-friend of yours.'

'That's absolutely untrue!' Sally was irritated. 'He never got as far as making even the mildest pass at me. But he did hang around rather.'

'That, my darling Sally, is an understatement. We've spent almost every weekend of the summer as a *ménage à trois*, not to mention evenings and odd days. I don't know when Peter did any work. In fact, except when we were at the Residence under your mother's critical eye, the only time we managed to get away from him was when Howard Farthingale took him out on his junk. The junk, much as you may hate to admit it,

47

was your one rival.'

'Rubbish! Anyhow, for all you know, you may have been the attraction, Bill, not me.'

'For God's sake, Sally! Don't start that rumour or my schoolmastering career will be over before it's begun.'

They laughed together. They were very much in love and, unless they had both won a gold medal at RADA, Peter was of no importance to them. But, granted that Bill was wildly exaggerating, they had been important to Peter; he wasn't in the habit of playing gooseberry. I wondered if Charles Crowne had known or guessed this when he decided I should pose as John Milment's friend. And what was the relevance of Howard Farthingale's junk? If it had any relevance. There were always so many loose ends, ends that never fitted. Lost in thought, I nearly missed what Sally was saying.

'. . . forget Monica. I think Peter was very taken with her. Which was why he suddenly shot off to London.'

I made an effort to control my voice, but it still didn't sound natural, not to me. 'And who is Monica?'

'Monica Cay – '

'Who?' I hadn't caught the name because Peter, damn him, had started to speak.

'She's a teacher.'

'A teacher?'

I was showing much too much interest. I couldn't ask them again what her last name was. I gave a weak smile.

'Sure, she's a teacher – like me. They're a funny lot in my profession, aren't they, Sally?'

'Extraordinary! They come in all shapes and sizes. So do their pupils.'

This seemed to be another in-joke, or they were pulling my leg. Maybe both. At any rate they were bubbling with amusement and I had to pretend to share it. If I'd not been so eager to read Charles Crowne's signal I might have changed my mind and gone water-skiing with them in Repulse Bay or wherever they were going, just to annoy them – and to find out some more about the teaching profession.

But Sally had drawn up with a flourish in front of my apartment block. I thanked her for the lift and said how nice it was to meet John's sister and in return she gave me a peck on the cheek for the apostle spoons. I got out and stood while

Bill scrambled in beside her.

I hoped the invitation would come from them, but when it didn't, I said: 'I don't want to emulate your old chum, Peter, but we'll meet again soon, won't we?'

'Of course. Thursday,' Sally said. 'You're going to Howard's party, aren't you?'

'Am I? He hasn't invited me.'

'He will.'

I waved them off. Thursday was four days away. I could scarcely wait to ask more about Monica. I cursed myself for having let slip my chance now and, in a chastened mood, let myself into the apartment.

The smell of incense was strong, but the silence was absolute. There was no one in the kitchen. I knocked on Ling's bedroom door and glanced in. It seemed that for the moment I had the place to myself.

I went into the living-room and automatically looked at the small pile of books carelessly heaped on a table by the sofa. For the first time they were not in the same order that I had left them. I fetched my attaché case and inspected the lock. There was the faintest of scratches. I couldn't be sure. But the hair I had arranged inside had disappeared. Teng, or whoever had searched my belongings, had been careless – and he had achieved nothing.

Planning to buy myself an ivory paper-knife like Sir David's, I slit the envelope he had given me with my nail-file and extracted Crowne's signal. It was long, which would mean quite a bit of work. I collected paper and pencil and got down to it.

My cypher is basically simple. It depends on transposition and, therefore, is theoretically breakable without a machine. But you need a brilliant cryptographer to make much of a single message, especially when there is no pattern, so that it's useless for him to count the number of times that a particular number occurs. Signals to and from me are cyphered from the book of a well-known author. I know the text by heart – I have a trained and nearly photographic memory – and the same page, indicated by the date, is never used twice. It's a little more complicated than that, but not much; and it's as fool-proof as any non-machine cypher can be.

However, it does need concentration, and this afternoon

my mind was not at its best. Either because the wine I had
drunk at lunch had made me sleepy, or because my thoughts
kept returning to what Sally and Bill had told me about
Peter – and Monica – I made a false start. Then I slipped a
line and had to start again. But eventually the signal was un-
buttoned. I sat back and read it. It was full of hopeful juice.

There was no actual info about Monica, but the Rolls and
the Chinese chauffeur she'd used to meet Peter at Heathrow
had been traced to a mews house in Kensington. The owner,
an eminent lepidopterist, was on a tour of the States combining
lectures with a butterfly hunt, his present whereabouts un-
known. The chauffeur, whose papers showed he was Hong
Kong born and had been in England over a year, said he'd
received instructions from his employer to expect a young
lady – he only knew her as Miss Monica – and to treat her as
an honoured guest. She had had several visitors but he didn't
remember a Mr Krail. He had driven her to the airport last
Sunday (the day after Dolly's party, the day after Peter had
been killed) but he had no idea where she was going from
there.

Jake was Jacob Leonard Dasser, Junior. He had returned
his car to Avis and left the country the same day as Monica.
He had taken a direct flight to Washington; no one fitting
Monica's description had been on that aircraft. The US
Embassy in Grosvenor Square had denied all knowledge of
a Mr Dasser and suggested he was just another tourist.
However, a contact had told Crowne that Jake was CIA.

There was nothing more on Dolly Bell-Pauson. During the
week she had been to her regular beauty parlour and had
shopped for food in the Marylebone High Street, but otherwise had not been out, which was unusual for her; she had
told her manicurist that she thought she was getting summer
flu.

Her neighbour, Major Minton, who had happened to meet
her in the greengrocer's, reported that she looked ill. The day
after this meeting he had received an anonymous telephone
call to say that if he didn't stop 'snooping and playing games
with the police' he would regret it. Special Branch had advised
him to forget Mrs Bell-Pauson.

At this point I was interrupted by Ling's return. I hadn't
even heard the front door when she came drifting in like a dry

leaf. She wanted to know if I would like some tea and if I would be in to supper. I said: 'Yes, please,' and smiled enthusiasm at her.

As soon as she had gone I collected all my bits of paper and took them along to the bathroom. I locked the door and burned every scrap over the lavatory pan – except of course the plain text of Crowne's signal. Later, when I had finished reading and could repeat the entire message word for word, I would burn that too. I urinated in the ashes, worked the flush, made certain that I had left no tell-tale marks and went back to the living-room. Ling arrived with the tray while I was licking the fingertips of my left hand which had got slightly scorched during the operation.

I ate the sugared cakes and drank the clear green tea that Peter had favoured, and read the rest of Crowne's signal.

An envelope addressed in Peter's handwriting had arrived at the office from New Delhi. Peter hadn't been there at the time of the postmark; probably he had asked a steward or air-hostess to post it for him. It contained a strip of paper which looked as if it had been carelessly or hurriedly torn off the bottom corner of a carbon. Crowne wanted me to give my interpretation and take action where possible.

As far as I could tell it seemed to be part of a list of words – some of them place names – and dates. The dates were all past except the last. The place names were Hua Bai and Chou Nol. And the one complete word in the first column was 'ROUGE'. Peter had produced another piece of the puzzle; I now knew that the scratch marks on the bottom of the tin box represented a date. I knew that 'ROUGE' was 'TO PLAY' at 6 Hua Bai the Thursday after next. It wasn't much, but at least it was something. I could take action.

Three

'I'm sorry I didn't have time for a real talk with you before the weekend. When the Colonial Secretary's on leave I'm always terribly busy.'

Howard Farthingale gave me a warm smile that washed away the worry lines in his sunburnt face. In repose his expression was sad, and this, with his grey hair and fattish, large-bottomed figure, made him appear older than his forty-two years. But he was a pleasant man and I felt myself respond to him. Simultaneously I experienced a sudden jerk of recognition. He reminded me of someone. Who? I couldn't remember.

'First, personal matters, Keith. Has Ian Hackard taken care of you properly and are you happy in that apartment?'

'Yes – to both questions.'

'Good. Housing's one of our chief problems in Hong Kong. You're fortunate not to have to spend months in a hotel. And Ling is a blessing. She's a good general *amah* and a first-class cook. If I were you, I'd give her a free hand. If she wants to use the supermarkets or stalls she likes or deal with a *comprador* – he's the grocer chap who calls daily – I should let her. Ian explained about the wages, did he?'

I nodded. I was a little overwhelmed by Howard's knowledge of and interest in my domestic arrangements. 'It was very good of you to think of taking a lien on that apartment for me,' I said. I didn't know if this had in fact been Howard's doing, but it was a fair guess.

'Not a bit. The sooner you're happily settled in here, the sooner I can get some work out of you. So, any other problems? Not schools at any rate, seeing you're a bachelor. And you had all the right shots before you came, didn't you? Cholera? Yellow fever? Hong Kong's a pretty healthy place but we get the occasional epidemic and it's worth taking precautions. Banking facilities fixed up? Good. What about transport? Are you going to buy Peter Krail's car?'

'No.'

I had been nodding my head like a Mandarin, and it was a relief to produce a firm negative. 'I don't mind it being second-hand, but I'd like something with more style than a Mini.'

'Yes. I understand. I drive a station-wagon myself because of all the stuff I lug to and fro from my junk. Incidentally I'll take you out with me soon, and you can have a look at the other islands. A lot of the people who come here to work think the Colony consists of Hong Kong island and the mainland, Kai Tak and the golden mile of Nathan Road. Some of them never get beyond acquiring a tan at Repulse Bay and going to cocktail parties on The Peak.' Howard leaned across his desk and regarded me with intent grey eyes. 'I don't want you to be like that, Keith. If you are, you'll be no good at your job. I want you to get to know the Colony and its people and its problems, especially vis-à-vis China. I want you to travel in the New Territories, to see the villages and the new towns and the university at Sha Tin. I want you to stand on the bank of the Shamchun River and think that on the other side live a quarter of the world's –'

'Wh – what?'

I was conscious that my reaction had been slow. But Howard Farthingale, my ostensible boss, had carried me away on his hobby-horse – Hackard had warned me about it – and I had continued to listen when he switched from English to Cantonese. I could only hope my understanding hadn't been too obvious.

'I'm sorry but I don't speak Chinese.'

Howard's mouth set. 'Nor does anyone else. There's no such language. That was Cantonese – and you didn't follow any of it?'

'No. I speak French and Italian, a little German, a little Spanish.' I shrugged off these talents. 'I thought I could get by here with English.'

'Keith!' Howard had regained his good humour. 'Haven't you listened to anything I've been saying? It's not enough to "get by". Cantonese is the mother tongue of eight out of ten people in Hong Kong, and if . . .'

He was off again, at the gallop. This time I paid the strictest attention. I didn't think he had been trying to trick me, but one never knew. Anyhow, I wasn't prepared to take the risk of being caught in a senseless lie if in his enthusiasm he once more burst into Cantonese.

I was saved by the traditional gun; this one booms from the waterfront at Causeway Bay every day at noon. Automatically Howard looked at his watch to check the time. He had just been telling me that I must learn Cantonese; there were plenty of good teachers – the word reminded me of Bill Reddington and Monica and I very nearly grinned at him – and night classes were available. I swallowed. The last suggestion wiped any incipient grin from my face; I had a better idea of how to spend my evenings.

'Damn! We'll have to stop now,' Howard said. 'I've got a date with the Honourable Lee Fook-Pin, who's a member of the Executive Council. But there's some reading matter for you to be getting on with.' He pointed to a heap of books and files on the corner of his desk, and obediently I picked them up, doing my best to look eager. 'And you'll find some detailed maps of the Colony there too. They'll be useful to you.'

'I'm sure they will,' I said sincerely; the maps I had brought from London hadn't mentioned either Chou Nol or Hua Bai Streets and I badly needed to locate them. 'Thank you very much – for all your help.'

'It's nice to have someone to talk to – or should I say talk at? – who isn't bored stiff with my love of this part of the world.' Howard smiled ruefully. 'I was born in China, you know, and I've spent most of my life out here. To me it's home. If the Foreign Office ever tried to post me to Europe or the States, I'd quit.'

I had heard 'old China hands' in London speak like that and I knew enough of the East myself to be aware of its fascination. I felt a lot of sympathy for Howard. But I wasn't expected to understand these things and purposely I made my face blank, uncomprehending. Perhaps I overdid it because he looked hurt. He nodded his dismissal.

'While I remember, Keith – '

I was at the door, one hand on the knob. Having to balance the stuff I was carrying, I turned slowly. And again, through a quirk of memory, I was struck by Howard's resemblance to someone I knew or someone I had recently seen. Again, like a haunting tune, my perception of the likeness grew fainter as I tried to concentrate on it.

'I'm giving a party next Thursday,' he said. 'Eight-thirty. I hope you can come?'

'I should love to,' I said truthfully; after Sally Milment's reference to it yesterday I had been waiting for this invitation. 'Thank you very much.'

'Good. I've a house on the top of The Peak. It's a hundred yards or so from the stop if you come up in the tram, or the Hackards will give you a lift. That's if you're not driving your own car.'

'Thanks again.'

Five minutes later, having forgotten all about likenesses, I was sitting at the desk in my office, poring over the maps Howard had provided. It was a futile task. There seemed to be every street name imaginable except the two I wanted. Then, in letters so small that they could have been fly-dirts, I found what I thought, hoped, could be Chou Nol. Before I could be sure I had to borrow a magnifying glass from Ian Hackard, who was highly amused at my enthusiasm for what he called 'Howard's getting-to-know-you fixation'. But Chou Nol it was, a long sliver of a street in the Wan Chai area.

Greatly encouraged, I set to again. I had to find Hua Bai. After all, Chou Nol was only of secondary importance; whatever had been going to happen there had already taken place. But in ten days' time, on Thursday, September 12th, 'ROUGE' was 'TO PLAY' – or be played – at 6 Hua Bai; and I had every intention of being present on that occasion.

Hua Bai, however, was not on any map that Howard had given me. There was no such street on the Island of Hong Kong or in Kowloon or the New Territories, or if there were it wasn't marked. After forty-five minutes of cross-eyed concentration I would have taken an oath on it. I had examined every mark, every inkstain, every fold in the paper. Hua Bai Street did not exist.

Abandoning my search I tidied my desk top, returned the magnifying glass to Hackard's office – fortunately he wasn't there – and accepted an invitation from another colleague to go and have a drink and a sandwich at the Yacht Club. Doubtless Charles Crowne would have expected me to dash off to Chou Nol, but the thought of a long, cool beer was too much for me. Work, my real work, could wait until the evening.

At the end of the day Ian Hackard gave me a lift back to the apartment. I didn't want it, but without telling lies about previous engagements, it was difficult to refuse. So I made the best of it, had a shower and changed my clothes. The balcony with its promise of the chaise longue, a slothful book and several gins and tonics tempted me, but I resisted. I ordered a taxi.

'The corner of Chou Nol Street.'

'Chou Nol?'

'Yes. You know where it is?'

'Sure. It's in Wan Chai.' He didn't sound too certain. 'You want a girlie bar? I can recommend—'

'The corner will do nicely, thanks.'

I let him concentrate on the traffic for the next few minutes and we were coming up to Victoria Barracks when I asked him if he knew Hua Bai Street. He had learned his lesson as far as I was concerned. He didn't hesitate.

'Hua Bai in Kowloon. You want we go there?'

'No. I just want to know where it is.'

'I told you. Kowloon.'

'Whereabouts in Kowloon?'

He tilted his rear-view mirror and took a long look at me. 'Where you want to go? Chou Nol? Hua Bai? You make up your mind. I take you.'

If I had trusted him, I might have said Hua Bai, but I could guess what would happen. He would drive me round Kowloon, stopping to question the occasional passer-by or to make enquiries at a favourite bar, until he got tired. Then he would stop and demand a huge fare. No, thanks. I might not have the right Hong Kong tan on my Western features, but I wasn't that sort of fool.

'The corner of Chou Nol.'

He stopped on Hennessy where it crossed Tonnochy. When I didn't get out, he waved a hand vaguely in the direction of Morrison Hill and Happy Valley Racecourse.

'Chou Nol start up there. One ways. I can't go.'

I paid him what he asked—which was the exact fare on the

meter – added the regulation tip and got out of the taxi. I didn't believe he knew where Chou Nol was either, but at least I had a map. And, in fact, I did him an injustice. Chou Nol was approximately where he had indicated.

It was a narrow ladder street, thronged with people. On either side hung apartments, above garish bars and massage parlours, shutting out the evening light. Neon signs in English and Chinese advertised liquor, cigarettes, palmistry, astrology, physiotherapy; and every exotic pleasure known to man was, I guessed, available.

A party of drunken sailors, each clutching a Chinese girl, her *cheongsam* slit up the thigh, jostled me as I climbed the steps. A pimp clattered beside me in his wooden sandals until I made it clear I didn't want his wares. A small boy – he looked about six, tried to sell me Mao's Little Red Book in English, French, German or Cantonese and, when I refused, added his sister for good measure; he was offended when I laughed.

The evening was sultry and I was sweating, but I didn't mind the heat. What got me down was the noise. It seemed to me that from every window a radio bleated Chinese music and from every doorway a jukebox blared the latest American pop song. The result was hideous.

Number 10, or what had once been Number 10, was at the top of the street, and my first reaction was disappointment. I didn't know what I had expected – a brothel, I suppose, under some guise or other – but certainly not the neat modern block of apartments that had replaced Number 10, and doubtless Numbers 11 and 12 too. Then I realized that the block itself was called Chou Nol – Chou Nol Mansions – which meant that '10' could apply to the apartment number itself; indeed I had to assume it did. My spirits soared again. I hadn't come to a full stop after all.

I went into the hall. There was no porter but a notice board gave me a list of tenants. Without exception their names were Chinese. Number 10 was occupied by a Madam Ko Tak-leen and, since it was on the first floor, I walked up the stairs. I rang the door chimes. After a minute I sensed that someone was peering at me through the one-way spy-glass. Then the door opened.

A Chinese girl in a short black dress, cap and apron, that made her look like a masquerading parlour-maid in a Feydeau farce, stood on the threshold. In spite of her puzzled frown she was very pretty. I gave her my best smile.

'What do you want?'

Slightly taken aback by her lack of response which didn't fit the costume she was wearing, I stammered something about a friend in Australia who had told me to be sure to call at Number 10 if I was passing through Hong Kong. At this gambit her frown miraculously disappeared. She tried hard not to giggle.

'If it isn't possible for me to see Madam Ko now, perhaps I could make an appointment?'

'Your friend was joking, having you on.' She could no longer restrain her titters. 'Madam doesn't make appointments with gentlemen.'

'No? Well. I'm sure you're right but –' I looked meaningly at the short skirt, scarcely more than an elongated frill, the black silk stockings, the exaggerated high-heeled shoes. This was no ordinary *amah*. 'My friend's a very serious person and I'm positive he said 10 Chou Nol.'

'Perhaps he did, but if so he pulls your leg. This place is for ladies only, not for gentlemen. Now do you understand?'

'Oh!' I said, as the penny dropped.

I leaned against the doorframe and laughed. The girl, still giggling, began to shut the door, but I thrust out a foot. In the entrance hall and on the stairs I had smelled plaster and fresh paint; this was a new building. Nevertheless, Madam Ko need not have been the original occupant of Number 10.

'How long has Madam Ko lived here?'

'Two months. Why do you ask?'

'Maybe before she came there was –'

She was a bright girl. I hadn't finished the sentence before she grasped my meaning. But she was shaking her head.

'No. We are the first here. Last year there was a big fire. Several houses were pulled down and where they had been Chou Nol Mansions was built. Madam Ko moved in as soon as it was allowed, like all the other tenants. Nobody wanted to find squatters already settled in their apartments.'

I thanked her profusely and was wondering if I ought to give her a tip when a gong sounded from an inner room. She gave me a broad smile and a wink and shut the door. Thoughtfully I walked down the stairs and out into Chou Nol Street, which seemed noisier and busier than ever.

At least I had found the right address. I was in no doubt about that. Chou Nol Mansions was the 10, Chou Nol Street mentioned in Crowne's signal. Whether or not Madam Ko's apartment had been the actual scene of whatever had occurred in the building on June 20th of this year was immaterial. At that date neither she nor anyone else – except probably a guard who could have been drunk or bribed – had been around. The block had been empty. But why should anyone want to use a brand-new apartment for a day or a part of a day? I could think of answers, however far-fetched they might be, but not one in which Her Majesty's SIS was likely to be interested.

Heavily broody, I almost didn't notice Jake. He had come out of a bar with some American sailors, though they weren't together, and their height disguised his as he walked down the street in front of them. But something in the way he moved stirred my subconscious, and I did a double take. Dodging an old woman – not unlike Ling – who wanted to read my fortune, and pushing past a threesome of Chinese girls arm in arm, I watched the sailors turn into another bar. Now, given an unimpeded view of the tall, lean man some twenty yards in front of me, I couldn't fail to recognize Jake. If, since I could only see his back, I had any doubt, it vanished when he turned his head to look at a particularly bright neon sign and I caught a glimpse of his profile.

Jacob Leonard Dasser, whom I had last seen in Montagu Square haring after Monica and who, according to Crowne, had caught the next direct flight to Washington, had resurfaced in Hong Kong. And, of all places, in Chou Nol Street.

I followed him as he descended the steps. At the bottom he turned right, left, right and right again. This brought us to another ladder street which, according to my calculations, climbed parallel to Chou Nol.

Jake started up it, seemingly without purpose. He glanced into the entrances of a couple of bars and spent a full minute studying a shop front which displayed bales of Thai silk. Casually, as he moved away, he looked back down the street. I didn't think he had seen me, but it was just luck he hadn't. I wasn't more than fifteen yards behind him; there were so many open doorways, alleys and passages that I couldn't risk letting him get too far ahead. However, I had kept a party of tourists between us and, as I caught the movement of his head, I had instinctively knelt to tie up a non-existent shoe-lace.

Jake strolled on – if one can be said to stroll up a ladder street. I followed, but more circumspectly than before. Which is why I lost him. One moment he was taking the steps in his stride, the next he had disappeared. I ran, pushing past the tourists, knocking a bag of lychees out of an old man's grasp, almost impaling myself on a large golf umbrella that a Chinese girl was demonstrating to her friends.

I had seen Jake go by the door of The Pussycat and was prepared to swear he hadn't gone inside but, in passing, I threw a hasty glance into the bar. As a result I almost missed the tunnel-like slit, scarcely wider than the shoulders of an American football player, which bored into the building. Hurriedly I side-slipped down it – not perhaps the wisest thing to do.

I was about six feet from the entrance when something hard and round, like the muzzle of a gun, jabbed into the flesh between my shoulder blades and a voice said:

'Hold it! Now – put your hands up, gently.'

I did as I was told, cursing myself for having fallen for the old trick of sheltering in a doorway to let the shadow pass and taking him from behind. I wasn't afraid – Jake had made no effort to hide his Bostonian nasality and I knew he wouldn't shoot – but I didn't like being made a fool of. As I lifted my hands slowly upwards I let my weight shift to the balls of my feet. Then suddenly, swiftly, I stabbed my heel backwards into his instep, at the same time bringing my elbow down and around so as to catch him in the chest.

But once again Jake had forestalled me. He was well out of reach, leaning against a wall of the passage and laughing his silly head off. There was no sign of a gun. I doubt he was carrying one.

'Hi, Mr Sterling!' he said. 'What are you doing here – apart from trailing me like a Boy Scout, of course – enjoying the delights of Suzie Wong land? You should be careful, my friend. This isn't exactly a healthy neighbourhood. And a paper dragon can get easily hurt.'

I wasn't sure if he meant it as an insult or a warning. Either way it didn't endear him to me but, since I couldn't think of a killing reply, I sensibly kept silent. Still playing his Humphrey Bogart role, he pushed himself off the wall.

'My name's Jake Dasser, if you didn't already know that, Mr Sterling, and you can find me at the US Consulate. Or call me at home. The number's in the book.' He grinned at me. 'Be seeing you.'

He gave me a wide salute and was gone. I didn't try to follow him. There was a file of questions I would have liked to ask him, but this was neither the time nor the place and I believed what he had said; we would meet again. I didn't intend, however, to seek him out.

Sore as hell, I removed myself from the passage and strode off down the ladder street. I found Hennessy without too much difficulty. And fortune began to smile again. A yellow and red minibus, empty, drew up at my signal and twenty minutes later I was sitting on my balcony enjoying my first gin and tonic of the evening.

Four

The tram toiled and moiled up the mountainside, inching its way under a tunnel of green humidity. The rain beat through the foliage and hammered on the roof above my head. Like everyone and everything about me this Thursday night I sweated gently. I also prayed. The gradient was one in two on the steepest part of the track so that we sat at an angle, pressed hard against the backs of our seats. I prayed that the steel cable, which was the tram's means of haulage, wouldn't break. I was glad when we reached Victoria Gap, the last stop; I had had my one HK dollar's worth of local colour.

The irony was that I was doing this to please Howard Farthingale. Having bought a second-hand Chrysler and fixed up a driving licence, I could have driven up The Peak to Howard's party in comfort, but I thought he would approve my enterprise. After all, the tram had been running since 1888 and was an essential part of the Hong Kong I was meant to be getting to know. But I hadn't bargained on the sudden storm and I arrived on the steps of his imposing old colonial house as wet as a retriever that had just rescued the stick his master had thrown into a lake.

The houseboy who opened the door to me was not welcoming. I had misjudged the time of the tram ride and was far too early for the party. Nor, in my half-drowned condition, can I have looked much like a guest. He left me standing in the hall while he went to fetch Howard.

For a long minute I waited. The air-conditioning had dried the sweat on my body and my clothes were sticking to me in a cold, clammy embrace before Howard appeared. But he beamed on me.

'My dear chap!' His smile lost a little of its warmth when he saw the puddle I was making on his beautiful Chinese carpet. 'Here, let Cheung take your shoes and we'll go upstairs.'

Obediently the houseboy knelt in front of me, slipped off

my shoes and my socks and dried my feet on a towel. Embarrassed, I murmured my thanks, which he ignored. I could have been a piece of furniture that Howard had ordered him to dust. Suddenly I felt the *frisson* of a shiver I couldn't control.

'Come along, Keith,' Howard said. 'You'd better have a shower and I'll find you some dry clothes. We don't want you getting a chill.'

In spite of the dreary state I was in, I was inclined to linger. There were some fine wall scrolls in the hall, a splendid lacquered chest inlaid with ivory, and two tall Chinese vases I yearned to look at closely. But Howard was springing up the stairs. As I went after him I saw a jade Buddha on the half-landing, and a great bronze dragon. I had no time to do them justice.

'Come down when you're ready,' Howard said, leaving me in what was obviously the main spare room.

Another houseboy appeared. He showed me into the adjoining bathroom, turned on the shower and produced warm towels. I stripped, dropping my slacks, shirt and jacket in a messy heap on the floor.

Under the shower I forgot everything, except the hot beads of water bouncing on my body. When I had had enough I turned the shower to cold, but thirty seconds of icy spray was all I could endure. Towelling myself down, I blessed my temporary boss.

My own clothes had been removed, but in the bedroom I found the contents of my pockets laid neatly on the bed and beside them underpants, a dark brown shirt, some white slacks and sandals. Each was a well-made, expensive item, and new, but I regretted my own things. Howard and I were not the same shape. On me the shirt mightn't be too bad – I could always roll up the sleeves – but the slacks, which would need a belt, were going to hang in folds over my bottom and reach a couple of inches above my ankles. I cursed my stupidity. It was my own fault. If I had to come by tram I could at least have brought a raincoat. Now I should have to appear at Howard's party looking like a clown.

Reluctantly I began to dress. I was reaching for the slacks before I realized how snugly the underpants fitted. The slacks themselves were a trifle too snug; but the rest of the gear was fine. Howard might have bought it for me; he certainly hadn't bought it for himself. I grinned at my reflection in the full-length mirror and saw my eyes suddenly widen in amazement, my grin fade. I swung round.

On a lacquered chest stood a bowl of Chinese porcelain filled with flowers. To the side of it, in one of those hinged, free-standing frames, were two photographs. It was these, reflected in the glass, that had startled me. They were photographs of Howard and a girl – a girl so like Monica that –

My hand shook as I picked up the heavy silver frame. I was right. It was a photograph of Howard, but a very much younger Howard than the man I knew. He looked about fifteen or sixteen, and touchingly vulnerable.

The girl, of course, wasn't Monica. Monica wouldn't have been born at this time. The girl in the photograph was about the same age as Howard. There was also a strong family resemblance. She was probably his twin sister who, I remembered, was dead. What relation she and Howard were to Monica I could only guess, but now at last I understood something that had been worrying me for days – who Howard reminded me of; improbably it was the beautiful, fair-haired, golden-skinned girl I had seen at Dolly Bell-Pauson's party.

Thoughtfully I went downstairs, pausing to admire the jade Buddha on the landing. I've taught myself a little about Eastern art but my knowledge of jade is negligible. However, I didn't need to be an expert to realize that this was a museum piece, and worth a mint of money. Howard Farthingale was a rich man, and he lived like one. There was yet a third house-boy waiting in the hall below to show me into the living-room.

Following him, I heard voices and laughter; some of the other guests had arrived. Howard came forward to greet me as if I were the one person he was waiting for, and led me into the room. A small private smile told me that he approved of my appearance but he made no comment on it, for which I was grateful. Cheung offered me a tray of drinks and I took my favourite tipple.

'Let me see,' Howard said. 'Sally, of course, you know, and the lucky character who's going to marry her.' Sally Milment kissed me as befitted an old friend of the family and Bill sketched a salute. 'And the Hackards.' Ian shook hands, though I had spent the afternoon with him, and Joan kissed me on the mouth, which I could have done without. 'The rest of my guests you won't have met. Let me introduce you — '

There were seven of them, a doctor and his wife, a couple who both taught at the University of Hong Kong, the Secretary for Social Services, and his daughter who was a lawyer. They were all Chinese and I'd never seen any of them before. The seventh, however, was Jake Dasser.

'Good evening, Mr Sterling,' he said. 'You ought to give me full marks. I told you we'd meet again. Howard, you didn't know Mr Sterling and I were acquainted, did you?'

'No, indeed I didn't. Is this of long standing?'

'Two weeks come Saturday, not what you'd call real long. Remember I told you how I saw Monica in a London taxi and followed her to a party? Incidentally, are you expecting her tonight?'

'Yes, but she may be late.'

'Fine. Anyway, as I was saying, Keith here — I can't go on with this Mr Sterling nonsense — ' Jake gave me a cheerful smile — 'Keith was at the same party.'

'Then you've met my niece Monica, Keith?'

'I don't really know.' It was difficult to keep my voice casual. 'There were a lot of people and nobody bothered with introductions much.'

Jake laughed. 'You'll remember Monica when you see her.'

'What an odd coincidence — ' Howard began.

'Not as odd as it sounds. Our hostess of that evening, a lady called Dolly Bell-Pauson, is a great party-giver — like you, Howard — and she collects anyone who knows Hong Kong. That's how she came to ask Monica. They were having coffee . . .'

Jake produced the same story to account for Monica's presence at Dolly's party as Dolly herself had given to the Special Branch. I listened, waiting for him to mention Peter Krail, waiting for Monica to come into the room. Neither happened. This whole triangular conversation between Howard, Jake and myself had become slightly surreal.

'Are you an old friend of Mrs Bell-Pauson?' Jake asked as Howard went off to welcome some new arrivals.

I didn't have time to answer. Sally and Bill had joined us and Sally picked up Jake's question.

'Oh, do you know La Bell-Pauson too? She's an extraordinary woman, isn't she? Bill says she's a menace but I feel rather sorry for her.'

'I've said no such thing! I do wish you'd stop putting words in my mouth, Sally.' Bill was taut. 'I've never heard of Belle whatever-her-name-is.'

'But, darling, of course you –'

'Ah, Howard's bought a new painting, I see,' Bill interrupted her, pointing to a large acrylic work on the far wall. 'Come and look at it, Sally.' He grinned at us. 'She needs educating. She can't tell a Lui Shou-kwan from a Graham Sutherland.'

We grinned back in male sympathy. Sally's lips quivered but she didn't manage a smile. She seemed disproportionately upset. She let Bill put an arm around her waist and lead her across to the painting where they stood, their backs to us, talking earnestly.

'There's more to that young man than meets the eye,' Jake said. 'He can be very forceful when he likes, as befits his father's son. But you were saying, Keith, about Mrs Bell-Pauson –'

'You were asking, Jake, and the answer's "no". She's not an old friend of mine. Some people called Cunningham, knowing her interest in Hong Kong, took me along that night. Actually I found it pretty dull. I sneaked away early.'

'How early?'

I pretended not to notice his quickened interest. He was wondering if it was possible that I had seen him search Peter's body and then roar away after Monica. It was a stupid situation. If Jake were CIA – and I took Crowne's word for it – then I was damn sure he knew or guessed I was SIS. Supposedly we were on the same side. But neither of us trusted the other; it was always possible that he or I might be a rogue.

'With the coffee,' I said. 'I had a word with Helen Cunningham, who's a very understanding woman, and lit out. What about you?'

Jake shrugged. 'I must have gone soon after.'

For the moment we had exhausted each other. Cheung, with a tray laden with bowls of various delicacies, was a welcome diversion. The Chinese doctor and his wife and Joan Hackard joined us. The talk was of food, a concert at City Hall, the prospects for racing when the season opened at Happy Valley in a few weeks' time, the crowds on the beaches enjoying the end of the summer. Joan slid her hand through my arm.

'Come and sit down with me, Keith. I can't stand up any more, not balancing this great brute of a baby inside me.'

I had no desire to get myself stuck with Joan Hackard but I couldn't refuse her request. I let her lead me across the room. She lowered her bulk carefully on to a sofa and patted the cushion beside her. I sat down reluctantly. At least I had a good view of the door. I would know the moment Monica arrived.

'When's the great day?' I asked.

'The day of The Wedding.' Joan nodded towards Sally and Bill. 'I'll probably be shucking my brat while they're saying "I do". Lucky Sally! How I envy her. All that lovely Redding-ton lolly. Mind you, Lord R keeps a tight hold, I hear. Poor Bill could do with some of it right now.'

She stretched her long, slender legs for me to admire. It was a natural gesture. For the moment she had forgotten how very pregnant she was.

'Do you have any money, Keith, apart from the pittance HMG pays you?'

'Not a penny, Joan.'

'No expectations. Not an heir-in-waiting like Bill?'

I thought of my father, who had been a gardener until he was crippled by arthritis. 'None!' The word exploded more sharply than I had intended.

'A pity. But never mind. Hong Kong's the place to make money. It's as corrupt as hell. Everyone leaves here richer than he came.'

'Really?' I wasn't sure if Joan was just gossiping or hinting at something specific. 'I'll have to ask Ian about that.'

'That won't get you anywhere.' She laughed scornfully. 'Hackard's the original incorruptible man.'

I laughed to cover my distaste for her remarks. 'What makes you think I'm not the second one?'

'I watched the way you were looking at all the beautiful things Howard has – inherited.' The last word was in italics. 'You yearned after them, Keith.'

It could be the truth, at any rate as Joan saw it. But there were alternatives. She could be sounding me out. She could be putting up a smokescreen to protect her husband. She could be trying to draw attention from Hackard and focus it on Bill or Howard or someone else. Whatever her intentions I had an unpleasant feeling she knew more about me than she should.

'. . . you're like me, Keith. I love beautiful things too. That's why I envy Sally – though only the Reddington money; I couldn't go for Bill. These types with dubious Middle-East backgrounds don't appeal to me. Nor old China hands either.' She leaned towards me so that I was gazing down the deep vee between her swollen, maternal breasts. 'Don't you wish you'd had poor and honest missionaries for parents – like dear old Howard?'

I forced myself to smile into her dreamy eyes. She terrified me. My God, if she could be like this when she was about to drop a baby what would she be like when she was beddable once more? Yet I was sure sex wasn't her only interest. She hadn't pressed so hard last Saturday, when I had dined with her and Ian and played that dreary bridge. Since then she had either made a decision or had one made for her, and been instructed. I would have bet on the latter.

Either way she had presented me with a peck of fresh problems. The most immediate was how to escape from my present position without antagonizing her. Fortunately this solved itself. Hackard brought some friends across to speak to her and I had every excuse to yield my place on the sofa.

'We must have another talk about – *objets d'art* very soon, Keith,' she said blandly as I got up. 'That was extremely interesting.'

'I'll look forward to it, Joan,' I said, which wasn't altogether a lie; I didn't think Mrs Hackard was important, but she could be useful.

For the next half-hour I made myself sociable, though I avoided the Hackards and Jake Dasser and Sally and Bill. And I watched the doorway. When Monica at last appeared I realized I couldn't kid myself any longer; my interest was not merely professional. I was as excited as any schoolboy about to meet the object of his dreams, and I was disgusted with myself.

'Keith, this is my niece, Monica Cayton.' Howard was introducing us. 'Keith Sterling, my new PA, who thinks he may have met you in London.'

She was wearing a white *cheongsam* tonight and she was

more beautiful than ever. We shook hands. I said my piece about Dolly Bell-Pauson's party and she brushed it aside as unimportant; she didn't pretend to remember me. Within a minute our exchange was over, Howard was introducing her to someone else and I was left feeling curiously deflated.

As if we had all been waiting for Monica's arrival, Cheung announced that supper was ready and we went into the dining-room. Here we were expected to help ourselves at a buffet and then find our allotted places at the small tables scattered about the room. From that point we were waited on by the two houseboys and Cheung, who served the wine. Everything was informal but organized and I had no chance to be near Monica. She had lingered in the living-room talking to Jake and now she was sitting with Bill Reddington and a couple of Chinese, their table nowhere near mine.

I sat between Sally Milment and Joan Hackard; the other man was the Secretary for Social Services. Mostly we talked about his work. Sally was subdued and Joan seemed to be on her best behaviour. I wondered how much trouble Howard had taken over the supper arrangements. Perhaps none; he might have left them all to Cheung. But neither Cheung nor fate had been kind to me.

However the food was very good and by the time we were drinking bowls of pale green tea I was feeling more cheerful. Then my luck stood on its head. As we came out of the dining-room I found myself beside Monica. Unsmiling, she said:

'Mr Sterling, Howard tells me you came up on the tram. Would you like a lift home?'

'Thank you very much. I'd love one – if it's not out of your way?'

'No, I live near Happy Valley Racecourse. But I'd like to leave soon. I only flew in from Paris yesterday and I'm feeling the jet-lag.'

'Whenever suits you.'

'Fifteen minutes, then?'

Slightly dazed, I nodded agreement. I couldn't believe it. Whatever the reason – and I wasn't such a fool as to imagine it was my *beaux yeux* – Monica Cayton had sought my company. The 'why' could wait till later.

She was certainly in no hurry to explain. She showed no inclination to say anything at all as we hurtled through the wet night down the black winding road of The Peak. Swaying from side to side I hung on to the seat with one hand and with the other clutched the parcel containing my clothes – freshly cleaned and pressed, I was sure – that Cheung had given me as I left. I asked some casual questions about Paris, but her answers were brief to the point of curtness. I let her concentrate on her savage driving.

When she swung the car on to the access arc in front of my apartment block – I hadn't told her where I lived – and braked to a shuddering stop, I thought she would say good night and drive away. Instead she invited herself in for a nightcap.

'I hope this isn't an imposition. I meant it when I said I was tired, but I need to talk to you, Mr Sterling.'

'Keith – please.'

'All right. Keith. I won't keep you long.'

'Monica, if I said that all night wouldn't be too long, would you be angry?'

We were getting out of the lift and she didn't answer, but she did turn her head to smile at me. She was used to compliments and used to dealing with the male animal. I guessed that with her men went as far as she wanted and that mostly this wasn't too far. She was very self-contained.

In the living-room I poured us each a brandy. She had sat herself in a corner of the sofa, her feet tucked beneath her. It made her look appealing, like a serious child. I sat myself across from her, in an armchair. I wanted to be able to see her face.

'Keith, I've done something horribly stupid and I don't want my uncle to find out. Howard's a dear but he does fuss so. He'll fret over it for weeks, months maybe.'

She stopped abruptly, the colour high in her cheeks like two bruise marks, and watched the brandy swirling in the bottom of her glass. I wanted to take her in my arms, kiss her, make love to her – forget the long signal to Charles Crowne I would have to encipher later.

'Monica, I can't tell Howard what I don't know,' I said gently.

'But you do know, now you've met me. You know I was the girl with Peter Krail when he was killed – and that I ran away afterwards. Oh God, it was dreadful! This car came tearing round Montagu Square and drove straight at us. I'd have been killed too if Peter hadn't pushed me into the gutter. Which is why I'm so ashamed that I – I bolted. I suppose it was shock. I'm not the sort of person who normally panics. But for some reason I was terrified. Then later I didn't know what to do, how to explain why I'd behaved like that – and nothing was going to help Peter.'

'What did you do?'

'I flew to Paris the next day, which was what I'd planned before – before it happened.' She sighed. 'Jake says the police won't catch up with me but I'm scared they will. Keith, what sort of questions did they ask you? I imagine they questioned everyone at Mrs Bell-Pauson's.'

'Monica, I never knew Peter Krail. I never knew he was the man you were with at that party. And I never knew that was the night he was killed. You see, I left Dolly's early, before the accident happened, and nobody questioned me.'

She stared at me, her grey eyes wide. 'You mean I needn't have – Oh hell!' She was furious with herself – and with me.

'Please, don't worry,' I said. 'Please. I promise you I won't tell Howard or anyone, ever.'

'Thank you.'

An hour later, having agreed to have dinner with me the following Wednesday, she had gone and I was busy breaking the promise I had just made her. Not because I didn't trust her – I did. I was sure she had told me the truth. There wasn't a single detail about herself or Howard or Peter or Dolly Bell-Pauson or the American, Jake, that didn't correspond with what I already knew, and the rest could readily be verified. But I was in Hong Kong to do a job. The ultimate judge of Monica and Joan Hackard and all the rest of them had to be Charles Crowne. Which didn't make me like myself any better.

Five

Saturday night, having spent most of the day in a vain search for Hua Bai, I went on the town.

I can't remember who first suggested that I should be shown the night-life of Hong Kong, but the idea originated somehow at Howard's party on the Thursday, was received with enthusiasm, died a natural death, and was revived at the office late on Friday. Someone had telephoned someone. It was not unlike one of those chain letters where the last in line are the losers.

To begin with I was keen myself. Howard had said he would come – with Monica, which was enough to encourage me. So had Sally, Bill, Jake, the Chinese couple from the University and a pleasant girl called Ruth Cecil, who was a secretary to one of the US Consuls. It promised to be a good evening, even profitable.

In the event it was disastrous.

After drinking tea at the house of the Chinese couple, who seemed to have taken charge of events, we set off in two cars. Since I was supposedly the *raison d'être* of the expedition they insisted I should ride with them, and I found myself sitting in the back of their Ford between Ruth and a third Chinese teacher, whom I hadn't met before. Sally, Bill and a friend of Sally's, the daughter of the Colonial Secretary, were in the Hackards' car; long Ian and his pregnant Joan had decided to join us at the last minute, which gave me no pleasure. To be honest, once I learned that Monica – I didn't mind about Howard – wasn't to come with us, I lost all interest in the evening.

One nightclub is very much like another unless you go in for exotica and, considering what an assorted bag we were, I thought it improbable that the Chinese had anything like that in mind. In fact, we started with a discotheque in Wan Chai, which is part of the standard tour. Here the noise beating on my old-style ear-drums made me so desperate I suggested to the Colonial Secretary's daughter that we went and sat in the car.

I had chosen her only because I was dancing with her when desperation overcame me. She was a nice kid, and wide-eyed for experience – two or three years younger than Sally, whom she greatly admired. She wasn't exactly my type, but sitting in the back seat with my arm loosely around her shoulders, I did my best to chat her up; and thus I acquired some useful information.

'Isn't it funny to think Sally and Bill might never have met if it hadn't been for me?' she said dreamily.

'You introduced them?'

'More or less. I took Sally to this party of Dolly Bell-Pauson's in London and Bill was there and they clicked – just like that.'

'Then you deserve to be the chief bridesmaid. You were a clever girl.'

'Thank you, Keith.' She put her hand on my thigh and leaned hopefully against me. 'To tell the truth, it was a string of coincidences. If Howard hadn't asked my mother and father to dinner . . .'

I kissed her gently, absent-mindedly. I didn't believe in coincidences, at any rate not of the multiple variety. It was far more likely that, as it had been arranged that Monica and Peter should go to the Bell-Pauson's, so it had been arranged that Sally should meet Bill there. Not that anyone could have foreseen the precise consequences of their meeting; a hit-and-run can be organized, but not a proposal of marriage, unless Bill himself . . . but that was a possibility I didn't want to consider. I liked Bill Reddington.

Liking, however, has little to do with my job. It didn't prevent me from manœuvring to go in the Hackards' car with Bill and Sally when later we set off for Kowloon. According to the Chinese professor, we were now heading for more sophisticated entertainment. Not that I believed him; the joints he had chosen in Wan Chai had been fit for Catholic converts, at least on the surface, which was all we had been allowed to see. I expected much the same of Kowloon. Meanwhile, as we roared through the four-lane tunnel that was taking us to the mainland, I seized my opportunity.

'You know, Bill, for a guy who's about to be married in a week's time you're pretty unromantic, aren't you?'

'Am I? I've not heard Sally complaining.'

'Maybe not. But most girls would have slapped you down for forgetting where you'd first met – at Dolly Bell-Pauson's. It ought to be a cherished memory.'

I felt his body tense. He began to make hesitant excuses. Sally intervened, too quickly, too fiercely.

'Bill didn't forget. When he said he didn't know Mrs Bell-Pauson he thought you were talking about someone called Belle – Belle with an "e" – not Dolly.' She gave a plastic laugh. 'She wasn't important to us. It was the only time either of us ever met her.'

I laughed in echo. 'He's exonerated then.'

And a voice from the front seat of the car, Joan Hackard's mocking voice, said: 'Bill's like Ian, Keith, *sans peur et sans reproche*. He's not a go-getter, like you, dear boy. If he's allowed, he'll make a happy little schoolmaster.'

'What's wrong with that?' Sally demanded. 'As we told Keith the other day, teachers come in every shape and size. Incidentally, what do you think of Monica Cayton now you've met her, Keith?'

'Monica?'

Sally's abruptness – she needed to take lessons from her mother – had thrown me, but she had achieved her purpose. We were suddenly a long way from Dolly Bell-Pauson, and Bill, off the hook, relaxed, unaware that he had betrayed any emotion at all.

'That is a woman I do *not* understand,' Joan said, glossing over my blankness. 'She could have any man she wanted. She could have money, position, beautiful things – anything she liked. And what does she do? She lives alone in that ramshackle old house her father left her. She refuses to get married, though I know she's over twenty-six. She refuses to take presents from Howard even though he's her uncle. And she works like hell at that University job of hers – as if teaching English to a lot of Chinks mattered.'

For the next five minutes I listened avidly while they argued about Monica's house – Sally rather liked it; her work – Bill and Ian both admired it; her age – Joan said she lied about it; and her boy-friends – there was no agreement. Next Wednesday with any luck I would be able to verify all this – plus any information that Charles Crowne might send me – at first hand. I was looking forward to Wednesday.

Hackard, following the car of the Chinese professor – Monica's colleague, I had to remind myself; it really was difficult to think of her as a dedicated teacher – had now reached Nathan Road and was driving us along the golden mile of hotels, shops, restaurants, clubs. Everywhere there were bright lights, eager people, strolling lovers or would-be lovers, drifting music and, behind this encouraging façade, everything for sale.

Still on Nathan Road, we came to Kowloon Park. We drove past the Mosque, turned sharp right and, confusing ourselves in a hinterland of roads, drew up in front of The Toothless Dragon. It was an inauspicious name for a nightclub. I remember thinking, as Hackard parked the car and we clustered on the pavement in front of the entrance, that its owner must be totally devoid of humour. Later I wondered if he mightn't have an excess of it.

At any rate the place seemed to have quite a reputation. It was known to Sally and the Hackards, though they hadn't been there themselves, and the American girl, Ruth Cecil, assured me that the floor-show was well worth the cover charge. First impressions were favourable.

The manager came forward to greet us, bowed low to the Chinese professor and his wife, and led us to a reserved table on the edge of the dance floor. The show, he said, was due to begin in fifteen minutes. In the meantime he suggested champagne cocktails – for such honourable guests as ourselves they were, of course, on the house. This was a bonus. As my eyes adjusted to the subdued lighting and I took in the rich elegance of the crimson and gold décor, I realized that prices here were going to be astronomical. My own share would go on my expense account, but I wondered about the others, Hackard with his overdraft, and the teachers – what did the University pay? – and Bill, who was said by Joan to be short of ready cash. I wondered if any of them had expense accounts for things like this, too.

Having just sat down, everyone got up again, determined to dance before the floor-show began. I found myself left with Joan Hackard. I sipped my cocktail and listened to the music.

The group was unusual for a nightclub, a piano, a clarinet, a trumpet and drums. They were very good, and strictly occidental. In fact, apart from the manager, the hostesses in their gold *cheongsams* slit to the hip, the waiters – and probably the kitchen staff – there was little Chinese about The Toothless Dragon. Even the clientèle – it being a Saturday night, the club was bulging – was ninety per cent European and American.

'This is a very high-class joint,' I said to Joan. 'I'm surprised we rate as "honourable guests", aren't you?'

For a minute she didn't answer and I looked at her. Her eyes were wide, her hands pressed tightly over her abdomen and beads of moisture glistened on her upper lip. Her breath came in short, hard gasps.

'Joan, are you all right?'

Suddenly her body relaxed, slumped. She wiped away the sweat on her face and managed to smile at me, but not even the roseate lights could disguise her pallor. My question had been moronic. Across the floor I saw Hackard dancing with Ruth, and made to stand up. Joan was his wife, his responsibility. But she put out her hand, digging her nails into my wrist, and stopped me.

'No, Keith. I'm okay. It was a – a cramp, nothing serious.'

'Are you sure?'

'Positive. For God's sake, don't make a fuss! Ian would never forgive me. He didn't want me to come tonight. We had a row about it. He's scared something might happen. Not to me – to the baby!' She snorted with laughter. 'Now, what were you saying? Oh yes. Why we're VIPs at this joint, as you call it. That's simple. Bill telephoned to say we were a party from Government House and the manager fell over himself to take the booking. What it is to have influence.' Envy mingled with malice; Joan was back in form.

The music ended on a triumphant trumpet note, but resumed in response to sustained clapping. I would have a few more minutes alone with Joan. I glanced at the tables nearest to us. They were empty; the customers dancing. I leaned closer to her and let my thigh press against hers.

'Sweetie, last Thursday at Howard's party, you said you and I were alike. Remember? You said we both loved beautiful things and were prepared to go to some lengths to get them.'

I fingered the emerald pendant she was wearing, pretending to admire it and letting the back of my hand stroke her breast. 'Did you mean it?'

Instinctively she responded. Then the cramp seized her again. My luck was out. I heard the sharp intake of her breath and her body went rigid. She thrust my arm aside.

'Christ!' she groaned. 'Jesus Christ!'

'Joan! What is it?' Ian Hackard was standing beside us. Abruptly he turned on me. 'What the hell have you done to her, Sterling?' For a split second I thought the foolish man was going to hit me. He must have seen his wife push me away and misinterpreted the gesture.

Ruth said quietly: 'Ian, Joan's sick.'

'What?' At once he was all inefficient concern. 'Joan, darling, it's me – Ian. Tell me what's the matter.'

'It's your – your – damned baby.' Joan got the words out somehow. 'The – the pains have started.'

'But they can't have.' Hackard was aghast. 'Baby's not due till next Saturday.'

It was typical of him that he spoke of his unborn child as 'Baby' and, while I edged away from her, I felt a spurt of sympathy for Joan. As a husband Hackard must be impossible, and surely too as a major enemy. Yet he was no more improbable than any of the other characters I had met since coming to Hong Kong – and I was sure that one of them was reponsible for Peter Krail's sudden flight to London, his urgent message to the Office, and his death.

'If someone doesn't do something soon,' Joan said through clenched teeth, 'I'm going to drop Junior right here, and that'll be an entertainment The Toothless Dragon will find difficult to repeat.'

After which a lot of things happened rapidly.

The group stopped playing. Those who had been dancing returned to their tables. Our party stood around Joan, arguing about what was best to do, creating a centre of confusion and holding up the floor-show. The manager arrived, all smiling teeth and anxiety. Things were sorted out.

Joan, who was temporarily feeling better, was helped from the room by Ian and Ruth. It had been agreed that one of the girls must go with her and the American as the eldest had become the reluctant conscript; the wife of the Chinese professor, herself a mother and therefore an obvious choice, had blandly refused. But the other Chinese teacher had at once volunteered to go with Ian, who was uncertain of the most direct route to the hospital.

When they had gone, amid a sea of curious eyes and a buzz of curious voices, I made my sole contribution. I suggested that the rest of us might call it a night. This, however, was badly received, not least by the manager who said it would be an inestimable grief to him if the honourable guests from Government House departed before they had seen the floorshow. I couldn't persist and the manager went into action.

The two tables which had been put together to accommodate our party were magicked into one, more champagne cocktails appeared – also on the house – and the curiosity of the other customers was assuaged by a brief announcement, in English but ending with a few words of Cantonese. There was a thin ripple of laughter before the applause. At our table only the Chinese laughed and the daughter of the Colonial Secretary. Sally smiled doubtfully.

'What was that?' I asked the professor's wife, who was sitting beside me. 'What did he say?'

'You do not know? I was watching you and I thought you understood.'

'That's because I have an intelligent face,' I said, giving her a wide grin; I'd hoped that I'd looked as blank as Bill. 'Actually I'm beginning lessons next week. Howard Farthingale's fixed me up with a teacher.'

'Good. I wish you success.' Her smile was without warmth. 'For now I translate. He said it was a pity that the nightclub was called The Toothless Dragon because it was not a suitable name to give to the lady's baby.'

I laughed dutifully and then, as I belatedly realized how appropriate Joan Hackard might consider the name, had to smother a real bellow of mirth. The lights were dimming. For a slow minute the room was in darkness. Voices sank to a murmur. The floor-show was about to begin.

The chanteuse wasn't Mireille Mathieu but she was a pretty good imitation and the audience loved her. She sang two songs, belting them out from where she stood on the small dais beside the piano. The third, a romantic ballad, brought a change of tempo and while she sang she moved languidly among the tables, lingering here and there as she picked out a particular man to share the refrain with her. It was the traditional approach, but nonetheless effective, and everyone enjoyed it – except some of the victims, such as Bill Redding-ton. When she perched herself on his knee, miming words of love and encouraging him to sing with her, he was shamefully unresponsive.

With a gesture of theatrical despair that caused a roar of laughter she stood up and moved behind him. Her eyes met mine. I thought I was to be next and made to pick up my glass to toast her; I didn't have Bill's inhibitions. But she stroked my cheek and passed on. I drank to her.

The next item was some temple dancers from Thailand. They looked about ten and I doubt if any of them had ever seen Bangkok, but I could have been wrong. Certainly my attempt to make any of them lose the expressionless mask that was characteristic of the dancing was a failure. Bored with their sinuous belly-buttons and long, long fingernails, I finished my drink. I yawned. And the pain hit me.

My first thought was of Joan Hackard. I seemed to have all the same symptoms. My abdomen was contracting. I was rigid with the effort to control it. My breathing stopped. Sweat broke out, on my face, everywhere. I blew air as the spasm passed. Common sense reasserted itself; I was not about to give birth. But I was certainly unwell. Perhaps it was some-thing I'd eaten. Maybe one of those bits and pieces I'd had in the course of the evening had disagreed with me.

The Thai dancers were returning to their temple amid polite clapping. To give the hostesses time to replenish drinks, the group had begun to play progressive jazz. I forced myself to relax, told myself that the horrible griping pain had gone and wouldn't return. I didn't believe it.

Suddenly three boys cart-wheeled on to the floor. They joked, they clowned, they performed casual acrobatics. It was a change of pace that delighted the audience. The fact that it was a strip-tease act was apparent only at the end, when it turned out that one of the boys was a girl. The applause was tumultuous. I clapped and cheered and added my praises to the rest.

My insides were churning. The griping returned.

Surely the attack was too sudden and severe for simple

food poisoning. Someone could have spiked a champagne cocktail – anyone sitting at our table, the chanteuse who had leaned over me, even one of the kitchen staff if a hostess had made sure I got the right glass. There was no point in trying to guess. In any case I needed to go to the lavatory. But I didn't want to go alone, and I didn't trust either the Chinese professor or Bill Reddington.

The chanteuse, wearing a diaphanous robe through which her body glittered, stood on the dais, half in shadow, and started to sing. Her voice was low and sweet and ripe with sex. In the spotlight a couple danced. They looked absurdly young, scarcely in their teens. They met, courted, embraced, started to explore each other . . . The music throbbed. This was going to be the grand climax of the show. If I could hold on a few more minutes, until the children were on the point of simulated orgasm and the spotlight was killed, until the applause had ended, the bows taken and all the lights were on again, if I could hold on until then I would be safe. The cloakroom would be full of over-stimulated men wanting to relieve themselves before the general dancing recommenced.

But I couldn't wait. The griping was getting worse, making me nauseous. I got to my feet, hesitated, nearly asked Bill to come with me and decided against it. I did mutter an apology, a part explanation, but no one showed any interest – they were concentrated on the performance – and I hurried through the semi-darkness, heedless of the exasperation I caused as I knocked against tables, trod on someone's foot and obstructed people's view of the two dancers.

It was like an obstacle course, the winning post the bamboo curtain that hung across the exit leading to the washrooms. When I made it, thankful now for the lack of both light and attention, I bent low and thrust my way through, immediately flattening myself against the near wall. But there was no one around. There was no one in the passage or standing at the urinals or in either of the toilets. I had been over-suspicious.

Secure behind a locked door I sat on the seat and let my bowels empty themselves. The relief was terrific. I felt cold, exhausted – and happy. I flushed the pan and waited to see if my insides would knot up again. When they didn't, I washed my hands and slapped cold water on my face. I thought about going back to the nightclub; the floor-show would be ending.

The idea didn't appeal to me much since my insides were still delicate, but neither did I want to stay in the washroom indefinitely.

As I came into the corridor one of the hostesses – she was wearing a gold *cheongsam* with a red dragon embroidered over her left breast – slipped through the bamboo curtain. She was petite even for a Chinese and very pretty in spite of the worry marks between her eyes.

'Mr Sterling?' She couldn't cope with the 'rl' in the middle of my name.

'Yes. What can I do for you?'

'Please. I am happy to have found you. There has been an accident and your friends need you. Mr Rouge has been badly hurt.'

'Mr Rouge!'

Nothing she could have said would have startled me more. Momentarily I was wide open, vulnerable. I sensed rather than heard the footfall behind me. I flung myself sideways. I avoided the full force of the chop, but I was much too slow. I had blacked out before I hit the floor.

Six

When I regained consciousness I was lying on my back on a low divan. The ceiling, crimson with gold stars painted on it, was a long way above me. The walls were crimson too and bare, except for a scroll depicting a dragon rampant. From where I lay he didn't look toothless, but no attempt had been made to disguise the fact that I was still in the nightclub. This worried me. If the enemy was indifferent to my knowing where I was, in all probability they never intended me to pass on the information.

But I had other, more immediate worries. I was stripped to the waist; my jacket, tie, shirt and watch had been removed. Two hooded men knelt beside me. One of them pulled off my shoes and socks. The second unzipped my slacks and began to ease them over my hips. I brought up my knee and he grunted as I made contact with his chin, but hampered by my clothing I hadn't put much force into the blow and he stopped only long enough to give me a double swipe across the face. Instinctively I jerked away my head and an excruciating pain shot up my neck and exploded in my temples.

By the time the nausea had subsided my pants had followed my trousers and I lay naked, the material of the divan pricking my skin. I hadn't realized before how closely connected courage and clothes are. Although the room was warm I had to bite on the gag in my mouth to prevent myself from shivering. And I yearned to let my fingers probe the source of that hellish pain, the tender place at the base of my skull where they had chopped me originally. I strained at the manacles that bound my wrists. The counter-pain was a help.

I forced my mind to concentrate. I needed to get my priorities straight. The comparatively minor damage I had suffered was less important than the people in the room and the room itself. Later I might get a chance to escape and, if I did, I would need to know where the doors were, how the lighting worked, what might prove a weapon – and the strength of the enemy. From my position on the divan I took in all I could without showing obvious interest. It wasn't a great deal. I struggled to sit up, but one of the men who had undressed me put his hand in the middle of my chest and pushed me down again. This time the pain in my head was bearable – just.

The men began to examine me. They looked in my ears and behind them, up my nostrils, under my armpits, between my toes, up my rectum and between the folds of my private parts. They inspected my hair, which is very thick, as if they were catching nits. They must have spent five minutes on my mouth, examining my gums and tapping my teeth; the taller man did the probing with long yellow fingers while the other held my balls, squeezing gently as a reminder of what could happen if I took the smallest bite at his companion. They were very thorough but they found nothing. To this day I don't know what they were looking for.

All this was done in silence. I tried to speak when the gag was removed, to protest, to demand to know what was happening and why I was being treated in this fashion – I had decided to play the innocent; it was the only part available – but a warning hand stopped me. And as soon as the mouth examination was finished the gag was thrust back in place. I lay there, hating them, hating myself. I felt as if I had been abused and had co-operated with my abusers. I wondered what was to happen next.

They didn't keep me in suspense for long. The man who had held my balls pulled me upright by the chain around my wrists and led me like a slave across the room. My legs were free and, had I been fast enough, I could have hooked him and thrown him, which at least would have given me some satisfaction. But, apart from his companion, there was another man who sat motionless in a high-backed chair, and a girl who was examining my clothes with the same meticulous care that had been given to my body; both were hooded. At four to one the odds were too high. I would have been overcome immediately and punished for my effort. What's more, I would have shown my own capabilities and learnt nothing in return.

I stood where I was put and allowed my ankles to be manacled. I took in the scene around me. It was obvious that

I was in a private dining-room of The Toothless Dragon. Five people had dined here; the remains of the meal were still on the table, though a space had been cleared near the seated man and the contents of my pockets laid out beside him. Before I could make a guess about the fifth person, there was a complicated knock on the door and the little Chinese who had given me that extraordinary message about Mr Rouge was let in.

'Everything okay,' she said. 'They were surprised Mr Sterling should go off like that, but they accepted.'

Even while she spoke she was taking off her *cheongsam*, which she folded and put carefully – with her sandals – in a suitcase. Then with equal care she got into the European-style dress and high-heeled shoes that the other girl brought her, and began to braid her long hair into a coronet. This changed her appearance so completely that I wasn't sure I would know her again.

As for the others I had no chance of recognizing them; their hoods covered their whole heads. I was positive they were Chinese, except perhaps for the seated man – the table hid his hands and I hadn't seen him walk – but they all wore clothes which aped the foreign devil, the men dark business-suits and the girl a plain silk dress. The only other facts about them of which I was sure was that they were all young – it was something I sensed – and ruthless. I steeled myself for the questioning I guessed was about to begin.

I expected the man at the table to take charge of affairs. There was no doubt he was the *taipan*, the big boss; the others turned to him constantly for his approval, which he signified by a fractional movement of his head. But I was wrong. The tall man, the one who had searched my body with such thoroughness, was to be the interrogator. He was equally thorough now. He waited while a spotlight was adjusted to his liking, signalled that a radio should be turned on and at what strength, and arranged his chair exactly where he wanted it. Not until then did he speak.

'Mr Sterling, we don't have a great deal of time so you'll answer my questions quickly, fully, and above all accurately. If you're foolish enough to lie you will be punished.' He motioned towards his chum who stood behind me and who had already given me a none too gentle kick for trying to speak

84

out of turn. 'Do you understand?'

'Yes, but – ' I winced as I received another kick at the base of my spine.

'You lie. You don't understand. You've no idea how severely we can punish you if we wish. I warn you, Mr Sterling.'

But I was in no position to heed the warning and, during the next fifteen minutes, I lied and lied. I swore that I didn't work for the SIS, that I'd never heard of Brigadier Crowne, that I wasn't a replacement in Hong Kong for Peter Krail, that friends of mine called Cunningham had taken me to Dolly Bell-Pauson's party, that I was a poor miserable First Secretary seconded from the FCO, and nothing more. And at every lie a finger, hard as a steel rod, jabbed into some nerve-point in my body. I was gasping with pain when – inadvertently, I think – the finger rammed into my original hurt and I blacked out.

I woke up in my own vomit. Here was my chance. I lay where I had fallen, making pathetic, slobbering noises. The toe of a shoe prodded me contemptuously. I screamed and someone hurriedly turned up the radio. Curling into a foetal posture, I made myself as small as possible, but hands seized me under the shoulders and pulled me to my feet. I managed to gouge my eyes with my knuckles and tears ran down my cheeks. I sniffed. I must have looked a woeful sight, completely unmanned.

'We shall start again, Mr Sterling, and this time you'll tell us the truth, the whole truth.'

I nodded, incapable of speech. 'Only don't – don't hurt me any more. Please.'

For a long, unpleasant minute the silence stretched. I was afraid I had overdone it. Then the *taipan* must have given a thumbs-up signal because the manacles were taken off my ankles and I was allowed to sit cross-legged on the floor. The hooded girl brought me a glass of wine. And I knew I had won. They had been defeated by their arrogance which wouldn't allow them to believe that a foreign devil could endure so much without breaking.

Yet I'm not particularly courageous. I just happen to have a high threshold of pain, my body's in excellent shape – or it was until tonight – and my mind has been trained to fight the trauma engendered by violence to one's person. The enemy had miscalculated.

The danger now was that I would fall a victim to my own arrogance and in turn underestimate the enemy. I concentrated on the interrogator, who was rephrasing his questions. I told the truth. I admitted to being SIS, to working for Charles Crowne, to having replaced Peter Krail in Hong Kong – all contrary to the rules. But I was telling them nothing they didn't already know. I admitted that on the Saturday he died Peter had telephoned an SIS number and demanded that someone should be sent to meet him at Dolly Bell-Pauson's party. I gave details, exonerating the Cunninghams from any complicity. Though I hated to do it, I told them about Monica.

'Why did you leave the party when you did?'

'Krail told me he'd panicked, he'd misjudged the crisis, he'd be in the office next morning.'

'What else did he tell you?'

'Nothing. There was no chance. We only spoke for a couple of minutes, casually.'

'Who is Major Minton?'

'Major Minton? Oh – he's a neighbour of Mrs Bell-Pauson. He saw the accident and reported it to the police.'

'Is he in the SIS?'

'No. I'm sure he's not.'

'What was the crisis Mr Krail spoke of?'

'I've no idea.'

'You must have some idea, Mr Sterling.'

'No – not really. I swear.' I let my voice rise. 'I supposed it was connected with his – his reasons for coming home.'

'And what were they?'

This was the moment I was waiting for and the moment I was dreading. Since my dramatic collapse, I had told them the truth, if not the whole truth. Now I was going to lie through my teeth, but I hoped that my behaviour, my obvious anxiety to please so as to avoid further punishment, and the veracity of what I had told them so far, would help to convince them. Their arrogance was again on my side. They wouldn't want to believe I had been playing them along.

'Krail thought he'd discovered a – a big deal that one of the Chinese bosses was trying to put over.'

'Chinese bosses?'

'Chinese. Malay. Hong Kong. I don't know. But definitely

an Asian *taipan*. The signal Krail sent wasn't very explicit. Explanations were to wait till he could speak to Crowne in person, which of course he never did.'

'And that is all you can tell us, Mr Sterling?'

'No, of course not!' Over-anxious, I trod on the tail of his words. 'Crowne believes it's something to do with the distribution of heroin, a sort of Hong Kong Connection, as it were. Normally that wouldn't concern the SIS, but Krail implied – or so Crowne interpreted it – that public servants are involved. My job's to find out who they are. We've had too many scandals lately. The British Government's running scared. If it was discovered that some sods – say in the Colonial Secretariat or the Trade Commission – were trafficking in drugs there'd be the devil to pay. After all, Hong Kong is still a British colony, though these days we try to avoid that dirty word.'

I stopped and looked anxiously from the interrogator to the *taipan*. I had told them a plausible story, as far as I could appreciate the situation. There seemed no reason why they shouldn't believe it, but those damned hoods hid any hint of their reactions. They could have been laughing their silly heads off or, if Crowne had been wrong about this not being a drug thing, could have been aghast at how much I knew. I rated my chances at evens.

At last the interrogator said: 'What success have you had, Mr Sterling?'

'Not much, but it's not two weeks –'

'How much?'

I told them of Joan Hackard's approach. If they knew about it, it would help to strengthen my case; if they didn't, little harm would be done. Joan herself was safe enough in hospital. I also said I had been enquiring into people's standards of living to see if they outstripped their incomes. I mentioned the Hackards again, Ian's overdraft, and Howard Farthingale, whom I had been able to exonerate since he had inherited money from his mother's sister; Howard himself had told me this when we were talking about Chinese art in the office. Eventually I wound to an end.

There were more questions. I answered them as best I could. They seemed designed to test the veracity of my story. At any rate none of them connected remotely with 10 Chou Nol Street or 6 Hua Bai, and there was no further reference to Mr Rouge. With an upsurge of confidence I turned my thoughts to my own safety which, I must admit, had always been at the back of my mind.

In a pause I said, stumbling: 'What – what are you going to do with me? I've told you all I know. I swear I have.'

'Don't worry, Mr Sterling. Luckily for yourself you've been sensible and no great harm's going to come to you.' The interrogator stood up; he was, as I had noticed before, tall for a Chinese. 'Indeed, we're grateful to you. You've relieved us of anxiety. Thank you, Mr Sterling.' He gave me a mock, formal bow.

And, in a sudden flashback, I saw the kitchen of my apartment and Teng, Ling's grandson, expressing gratitude for the offence I had deliberately given him. Here was the same contempt, the same tall young body, the same hatred. Hidden behind the hood, which not only covered his head but distorted his voice, I saw Teng's oriental features and black hair. This was Teng.

To hide a spurt of triumph I shut my eyes and let my head droop. It wasn't difficult to feign exhaustion and the last thing I wanted was to let Teng know I had recognized him. That might well make them change their minds – if, that is, they really intended to let me go.

The two girls had brought me my clothes. Disconcertingly, they started to dress me. They did this as if I were an unloved child, peeling off pants when they put them on backwards, and slapping my legs to make me step into them again, hoisting up slacks and thrusting socks and shoes on limbs that were presumed to have no feeling. When they finished with my lower half, they changed the manacles from my wrists to my ankles and put on shirt, jacket, tie; after this they re-handcuffed me and made me return to my cross-legged posture. Ignominious as all this was, I was absurdly grateful. At least, without the insecurity of nakedness, I could face the enemy on comparatively equal terms.

The interrogator – Teng – said: 'Mr Sterling, listen to what I'm going to say. Listen very carefully. Your life will depend on it.'

'But you just said no harm –'

He ignored my whining protest. 'You are going to be given

a drink which will put you to sleep. When you wake up you'll find yourself lying in some back street a short distance from The Toothless Dragon, unless of course the police have found you first and taken you to hospital – or to gaol. Your explanation will be that when you went to the cloakroom here you didn't feel too well and decided to go home. That was the message your friends received, so they're not worrying about you. You'll say you left the nightclub by a side door and intended to get a taxi, but you were mugged before you found one. It's a reasonable explanation. Nobody will query it. And that's what you're to tell everyone, Mr Sterling. Do you understand?'

'Yes, I understand, but –'

'No buts. No exceptions. I said everyone and I meant everyone, including your boss, Charles Crowne. If you even hint at what happened in this room tonight, you'll die. That's not an idle threat, I promise you. Remember Mr Krail. He was knocked down by a car and killed. For you, we would arrange a much more painful "accident". And don't think we shan't know, Mr Sterling, because we most surely will.'

'I'll do what you say, exactly. Is – is there anything else you want?'

'No. Go on with your enquiries into corruption, do enough to keep Crowne happy, and enjoy Hong Kong. That should be easy for you. After all, if anything comes up we'll always be able to find you.'

There was a note of grim humour in the last remark and I wondered if, in spite of assurances, they did intend to kill me. I comforted myself with the thought that they were too businesslike to have wasted time deceiving me and they had nothing to gain by my death. Even if I ignored their threats and made a fuss, I would have no means of identifying them to the police – Teng couldn't know I had recognized him – and the management of The Toothless Dragon would plead ignorance, perhaps justifiably. Besides, how was I to explain their interrogation without explaining my 'mission'? No, I could do them no harm and now they knew me – as they thought – in all my weakness, I might be useful leading Charles Crowne down the garden path.

Secure in this belief I should have downed in one the drink that had been put in my hands, but somehow I had a great reluctance. I looked with distaste at the colourless liquid in the wineglass and then at the *taipan*. I swallowed my saliva. I knew I had no choice. To have dropped the glass or spilt its contents – easily excusable since my hands were still manacled – would have caused only a petty delay. So, slowly and carefully, I lifted the glass. I smelt gin, but the liquid was cloudy. I drank.

Immediately, as the warmth of the spirit spread through my stomach, a wave of darkness engulfed my mind. Screwing up my eyes and gritting my teeth, I fought to remain conscious. It was a waste of effort. The second wave drowned me.

My next recollection was of extreme discomfort. I was heaped untidily at the side of some evil-smelling alley, like a sack of potatoes fallen from the back of a van. One leg stuck out at a disconcerting angle and, when I shifted to try to get more comfortable, I realized my head was pillowed on a doorstep. The stench from a nearby drain was revolting. I thought about moving but decided it required too much effort. I was horribly tired. If I could sleep for a little perhaps I would feel better; nothing was as important to me as sleep.

This fact was imbedded in my mind with such firmness that when hands plucked at my jacket and began to pull off my shoes I was furious at being disturbed and lashed out. My fist hit air, but my foot made contact with something soft. There was a yelp of pain and a chatter of Cantonese. The hands returned, no longer probing delicately, but rough and ruthless. For the second time that night, my clothes were being forcibly removed. I struggled, believing I was putting up a tremendous fight; in retrospect, I think my efforts were futile, though they may have had a delaying effect.

Suddenly there were angry shouts, pounding footsteps. The hands abandoned me, and feet, which I associated with the hands, scurried away like fleeing rats. Someone bent over me. Brut after-shave competed with the smell from the drain. At least this was one of my own kind. But he wouldn't let me alone either. He too insisted on moving my limbs around and doing things to my jacket, which seemed to be inside out; but he replaced my shoes. It was all a mystery.

Resentfully I slit open my eyes. Close above me in the surrounding darkness a face floated, a thin intelligent face that looked familiar. Jake Dasser, the CIA man. The effort of remembering was very great. My eyelids collapsed. I wished he'd go away and leave me alone.

Yet, moments after he had gone I withdrew the wish. For no particular reason I was suddenly scared. I began to shake, to judder like a Formula One car with its engine running. Car. Yes, that was the emotive word. I was lying here on the ground, and a car was coming. I knew I ought to crawl into a doorway but there wasn't time. I heard the engine roar as the car turned into the alley and accelerated. I opened my eyes to see headlights beaming down on me. It was a big, heavy car — like the one that had killed Peter Krail. It was within feet of me when I screamed, and it stopped.

Seven

I lay still in the bed, allowing only my eyes to move. When I was sure I was alone I eased myself into a sitting position. This required an effort. I was in bad shape. I felt like a battered baby, or how I imagined a battered baby feels. Added to which, I seemed to have a gigantic hangover.

But the room was reassuring. I wasn't in prison or in hospital. No prison had such comfortable beds, or curtains patterned with poppies. No hospital would permit the charcoal drawing of a voluptuous nude that hung on the wall facing me. This was a bedroom in a private house or apartment. But whose?

Recollections of last night deluged my mind – the night-club, the floor-show, that incomprehensible reference to Mr Rouge, the hooded Chinese, Teng, questions, pain. It wasn't surprising that I felt as I did; even my hangover could be explained by the knockout drops they had given me. Afterwards, Teng had kept his promise. They had loaded me into a car, driven a few blocks and thrown me out into some quiet gutter. I remembered the stench in the alley. I remembered hands searching me – but they had been interrupted. I remembered Jake Dasser. Or did I? What was he doing there?

I looked about me. There was nothing on the bedside-table, no sign of my watch, my wallet, my keys, which was fair enough after the mugging. But there were no shoes in sight either, no suit, no underclothes. At the moment I was wearing pyjamas. They were striped scarlet and white, very natty and not too bad a fit, but I had never seen them before. Someone had cared for me. The very fact that I was here – wherever here was – clean and tidy and sweet-smelling, was proof of it. There was also the tight bandage round my ribcage.

The last thing I remembered clearly, it seemed to me, was lying defenceless in the path of a car that was roaring towards me. No, it was Peter Krail who was . . . I shook my head to clear it. Immediately I wished I hadn't. The room tilted at a sharp angle; it started to revolve and I had to cling to the sides of the mattress until gradually everything grew steady once more.

The door opened as the vertigo passed and Jake Dasser, looking disgustingly healthy, came into the room. He stood at the bottom of the bed and grinned at me.

'Good afternoon. How are you feeling?'

'Afternoon?'

'Sure. It's ten after twelve. But today's Sunday, so take it easy.'

'I don't think I could do anything else.'

'Come now, Keith, don't be a defeatist. I'll make you one of my pick-me-ups and you'll be rearing to fight the dragon again in no time.'

'What dragon?'

'That's what you're going to tell me – I hope.' Jake had his hand on the doorknob. 'Back in five minutes. Give you a chance to dream up a good story.'

I didn't need to dream up a story, good or otherwise; I was already provided with one. Instead I used the respite to judge the extent of the damage I had suffered last night. It wasn't as bad as it might have been. Apart from the hangover and my body's general soreness – either would by itself have demanded fortitude from a saint – one side of my face was badly bruised, and several ribs felt as if they had been kicked into my chest. I took a deep breath, expanding my lungs. The pain made me gasp. Sweat started on my skin and the room reeled about me. I shut my eyes tight.

When I opened them Jake was beside the bed. I had been so concentrated on myself that I hadn't heard him come into the room. He was holding a highball glass which looked as if it contained an oversized Bloody Mary. I fought down my nausea.

'Keith, do you want a doctor? Ruth said you ought to be okay, but – '

'No doctor.' Somehow I managed to get the words out and, pleased that I had remembered not to shake my head, I even achieved a travesty of a grin. 'I'll live – just.'

Jake laughed. 'Drink this. It's guaranteed to improve the outlook.' He held out the glass. 'It's my special for the morning after.'

I took it reluctantly. 'What do you bet I'll bring it up before it's half way down?'

'You won't. It'll settle your insides and blunt your headache. You'll see.'

He was right, at any rate about my stomach. By the time I had drunk three-quarters of his bloody concoction I no longer felt nauseous and the nude on the opposite wall no longer showed an inclination to stand on her head. The world was a solid place. Admittedly the throbbing in my skull hadn't disappeared, but then I wasn't hung-over, or not in the way that my host appeared to believe. I wondered what he really did believe.

'Thanks, Jake. Thanks a lot.'

'You're welcome.' He sat himself on the side of the bed and regarded me like a stern parent. 'But let this be a lesson to you, young Keith. If I hadn't happened along when I did, you might have come to a sticky end. Hong Kong can be a dangerous place, and small boys shouldn't play with big bosses.'

'I wasn't playing with anyone.'

'What were you doing, then? Or have you conveniently forgotten?'

'I don't know what you mean. We were at a joint called The Toothless Dragon and in the middle of the floor-show I began to feel sick – too much rot-gut liquor, I expect. I didn't want to spoil the party so I decided to slope off by myself. I asked one of the hostesses to take a message to our table, and went to look for a taxi . . .'

I reproduced Teng's story precisely, and Jake listened without interruption, his face expressing only amused interest. I would have dearly liked to know what he was thinking. Though it was clear he'd rescued me from the horrible searching hands that had been stripping me, I didn't altogether trust him. Whatever he might say he hadn't just 'happened along' at the right moment to save me; that would have been too much of a coincidence. So, how did he come to be there?

'. . . when I woke up someone was trying to pull my shoes off. I began to struggle but it was a feeble effort. Then they left me. You must have interrupted them. I remember running

94

footsteps and your face bending over me – and a car tearing towards me.' Involuntarily I shivered. 'I thought it was going to be the end of me.'

Jake nodded sympathetically. 'That was my car, and I had a devil of a job getting you into it. In fact I doubt I'd have succeeded but a couple of sailors rolled into the alley. They were pretty pissed, but when they'd relieved themselves of a couple of gallons of beer each, they helped. And when I got back here the night porter was happy to lend a shoulder to my drunk friend.'

'I wasn't drunk. I was mugged.'

'That I believe. I saw it myself. Brother, they'd have had the pants off you if I'd not intervened. By the way, your clothes are in the kitchen. My *amah*'s doing what she can to them.'

'Not my watch, I suppose, or my wallet?'

'I'm afraid not. They'd have cleaned out your pockets and taken your watch before they started on your clothes.'

I grunted. I didn't mind about the wallet – there hadn't been more than HK$200 in it – but the missing ID cards and passes and credit cards could be a nuisance, and the watch I hated to lose. My dad had given it to me when I got my degree – he had saved for it from the first day I went to London University – and I was fond of that watch. I cursed Teng, and the *taipan* who had ordered my disposal.

'You'd better report the mugging to the police. Not that they'll be able to do anything about it, but it'll help to keep their statistics straight.'

'Okay. But what do I tell them about you? Do I say Mr Dasser was taking a stroll down the evil-smelling alley when –'

'Tell them I was driving along Phon Tak Street and saw two youths, Chinese, in jeans and T-shirts, hoist you out of the gutter and carry you off. I thought I recognized you, but anyway you were a Westerner and, by the looks of it, in deep trouble, so I followed you. For which, Keith Sterling, you should be eternally grateful.'

'I am, Jake, I assure you. I am. And if there's anything I can do for you in return . . .'

'You could tell me what you were doing on Chou Nol last Monday.'

The unexpectedness of the thrust startled me. To gain a moment I coughed, wincing as my ribs hurt. I smiled ruefully.

'I was visiting a – lady in Chou Nol Mansions. A friend of mine gave me her address. Unfortunately she's moved since he was in Hong Kong.'

'Too bad! Did he give you any other addresses?'

'Let me see. Yes.' I decided to take the risk. 'He mentioned the Chinese Communist Store for jade and ivory and cloisonné, but of course prices have sky-rocketed since you Americans were allowed to buy goods made in the People's Republic. And he said that anyone interested in up-and-coming painters might pick up something worthwhile at the gallery on Hua Bai.'

'Where?'

'Hua Bai. I really must go there. Do you know where it is?'

'I've never heard of Hua Bai.'

Jake's eyes, no longer friendly, seemed to bore into me. It was an effort to appear nonchalant. Until now our verbal sparring had been light, ironical; we were both playing a game. Suddenly things had changed. He was suspicious and inimical. And my gain was slight. All I had got from my probe was a fairly firm conviction that Hua Bai meant less to Jake than it did to me. I could have made a bad mistake. I gritted my teeth.

In the silence I heard the doorbell ring and Jake stood up. He opened his mouth as if he were about to say something interesting, but changed his mind.

'That'll be Ruth. She's having lunch with me. I'll bring you a tray – cold meat and salad. You'd better try to eat.'

'I'd love some coffee. And – Jake – I can't be a very welcome visitor in this condition. I'm sorry.'

'Forget it. You'd do the same for me – I hope.'

As soon as he had gone I threw back the bedclothes and gently swung my legs on to the floor. I paused. Nothing disastrous happened. With the utmost care I stood upright. Slowly I walked over to the nude, who lay in her frame and taunted me. It was a splendid drawing. Unfortunately it didn't do a thing for me. I felt infinitely old. However, I was at least mobile again.

I was back in bed when there was a tap at the door and

Ruth and Jake came in. Jake was carrying a tray. Even to my jaundiced eye the food looked good and there was a large pot of coffee. I was suddenly hungry and, considering what I'd been through, I could have been in worse shape, a lot worse. My welcoming grin was genuine.

'Hi! How's the invalid?'

'Hallo, Ruth. I've just decided I'm going to make it.'

'That's great. I wasn't too sure when I first saw you in the wee hours of the morning.'

'Ruth helped me clean you up and strap your ribs,' Jake explained. 'She's an apartment across the hall and as soon as I'd got you in here I went and leant on her bell.'

'I see.' I tried not to sound speculative. I assumed Ruth was part of the CIA set-up in Hong Kong, but it certainly wasn't my business if she was also Jake's girl-friend. 'Many thanks, Ruth.'

'You're welcome, Keith. I guess it was my night for being the Good Samaritan, what with Ian and Joan, and then you.'

Joan! I had completely forgotten the Hackards. 'Of course, you went to the hospital with them. What happened? How is Joan?'

'She had a baby boy at ten o'clock. The kid's fine but it was a breech birth and Joan's in a bad way. I called the hospital a half-hour ago. I got the usual "doing as well as expected", but I spoke to Ian. Poor old Ian! Is he ever frantic?'

'I'm sorry.'

And I was sorry, though I must admit the words had come automatically. My mind was back at The Toothless Dragon, adding more facts to the little pile I had collected last night. But fact and fancy were woefully intermingled. I would have to sort them out later, when my brain was less addled – and I was no longer under observation by the CIA.

In the late afternoon the CIA, in the person of Jake Dasser and, I rather suspected, Ruth Cecil, drove me home. They had been extraordinarily kind, but Ruth had asked a lot of wide-eyed questions, not easy to parry, and I was glad when they refused the drink I felt bound to offer.

With a host of admonitions to take care of myself they left me at the entrance to my apartment block. I stood and waved them goodbye. Suppressing a sudden regret that I couldn't trust them enough to tell them the whole story, I made my decrepit way to the lift. As it carried me up I thought with pleasure of lying on the balcony and having Ling bring me a long gin and tonic – probably the wrong thing for that bump at the base of my skull, but excellent for morale.

I was standing on the doormat before I realized that I no longer had my keys and, if Ling weren't at home, I shouldn't be able to get into the apartment. Somehow it seemed the last straw. I jabbed a thumb on the bell and kept it there. The door was opened at once – by Teng.

'Mr Sterling, sir.'

Blank with amazement I walked past him into the hall – my hall. In God's name, what was Teng doing here? Mindless anger, rooted in fear, welled over me. I swung round to confront him and was on the rim of hurling myself at him when I took in his appearance. He was wearing black trousers and a white Mao jacket – the uniform of the high-class house-boy – and, with his head slightly bowed, he looked a parody of the perfect servant awaiting his master's orders.

Digging my nails into the palms of my hands, I fought to control myself, my body trembling with the effort. And inevitably my distress communicated itself to Teng. He jerked up his head and his eyes, dark with dismay, met mine. It was now, if ever, that I justified my training and the not inconsiderable salary the SIS paid me.

I made a supplicatory gesture. 'Hallo, Teng. Teng, I'm sorry but I'm in a bad way. I was robbed and beaten up last night. I'd come out of a nightclub in Kowloon and I was trying to find a taxi. It was a hell of an experience.' I gave a weak laugh. 'Help me on to the balcony, will you, and ask Ling to get me a large gin with a splash of tonic.'

I had a moment of agonizing suspense. Then I heard Teng expel his breath in a hiss through his teeth as he relaxed. A surge of relief overwhelmed me. Not only had I just earned my keep; in all likelihood I had just saved my life. I'm sure that if I had lost control and gone for Teng he would have tried to kill me. In the circumstances, he would almost certainly have succeeded; whatever my instincts, I wasn't in the best of fighting form.

Teng offered me his arm. Cloaking my reluctance I took

it; I even made myself lean against him, though the last thing I wanted was any further contact with him. The warmth of his body revolted me and I deliberately kept my eyes away from his hands. But it wasn't far to the balcony. Soon, propped up with pillows, I was lying on the chaise-longue and feeling almost human.

'I will get you your drink at once, Mr Sterling.'

'Thank you, Teng. But where's Ling?'

'Ling has gone.'

'Gone? Gone where?'

'She became ill yesterday evening after you went out and the family came for her. I am to take her place.'

'I – I see. Poor old Ling. Let me know if there's anything I can do for her.'

'There's nothing you can do, Mr Sterling.'

It was a flat statement and I accepted it, but that's not to say it gave me any joy. With Teng living in the apartment I should be under much closer supervision. I sighed, and winced as my ribs hurt. Something warned me I was going to regret the smell of Ling's joss sticks.

'Your drink, Mr Sterling.' Teng put the glass on the table beside me and next to it a slip of paper and a small parcel, neatly wrapped in brown paper. 'This is a list of your telephone calls during the day. If you wish to return them I'll bring the instrument.'

I glanced at the list. Sally Milment had phoned three times and Howard Farthingale once. Howard hadn't asked me to return his call, but Sally had demanded I phone back as soon as I came in.

'Yes, please. Bring it.' I pointed to the parcel. 'What's that?'

'I don't know, sir. About half an hour before your return the bell rang. When I answered the door there was no one there, but I found that packet on the mat.'

Teng went to get the telephone and I took several swallows of my gin, letting the cold liquid bathe the inside of my mouth. The taste was marvellous. I picked up the parcel, which bore neither name nor address, and took off the wrapping to reveal a cardboard box. Teng had lied when he said he didn't know what it was. The box contained my wallet with money, credit cards and passes intact, my driving licence, my keys for the apartment and the car, my watch, my Parker pen, a letter that helped to support my cover-story, and an engagement book – all the things that had been in my pockets when I went out the previous evening.

I was glad to see them again, especially the watch. Nevertheless I knew that their return was intended as a warning. It was a demonstration of the enemy's power over me and, though this may not have been intended, of the *taipan*'s discipline. I was wondering about that *taipan* when my new houseboy brought the phone.

'Anything else, sir? Supper is cold and ready when you wish.'

'Good. I want an early night. But now I need another drink.'

I didn't wait for Teng to go. I dialled Government House. It was impossible to guess if Sally's call was merely social or H.E.'s way of getting hold of me. Whichever it was, it sounded urgent. Sally answered the phone herself.

'Keith! At last! Where have you been? Bill said you'd turn up all right, but I was worried about you after that abrupt departure from The Toothless Dragon.'

'Didn't you get my message? I asked one of the hostesses – '

'Yes, I know. But when I rang this morning to see if you were feeling better your houseboy said you hadn't been home all night!'

'Sally, my love, don't sound so indignant.'

'I'm not your love, Keith Sterling. If I were I'd be giving you hell.'

I laughed and caught my breath with the pain. Hurriedly, to avoid more questions, I told Sally the story I had been instructed to tell. I knew I should have to repeat it again and again, like a recording. I was already bored with it. I cut short one of her more fatuous comments and she took the hint.

'Well, I won't keep you, Keith. You'll be all right for tomorrow, won't you?'

'Tomorrow?'

It was Sally's turn to be impatient. 'You're meant to be dining with us. Don't say you've forgotten. John and his wife have arrived – and my future pa-in-law. It's going to be quite a week. I'll probably have to drag Bill to the altar on Saturday.'

'Nonsense. Don't fish for compliments.'

'I'm not. Honestly, Keith, he's as jittery as hell. Even John remarked on it.'

'How is John?'

'Fine. He sends his regards and says come early so that you and he can have a natter together before the party begins.'

'Tell him I'll do that, and thanks for phoning, Sally. Until tomorrow then. Goodbye.'

I put down the receiver and sipped my second drink. I had thought John Milment might bring me news from Crowne, but if he had, it was clearly non-priority. I wasn't sorry. In my present state I didn't relish the idea of driving over to Government House, and the telephone wasn't safe. As if I needed to be reminded of the need for security, I caught from the corner of my eye a flick of Teng's white jacket in the living-room behind me.

Smothering a yawn, I dialled Howard's number. Cheung answered. Mr Farthingale was out on his junk and wasn't expected back until late; he had left no message for me. I thanked Cheung and said it wasn't important, which was probably true. I couldn't imagine why Howard had telephoned me on a Sunday. And I had other things to occupy my mind. There were only three days left now until Thursday and, in spite of all my enquiries, I still had no idea where Hua Bai was, or what – who – ROUGE was. Last night hadn't given me any clues. The mention of 'Mr Rouge' by the phoney night-club hostess certainly hadn't helped . . .

My eyes were closing, and I slowly drifted into sleep.

Eight

The next morning, feeling like hell, I staggered into the office. It was black Monday and the beginning of my second full week in Hong Kong. Sitting at my desk in the Colonial Secretariat, I pretended to read and makes notes on what the English-language papers in the Far East had to say about the People's Republic of China. In theory my efforts were designed to help Howard Farthingale prepare his monthly report for London. But in practice Howard needed no help, as everyone knew, and anyway my heart wasn't in it.

There was too much else on my mind. It was ten days since I had first heard of ROUGE, and eight since Charles Crowne's telegram about Chou Nol and Hua Bai with its instructions to 'take appropriate action'. The time had zipped by. The demands of the Secretariat, the essential façade of my social life and practical needs such as getting a car and a driving licence had kept me busy. As far as what really mattered, I had made some headway; but Chou Nol had been a dead-end and I still hadn't located Hua Bai.

By now I was almost prepared to believe the place didn't exist. It was not on any map or in any directory and my determined enquiries had drawn a blank. Posing as a tourist I had asked at the Public Library in City Hall, at the Telephone Exchange, at the Hong Kong Tourist Bureau, at the main Post Office and at all the obvious and less obvious places. Chou Nol had been a street, but there was no certainty that Hua Bai was also one. It could be an obscure building, a boat, a private house, anything.

Abandoning all pretence of work, I propped my feet on the desk and let my imagination roam. Teng was the one person I knew who could tell me where Hua Bai was, and what ROUGE TO PLAY meant, but he was the one person I couldn't ask. However innocent I made my questions, the *taipan* would know at once that I wasn't following instructions.

Undoubtedly, he would try to keep his word. I shuddered. I had had a foretaste of what could be done to me; apart from my ribs and my bruised face, my whole body this morning was a mass of sudden sharp pains. A quick movement —

I jerked my feet down from the desk as the door of my office was swung open. I had acted instinctively; it wouldn't do to be caught with my idleness showing. A moment later I would rather have been caught playing with myself than endure the agony as every muscle I owned went into spasm.

'God, you look awful!'

'Hallo, Ian,' I said, when I was able.

I might well have added, but I didn't, that I couldn't look worse than he did. His skin had a jaundiced tinge beneath its Hong Kong tan. His eyes were black-rimmed and sunken with fatigue. His Adam's apple was working overtime and he exuded nervous energy like an athlete high on pep-pills. However, it didn't need a Sherlock Holmes to see that he was happy. With a triumphant gesture worthy of an old-time Hollywood movie he carefully laid a cigar on the desk in front of me and waited for my admiration. It was certainly a big, fat, expensive cigar, but I never smoke.

'Thank you, Ian. That's very generous of you. How is — the family?'

'All right. Joan's going to be all right. I had to go home to shower and change, but otherwise I've come straight from the hospital and they say she'll be fine. But it was touch and go, poor girl. She had a dreadful time.' He pulled a grubby handkerchief from his pocket and blew his nose. 'Baby's fine too. He weighs eight pounds two ounces. Joan did me proud. Incidentally, drinks on the Hackards for everyone, one o'clock at the Yacht Club. You'll be there?'

What could I say? I had intended to go to the police at lunch-time, as Jake Dasser had advised, and tell them about my mugging. At least Hackard's invitation would be a good excuse for putting off that visit. I assured Ian that nothing was more important to me than drinking to his son. I did my best to sound as if I meant it.

'Good,' he said. 'I'm glad you can make it. When I heard you'd been beaten up I thought you mightn't be able to.' Suddenly he laughed. 'What a day for the office gossips — news of Baby, this extraordinary story about you being mugged and

103

Howard missing.'

'What do you mean? Howard missing?'

'Howard's disappeared. Nobody knows where he is, and with the CS away everyone wants him. And that goes for his niece, Monica. She's phoned a couple of times. According to his houseboy, Howard went out in his junk on Sunday morning and he's not been seen since.'

The 'mystery' of Howard's disappearance was short-lived. We met him on the causeway that leads to Killet's Island when we were going over to the Yacht Club. He looked tired and dirty and was not in the best of tempers. He said that he had spent the night trying to mend the engine on his junk and praying for a breeze so that he could use the sails. He flatly refused to 'drink Baby's health' and, though he was startled by my swollen, discoloured face, he didn't want to discuss it. Obviously he had problems of his own.

He had turned his back and was on his way when I remembered his telephone call. I told Ian to go on and ran — shambled would be a more descriptive word — after Howard. At my shout he stopped and waited for me.

'What is it, Keith?' He didn't bother to hide his impatience. 'I've missed a whole morning's work and I've an enormous amount to do.'

'Sorry, Howard, but — you phoned me yesterday, at home. Was it anything important?'

'Important? No-o, I don't think so.' He bit his bottom lip, forced himself to concentrate. 'Oh, I know. It was about that shop — the art dealers someone had recommended to you. You asked me if I knew where Hua Bai was. You remember? On Friday. And I'd no idea.'

'Yes, I remember. No one seems to have — '

'Well, I found out for you. A friend of mine, a professor at the Chinese University at Sha Tin in the New Territories, says Hua Bai used to be a narrow street in Kowloon. Most of it was engulfed by one of the new building projects ten years ago, so you're a bit late.'

'Too bad!' I laughed to hide my disappointment. 'Anyway, many thanks for your help, Howard. I didn't intend to be a bother.'

'No bother.' He glanced at his watch and groaned. 'Oh, God! I must go. Look, Keith, I'll show you on a map later.

There's an outside chance your shop's still there. The part that wasn't demolished became an arcade – behind the Hung Shing Temple on Phai Lip Street, and it would be the right kind of place for it.'

Howard was loping down the causeway before I could repeat my thanks. Thoughtfully I followed Ian to the Yacht Club. My spirits, which had sunk to the ground, were see-saw high again. The surviving arcade behind Phai Lip sounded promising. If Howard's information was accurate this was the closest I had got to the smell of Hua Bai.

In spite of my appearance – my new white dinner-jacket seemed only to draw attention to the discolouration of my face – and in spite of my body's remaining aches and pains, I was still in a good mood when I arrived at Government House that evening. The afternoon had gone well. Having increased the Hackard overdraft by the price of three double gins, I had managed to display ignorance through my first Cantonese lesson, given an interview to the police, who had been kind enough at Howard's request to send a couple of their representatives to the office, and been shown on a map of Kowloon precisely where the unmarked arcade was said to be. It was the last that really gave me joy. Nevertheless, my visit to 6 Hua Bai – if it really were there – had to be postponed; my dinner date at Government House took priority.

As Sally had suggested, I was the first arrival. However, Macfar, H.E.'s chauffeur, was already on duty waiting to park the cars, and we chatted for a minute or two. I asked if he would be driving Sally to the church on Saturday and was listening to a long flow of words in reply when John Milment hailed me from the front door. My attention distracted, I caught only the tail end of Macfar's wordiness, and that not very distinctly.

'. . . I said, Mr Rouge, I said –'

'What? What was that?'

I swung round on Macfar. Startled, he took a half step back and snapped to attention. His face wore the set expression of a sergeant-major about to be reprimanded by a brand-new second-lieutenant. He looked stuffed. Carefully I arranged my features into a casual smile.

'What were you saying, Macfar? I didn't quite get it.'

'Saying, sir? Nothing special, sir. I was just talking about the wedding. We're all very fond of Miss Sally, sir, and we hope everything will be perfect on the day. Yes, sir, I shall certainly be driving Miss Sally to the church. I hope I haven't spoken out of turn, sir.'

I stared at him. His gaze drilled a hole through my right ear-lobe. I sensed John Milment coming down the steps towards us. Nodding at Macfar, I left him. It was hopeless to try to get anything more out of him now. But why, why hadn't I listened to him before? Surely I had heard him mention 'Mr Rouge'. I could swear it.

'Keith, how nice to see you again.'

'Hallo, John.'

We shook hands and I clapped him on the shoulder. After all, we were old friends – and Macfar was watching us. I thrust thoughts of Macfar to the back of my mind.

'Let's go and have a drink before the others arrive and you can tell me about your first impressions of Hong Kong.'

'That sounds an excellent idea. Did you have a good journey?'

'Not too bad. The usual delays and frustrations.'

Making general conversation we went into the house and John led the way to the small book-lined room where I had first met H.E. The Milments seemed to use it as a sort of inner sanctum. As soon as the door was shut the questions burst out of him.

'What happened? Are you all right? Your face's ghastly and you're walking like a cat on hot bricks.'

'Thanks, chum.'

He ignored the interruption. 'Christ, but you don't know how worried I was. To be told, casual-like, by Sally that you'd disappeared from a nightclub and couldn't be found, then that you'd been mugged and left in a gutter somewhere. Were you mugged? Or is it part of – part of – ?'

'I was mugged. And I'm fairly fragile.' I sat down carefully in a voluptuous armchair. 'What about that drink you promised me, John? I could do with a strong pink gin.'

'Yes, of course. Sorry.' He began to occupy himself with drinks. 'I just pass on information and not ask questions. Is that it?'

I grinned at him. 'I'm happy to hear you've got some

106

information to pass on.'

'I have, yes. I saw Crowne the day before we left London. And while we were waiting for our flight at Heathrow a special messenger brought me this.' He extracted a buff OHMS envelope from his wallet and handed it to me. 'I've been scared to death of losing it ever since.'

'Thanks.'

I slit the envelope and took out the flimsy. Since the message had come by hand of John Milment I thought it might be in clear, but it wasn't. I would have to decipher it tonight behind a locked bedroom door, safe from Teng. There was no immediate urgency. I put it in my inside pocket, from which I took another envelope. I held it out to John.

'Would you mind asking your father if he'd be kind enough to get this sent off as soon as possible?'

An inflection in my voice must have alerted him. He laughed. 'Dad been giving you a bad time?'

'Let's say that as a postmaster he doesn't encourage voluminous correspondence.'

John looked at his watch. 'Shall I take it right away? It would be a good moment. Mother'll be fussing over his bow tie and he'll welcome an excuse to escape.'

'Okay. Crowne's news can wait.'

When John had gone I pushed myself out of the chair and went across to the window. I was glad to have got rid of that signal to Crowne. I had planned to give it to H.E. in the course of the evening, but this was a much better plan. Pleased, I sipped my gin and thought dismally of my mishandling of Macfar.

The window of the sanctum gave on the garden and, while I thought my grey thoughts and watched the warm, peaceful evening, two men came into sight. One I recognized from television and newspaper photographs: Lord Reddington was well known to the public. The other was Bill. They made an incongruous couple as they marched backwards and forwards across the lawn. Lord Reddington was a short, fat, sad-looking Levantine Jew, whose enormous ability was matched by his achievements. Bill was a head taller, elegant, good-looking, Eton and Cambridge – all the privileges and so far nothing to show for them. Yet no one could have mistaken their relationship.

At the moment they seemed to be having an argument. This ended abruptly, as Lord Reddington shook his fist under Bill's nose and stomped towards the house. Bill made an obscene gesture at his father's back and strode off in the opposite direction. To an observer like me it was an absurd scene—absurd but for some reason not laughable.

I turned away from the window; John had come into the room. 'Success?' I asked.

'Yes. No trouble. Your signal has top priority.'

'Thanks. That was good of you.' I shook my head as he gestured towards my empty glass. 'Tell me what Crowne had to say.'

'Not much actually, but he gave me a very good lunch.'

I perched myself on the arm of my chair; I didn't want to have to heave my frame again from its cushioned depths. John topped up his whisky and sat down opposite me.

'Crowne said you'd be interested to hear about a lady called Dolly Bell-Pauson.'

'I am indeed. Do you know her?'

'Me? No! Why ever should I?'

His amazement was genuine and I had to explain that Dolly had a penchant for collecting people associated with Hong Kong. I mentioned Monica and Jake Dasser and the Colonial Secretary's daughter, and Sally. John frowned. He seemed perturbed.

'I had no idea. Crowne just said she had Hong Kong connections. I do know Monica Cayton. She's a friend of Sally's. As a matter of fact she's dining here tonight. So's the other girl. But who's Dasser? You've got to remember this is only my second visit to Hong Kong since Dad was made Governor.'

Hiding my delight that I should soon be seeing Monica — I had known Howard was to be a guest but he had said nothing of his niece and this was a bonus indeed — I told John about Jake Dasser. He wasn't really interested; he was too concerned for Sally.

'Crowne gave me the impression the Bell-Pauson woman wasn't a very salubrious character. I don't like to think of Sally — ' He sighed. 'Oh, well! What I was to tell you, Keith, is that Dolly Bell-Pauson is dead. She appears to have taken an overdose of sleeping pills and the verdict will be accidental death. However, the house had been thoroughly searched.

There were no private papers anywhere, no engagement diary, no address book. And the major who lives next door saw a young Chinese leaving the Bell-Pauson house early in the morning with a heavy briefcase. The major, incidentally, has gone for a holiday in the country.'

Personally I thought that Major Minton should have been moved out of Montagu Square when he first received threats; but Crowne's decision to leave him there had been justified. Nothing had happened to the major. It was Dolly who had been killed, and almost two weeks after that party of hers. Why now? Why wait so long? Suicide, right after her questioning by the police, would have had a more logical face. But no, her disposal had been delayed until the Peter Krail incident was closed, and she was once more leading an apparently normal life. It didn't make sense to me.

Crowne wasn't of the same opinion; he always expected things to make sense, some sort of sense. There was an addendum to the message he had sent me.

John said: 'Crowne's happy about the way things are going. I'm to tell you he thinks you're goading the dragon very prettily.'

'How kind of him.'

There was an edge to my words. It hadn't occurred to me that I might be responsible, albeit indirectly, for Dolly's death. Yet, from that remark, Crowne seemed to think I was. But what had I done for which Dolly might be blamed? The obvious answer was gate-crashing her party, but that was past history, unless – My mind raced. Dolly had told the Special Branch about her gate-crasher, probably because she thought I was some kind of policeman sniffing after drugs, but maybe she hadn't admitted my presence to her masters. Perhaps it was only later – at Howard Farthingale's party? – that Keith Sterling, a suspect character in Hong Kong, had been connected with the 'friend of the Cunninghams' in London. I remembered my conversation with Jake. It hadn't been exactly private.

'I must go. The guests will be arriving and my wife will wonder what's happened to me.' John drained his whisky and stood up. 'If you want to stay here and brood on Charles Crowne's problems, by all means do, Keith. No one will interrupt you.'

I smiled and shook my head. 'No, thanks. I'll come with you.'

'Okay.'

And as if to signal that we had completed Crowne's business and could now enjoy a normal evening, he began to talk about the wedding. Thank God he had waved me through the door ahead of him so that he didn't see my face.

'. . . extraordinary to think that this time next week my kid sister'll be Mrs Rouge.'

'Mrs Rouge?'

It was astounding how mildly I managed to enunciate the two words. But John was already in the middle of his next sentence and was puzzled by my interjection.

'Yes. What else?'

'I thought – as she was marrying Bill – she was going to be Mrs Reddington.'

'No, no! Rouge is the family name. At least it's the name the old boy gave when he first appeared in England after World War II. Ten years later – when he got his title – he became Lord Reddington.'

'How stupid of me! I should have realized.'

'Not all that stupid.' John gave a wry laugh. 'Much as he hates it, people always refer to poor Bill as "Lord Reddington's son", so you can't be the first to think of him as Bill Reddington.'

I nodded dumbly. Thoughts were snowing my mind. ROUGE TO PLAY. Bill Rouge. In spite of what John said, everyone knew that Bill was Bill Rouge, except me. Peter Krail had known. It was Bill that Peter had been pointing to when he scratched Rouge on the bottom of that box in which he kept his spare car keys. As for Crowne, he must have assumed I understood the reference on the torn piece of paper that had cost Peter his life. And the pseudo-hostess at The Toothless Dragon had naturally spoken of Bill as Mr Rouge. God, how ironical! What a fool I had been! What an incompetent fool! Poor Macfar, standing to attention. What a balls-up I had made!

And I could blame no one but myself for it. No one had tried to deceive me. Bill Rouge was just one of those chaps that people always called by their first names. He was Bill or Lord Reddington's son or Sally's fiancé. Suddenly I was back in Crowne's office and Crowne was saying: 'The

Governor's daughter, Sally Milment, is engaged to old Reddington's boy. You'll be in Hong Kong for the wedding.'

The wedding! Depending on what happened at 6 Hua Bai on Thursday there might be no wedding. Perhaps Bill had never intended – He had met Sally at Dolly Bell-Pauson's, though he chose to forget the fact. He had insisted that the marriage should take place in Hong Kong, rather than London as Sally would have preferred. Now, having got his way, he was nervous and on edge, making Sally miserable and seemingly quarrelling with his father. It could be pre-wedding jitters. But I thought it more likely that he was worrying about Thursday rather than Saturday. Nevertheless, I could have sworn that Bill was as much in love with Sally as she with him. What's more, unless he'd flown in secretly – which was hard to believe – he hadn't been in Hong Kong when the 'incident' at 10 Chou Nol had taken place. In God's name what, I asked myself, had Peter meant by ROUGE TO PLAY?

Followed by John Milment I walked into the splendid drawing-room of Government House. I was welcomed by H.E., allowed myself to be pecked on the cheek by Lady Milment, kissed Sally – and shook hands with Bill Rouge. Somehow I made conversation, answering their questions about my injuries. I couldn't look Bill in the eye. Across the room I saw Monica, in a pale green dress, talking to Lord Reddington. But for once the sight of her did nothing for me. It was going to be a long, long evening.

Nine

I could have enjoyed the Milments' dinner party had the circumstances been different, but tonight I had too much on my mind. I found myself detecting hidden meanings in the most casual remarks, being suspicious of behaviour that was absolutely normal and rudely lapsing into inattention as I struggled with my thoughts. Luckily my battered face and cracked ribs would excuse my solecisms, but I had to watch myself.

It was a largish party. Discounting immediate family, I judged there were about forty guests and they were a mixed bag. Some were easy to place as friends of Sally and Bill, though it was by no means clear whether Howard Farthingale fitted into this category or was there to represent the Colonial Secretary. There were the usual senior Hong Kong officials – the Commander, British Forces and the Commissioner of Police, for instance. Others were from the business community, and a couple of Trade Commissioners were doubtless delighted at the opportunity to meet Lord Reddington. Some I never placed, but two rather puzzling ladies of exalted age turned out to be His Excellency's aunts, come from England for the wedding; I should have guessed.

However inharmonious the people might seem, there was nothing discordant about the party itself. It was a mixture of protocol and informality, just right for the occasion. I said as much to Celia Milment, John's wife, a pretty dark-haired girl, who was sitting on my left at dinner.

'That's thanks to my mother-in-law,' she said at once. 'She's a wonderful woman. You can't produce this sort of result without flair and effort, and she's got enormous flair and takes infinite pains.'

'You sound fond of her.'

'I am. I consider myself extremely lucky. I couldn't have

picked a nicer, more helpful mother-in-law. Bill will agree with me later.'

Later? What did she mean by that? I glanced along the table to where Bill sat with Sally. Sally was chattering away in a bright, nervous fashion. Bill was concentrating on his food. Neither of them looked very happy, and it wasn't just my imagination. Before dinner I had avoided Bill but I had talked with Sally. She was wearing more make-up than usual but it didn't completely hide the red rims of her eyes. She had clearly been crying. I wished I didn't like them both; in my job it's easier if you don't like people.

'It's a pity Bill isn't going to be an ambassador,' I said. 'Then Lady M could give him and Sally all sorts of useful tips.'

'But, heavens, how he'd hate it!' Celia's laugh derided my suggestion. 'It's definitely not his thing.'

'John will enjoy it though, and so will you?'

'Yes – if we make it. There's a long way to go yet.'

'What's to stop you?'

She shrugged. 'On the face of it, nothing. John's doing splendidly. But – things can happen.'

'Such as?'

I dabbled my fingers in the finger bowl and dried them on my table napkin; the late asparagus had been delicious. I waited while the fish was set in front of me and turned again to Celia.

'Such as?' I repeated.

She didn't answer directly. 'Diplomats are even more vulnerable than politicians. I know of at least one man whose expectations have been disappointed, and through no fault of his own whatsoever.' Her voice was cool. 'His sister married an eminent scientist, and three children later the scientist defected. That was virtually the end of the diplomat's career. It was certainly the end of promotion for him. So you see – it's not wise to count on reaching the top.'

'No. I suppose not.'

I was shaken. Surely Celia wasn't implying that Bill Rouge . . . She gave me a small smile. Was she a little surprised that I hadn't said that such a thing could never happen to John Milment? But the conventional reply had stuck in my throat, with the forkful of sole that suddenly tasted of sawdust. I'd only just taken in the fact that not only Sally but the whole Milment family was at risk if Bill went through with the wedding and then – Then what? I hadn't the faintest idea. Heaving a gusty sigh, I again attacked my fish.

'You sound unhappy.'

All the while I was talking to Celia Milment I had been conscious of Monica Cayton sitting on my right; Lady Milment had been kind to me when she made her seating plan. Monica hadn't been so kind. As soon as we sat down she had turned to her other neighbour, and these were the first words she had spoken to me during dinner. Nor had she been particularly friendly earlier, when I had interrupted a conversation about Chinese painting she was having with Lord Reddington. I had to remind myself that, though she had been constantly in my thoughts since Dolly Bell-Pauson's party, we had only met once, at Howard's. Yet she imagined she owed me a favour and she had made a date with me for Wednesday night . . . I was a little hurt by her attitude.

'How could I be unhappy when you've promised to have dinner with me on Wednesday?'

'Oh, Keith, I'm most dreadfully sorry. Something's come up at the University and I can't make Wednesday now. I was going to phone you.'

I wanted to believe her but I've got a suspicious nature and, disappointed, I was prepared to accept that she had never intended to keep the date. I had more or less blackmailed her into it anyway.

'Keith, would Thursday be okay instead?'

Thursday? Immediately I banished my suspicions. She hadn't deliberately broken the date; on the contrary she had suggested the very next night. Then I remembered. Could she conceivably know that I had another engagement? Much as I wanted Monica to myself for an evening, I knew I could do no less than try to play with Rouge on Thursday.

Against my will I heard myself say: 'Please do forgive me, but Thursday's impossible.'

'I'm sorry.'

Her wide grey eyes smiled into mine and, while I swallowed my emotions, the chap on her right collected her in conversation. I willed every curse on him but it made no difference. The moment had passed.

114

On my other side Celia Milment said: 'Have you met Lord Reddington yet?'

'I've kissed hands,' I said, still swearing to myself at the way things had turned out with Monica.

Celia smiled. 'I agree. He does rather give the impression he's royalty.' Her smile widened. 'About to send for the PM to tell him the Chancellor of the Exchequer must be made redundant. But he's really an old dear. He's been very kind to John and me.'

I gave her a doubting look. 'I distrust all rich and powerful men. Maybe it's because I envy them.'

'Well, don't envy Lord Reddington. He's the most unhappy man I've ever known.'

'I find that difficult to believe.' Forgetting my personal problems, I gave Celia my full attention; her certainty had startled me. 'Do you mean it?'

'I wouldn't have said it otherwise.' Her clear, authoritative tone reminded me of Lady Milment. She lowered her voice. 'You know about his wife, don't you?'

'I thought she was dead.'

'She is, yes. But she was an invalid for years before she died. She had some strange collagen complaint, unbelievably painful. She had to live on drugs and in the end she took an overdose. That's partly why Lord Reddington was so furious when Bill got into that trouble at Cambridge. He hates and detests any kind of drug.'

There was a burst of laughter across the table, disturbing our quiet confidences, but Celia was happy to have made her point; Lord R had his worries, like all of us. It was Bill's worries, however, that interested me. I could guess what the 'trouble at Cambridge' had been, but I should need the details. It might be useful to know how far he had penetrated the drug scene.

I cut carefully into my steak. The story that had caused the merriment was being repeated for the benefit of those who hadn't heard it. I laughed with everyone else, though I hadn't taken in a word. I was asking myself why, if the thing Peter Krail had got on to really was some drug connection, the *taipan* at The Toothless Dragon had been indifferent to the yarn I had spun him. Surely he would have thought I was too close to the truth for comfort. Yet the impression I had got was amusement and . . .

'Can you swim, Keith?'

'Sorry. What did you say?'

'I asked if you could swim.'

With an almighty effort I focused on the question. Monica was laughing at me. I pretended to be considering the matter.

'Yes, I can swim – but not up to Olympic standards.'

'You were miles away,' she said reproachfully. 'That doesn't do much for my ego.'

'I apologize humbly. Forgive me and tell me why you want to know.'

'Because I refuse to take anyone who can't swim out on a boat, and I was wondering if you'd like to come sailing with me on Sunday.'

'Monica, I qualify. I swear to it. I can sail and if I turn the boat over I can swim. You've got a date.'

We made arrangements. Monica would get a Yacht Club boat and we would meet there. She would bring the food and I would be responsible for the drink. It sounded as if it could be a blissful day. But Sunday was a whole week away and I knew I should be a fool to count the hours. Thursday had to be got through first, with whatever that might bring, and the wedding on Saturday. I wasn't optimistic.

Two o'clock in the morning and I lay on the bed, brooding over the signal from Crowne that John Milment had brought me. I had deciphered it as soon as I got back from Government House. It was, as I expected, a reply to the one I had sent after Howard's party but it wasn't very illuminating; it either confirmed what I already knew or raised more questions than it answered.

I read it through again, for the umpteenth time. Howard Farthingale had told me he had inherited some money from his mother's sister and this Crowne confirmed; the sister had married a rich business man and the amount had been substantial. Howard could well afford to live in the style he affected, surrounded by beautiful things. Joan Hackard's innuendo was totally without foundation.

She had been right, however, about Bill – at least about his finances. He had a healthy overdraft and a fair number of debts. Nobody pressed him because he was Lord Reddington's son, even though, according to Crowne, he was living on a small income left him by his mother and received nothing from his father. It seemed that after Bill had been given a suspended sentence for the pot-smoking incident at Cambridge there had been a family row, and Bill had left home. That was more than two years ago, and the breach was said to have been healed recently – by Lady Milment. I had my doubts. From what I had seen yesterday evening, the breach between Reddington and Rouge was still wide open.

I winced. The request for information on Bill *Reddington* in my last signal had been duly noted. 'Assume slip. Please confirm.' I would most certainly confirm. There was no need for anyone but myself to know what a fool I had been. I didn't want to become the butt of a joke told as a horrid warning to SIS recruits.

I turned my mind to more pleasant thoughts and reread what Crowne had to say of Monica. Monica Hilda Cayton had been born in Hong Kong twenty-six years ago – so Joan Hackard had been right about that too. I was surprised; I shouldn't have thought that Monica would have bothered to lie about her age. Her father was Joshua Cayton, deceased Scottish business man; her mother, also deceased, had been born Hilda Farthingale. Suddenly the connection hit me.

I pushed myself up on my elbows till I was sitting upright. I stared at my reflection in the mirror on the opposite wall and saw the wide grin spread across my face. Mental arithmetic wasn't my strong point, but this was a simple sum. I should have done it before. Monica had been born in February; Howard and his twin sister had been born in August; Howard was only forty-two now. Whichever way one counted, when Monica was conceived her mother had been at most fourteen and ten months. Which must have been one hell of a shock for the missionary Farthingales. They must have been very grateful to Joshua Cayton for marrying their daughter. And, remembering Joan Hackard's venomous tongue, I was no longer surprised that Monica lied about her age.

The question was whether she had lied about anything else. Crowne had had her story checked as carefully as he could. After all, it was Monica who had taken Peter to Dolly Bell-Pauson's party, and it was on leaving it that Peter had been killed; but the actual time and place of the hit-and-run didn't have to be significant. If Peter had gone straight from Heathrow to the house of the lepidopterist where Monica was staying, and from there by taxi to Dolly's, his departure from the party might have been the enemy's first opportunity to attack. What did require explanation was Peter's telephone call. It was difficult to understand why, if Peter had trusted Monica, he had been so very circumspect when talking to 'his sister in Wimbledon'. But then Peter had never been inclined to trust anyone overmuch.

Simultaneously I sighed and yawned. I was tired. It was going to be a short night anyhow, and at the moment all I was doing was wasting sleeping time. But sleep didn't come easily. Three-quarters of an hour after I had put out the light I was still awake, thoughts bombarding my brain; uppermost among them was the realization that today I had to find Hua Bai.

And find Hua Bai I did, 6 Hua Bai. In the event it was a very simple business though, being me, I didn't do it the simplest way.

To tell the truth I was a little nervous, though I didn't admit it. I told myself it was sensible to take precautions; there was no point in waking the dragon if it could be avoided, not after Teng's warning. So, when I left the office at lunch-time, I didn't take the car and drive over to Kowloon. Instead I made straight for the Hilton.

It was a hot, humid day, the temperature in the low nineties, and I would gladly have lingered in the air-conditioned rooftop bar, sipping a long gin and watching the bustling activity of Victoria Harbour. But I allowed myself only ten minutes before I looked at my watch as if to check on an appointment and made for the Gents.

No one seemed to notice me. At this hour the bar was doing a flourishing trade and there was a lot of coming and going as people met for pre-luncheon drinks. I was just another European, probably a business man to judge by my conservative clothes. There was nothing eye-catching about me. I wore beige trousers, a white shirt with long sleeves and a nondescript tie. I had left my jacket in the office but I carried a cheap plastic briefcase, the kind of thing that some firms use as give-aways to their better customers.

The Gents was full, a row of backs at the urinals, and the

wash-basins being put to good use. Three or four of the men seemed to know each other and there was a certain amount of badinage. The cubicles were all occupied but someone had just flushed a pan and I stationed myself in front of the door. As he came out, I went in.

While I was snicking the lock with my right hand, my left hand was already pulling off my tie. I sat on the seat and unzipped the briefcase. I had to be quick, but not too quick; it would be best if the clientèle outside had changed before I emerged.

Less than five minutes later I worked the flush and came out. I didn't recognize anyone I had seen there earlier. And I hoped that no one would recognize me. I now wore a loose green silk shirt over my white one, the sleeves of both rolled above the elbows. I was tieless but had a yellow sweat-cloth knotted round my neck. A floppy brimmed hat, such as small children wear on the beach, was perched carelessly on my head; the mirror above the wash-basins confirmed that the hat was dead straight and tilted over my nose. Sun-glasses hid my eyes. A camera hung over my shoulder. I was ready to go.

Not seeming to hurry but with a fair turn of speed, I made for the lifts. I didn't want the man who had gone into the cubicle I had used to come dashing after me with my abandoned briefcase. He was welcome to it, and to my copy of the *Hong Kong Standard* which was all it contained. I went down in the express lift, through the lobby and out of the main entrance. Here I spent an uneasy couple of minutes waiting for a taxi; the Hilton's a popular hotel and the last thing I wanted was to run into someone I knew, like Jake Dasser or Bill Rouge. But my luck held.

Safe in a cab I told the driver to go to Kowloon. To be in strict tourist character I should have got him to take me down to the ferry and gone across in one of the Star boats to Tsim Sha Tsui, but I couldn't spare the time. Howard Farthingale would be expecting me back in the office before too long. So we raced through the tunnel, which at least gave me a chance to study the traffic behind us. Nobody had followed me from the Hilton, as far as I could tell.

'Kowloon's a big place, boss. Where you wanna be dropped?'

'Do you know Phai Lip Street?'

'I sure do. I used to live near there. That was before they pulled down that whole area and rebuilt it, about ten years ago.'

I took a deep breath. Of all the taxi-drivers I could have chosen, here was one who would know about Hua Bai. But I had chanced on him too late, when I no longer needed his help.

'Anywhere on Phai Lip will do.'

'Okay.'

As I expected he put me down at the far end of the street and overcharged me, though not unreasonably. I didn't argue. I watched while he drove off, stopped after fifty yards to pick up a couple of Chinese and went on his way. I wished I had met him days ago.

Phai Lip was a modern street of shops and restaurants and bars, above which was layer on layer of apartments, bright with washing hung from poles. It had its complement of traffic and neon signs and beating sound and visitors from every corner of the world, but it wasn't as garish or as glittering as Nathan Road. And somewhere near the middle of its length there was a gap between the high buildings. Here, overshadowed by trees, was an ancient temple of Hung Shing – god of the South Seas and a weather prophet – which had been carefully preserved. Beside the temple there was the entrance to a lane.

If Howard Farthingale hadn't warned me I might have walked past the end of it without a glance but, knowing what I was looking for, I had no problem. The lane was called Temple Lane and on the map it was marked as a cul-de-sac, so that the reason for the thin two-way trickle of pedestrians making use of it wasn't at first self-evident. However, a tourist wandering down the lane would have found, as I did, about twenty yards along on the right-hand side, an arcade. Its name, according to the street sign, was Temple Arcade.

Like the Hung Shing Temple, the arcade is old, though not nearly as old as the temple itself. My guess was that it had originally served as a covered market. Why it had been saved when the rebuilding and modernization of the district took place I had no idea. Perhaps the land belonged to Hung Shing. At any rate, providing I had at last discovered what had once been Hua Bai, I was happy to give him the credit.

I stood at the threshold of Temple Arcade and made a great show of adjusting my camera. I took a couple of general shots. This gave me the perfect excuse to size up what lay in front of me. I wasn't sure I liked it.

The arcade was a narrow walking street which ran parallel to Phai Lip directly behind Hung Shing Temple. It wasn't long and, unusual for Hong Kong, on neither side were the buildings more than two storeys high. On the ground level there were the usual Chinese shops, a bar, and one of those anonymous-looking restaurants that often turn out to be both select and expensive. On the next floor were apartments, doubtless housing a miscellany of affairs. The arcade was clean and quite smart, neither too full of people nor too harsh with noise. But it was a dead-end, which meant it could easily be turned into a trap.

That was my first impression. I didn't modify it much as, pausing to gaze idly into a shop-window or take a photograph, I strolled down one side and up the other. I spent a full minute studying a display of jade – and the reflection in its window of the art shop opposite, which seemed to be somewhat unimaginatively called 'Temple Gallery'. I took a photograph of two old men intent on a game of mah-jong; they were photogenic enough to tempt any camera buff and they were sitting outside an incense shop by the side door of the gallery. The door had a metal '6' pinned on it. There was also a plate with the name S. Wang. Unlike the plates on the other doors, which advertised such trades as palmistry, astrology, tailoring and leather work, there was nothing to indicate Mr Wang's profession, but I assumed he was the art dealer. If so, and if 6 Hua Bai was indeed an art gallery, the cover I had chosen for my search had been almost too true to be good.

In fact, the gallery had a dead, shut look. There was an easel in the window supporting a large acrylic painting, the sort of thing that no one would bother to steal and which I doubted Mr Wang expected to sell. There was no light visible in the shop and the blind behind the door was drawn. I tried the handle.

As I had expected the door was locked. And I was standing there, wondering about back entrances through Hung Shing's garden – the gallery was immediately behind the temple – when a shadow appeared on the glass in front of me. I turned slowly, warily, the adrenalin pumping. The shadow was small, but it could be dangerous.

'You are looking for Mr Wang, sir?'

'Am I? Well – I don't rightly know.'

My smile was as broad as the American accent that would have made Jake Dasser wince. The Chinese girl smiled in return, reluctantly; the smile didn't reach her eyes. She was slim and pretty, with a perfect skin. I didn't think I had seen her before, but . . .

'A compatriot of mine told me about Temple Gallery. He said it had some interesting things and I was hoping to have a look-see. Perhaps pick up a little painting – nothing expensive, mind you – just a memento of Hong Kong to take home to the States next week. When does your Mr Wang open shop?'

'The gallery is closed until October.'

'October! I'll be back in Colorado way before then. I – I suppose Mr Wang wouldn't let me have a kind of private view. You couldn't ask him for me, could you? Is he upstairs?'

'No, no, certainly not.' The girl was rattled by my persistence. 'Mr Wang's not here. He's in Peking, visiting his family. And the gallery is closed. I told you.'

'Until October, you said. Yes. Too bad. These long vacations can play havoc with a business. Ah well, thanks.'

I grinned at her, touched my floppy hat in a mock salute and sauntered off. When I reached the end of the arcade I glanced back over my shoulder. The girl was standing outside the gallery, watching me go. She was still clutching the red and white poster – its paint not yet dry – that she had so unsuccessfully tried to prevent me from reading.

Mr Wang might or might not be in Peking, but the poster advertised an Exhibition of Contemporary Chinese Art at the Temple Gallery, Grand Opening at 8.00 p.m., Thursday – the day that ROUGE was TO PLAY. I seemed to have found 6 Hua Bai all right.

Ten

'But she wants to see you.'

I looked at Ian Hackard with exasperation. It was six o'clock on Thursday evening. I had just finished some work for Howard and was about to go home. I had ample time to bath, change, have a drink and get to Temple Arcade (or Hua Bai, whichever you liked to call it) before the Exhibition of Contemporary Chinese Art was due to open – but not if I had to go to the hospital en route.

'Joan wants to see you.'

'So you said, Ian. But –'

'Don't you understand? She's been desperately ill. She nearly didn't make it. This is the first day she's been allowed to have visitors, other than me, and she's asked for you. How can I tell her you refuse to come?'

'I'm not refusing!' I was getting angry; where Joan was concerned Ian could be both stupid and stubborn. 'I'll go tomorrow. She'll be feeling even better and –'

'You've got a date tonight, I suppose. With some girl.' He leered at me. 'Won't she wait for you, then?'

'It isn't a girl. I have to –'

'I don't care who it is. Nobody's as important as Joan, not at this moment. Keith, please!' He was leaning over my desk. His great height was pushing his face close to mine; his breath was faintly sour. 'You must come. The doctor wasn't keen on her having visitors so soon but Joan was determined and he gave in. She really wants to see you.'

'Ian, why me? Surely one of her woman friends –'

'Joan doesn't have woman friends. It's you she wants, no one else. I don't know why.'

The words came out flat, expressionless. Ian Hackard wasn't a fool; he saw his wife through rose-coloured spectacles but he wasn't completely blinded by them. Either way he couldn't believe that Joan, having just unburdened herself of a child,

123

was already panting after another man. There are limits, even for a nympho. I couldn't believe it myself. Why then was she being so insistent? And why me? Somehow I didn't think it was anything to do with sex.

'Okay, Ian. I'm sorry. Of course my date can wait. I didn't mean to be difficult. You and Joan have been terribly kind to me since I got to Hong Kong and I'm not unappreciative. But you took me by surprise. I should have realized that after what Joan's been through she's likely to be – to be subject to whims.'

I was sending loud and clear, and Ian seemed to get the message. When we reached the hospital there was no nonsense about him staying in the room to hear what Joan and I had to say to each other. He went in alone first, leaving me to wait in the corridor, clutching my sheaf of flowers done up in plastic. Two or three minutes later he reappeared, a smear of lipstick by his mouth. 'Joan's ready for you now. She's delighted you've come. I'll go along and see Baby and you two can have a chat.' Beaming as if he were conferring a great favour on me, he urged me into the room and shut the door behind me.

'Hallo, Joan. How are you? You look wonderful.'

I lied. Joan owed her normal attractiveness to her chic and her vitality, and at the moment she was bereft of both. Supported by pillows like a doll on a pile of cushions, her hair dull with sweat, her make-up smudged and an egg-stain on her bed-jacket, she had a certain raffish air; but only her eyes seemed alive. I had never liked her so much. Bending, I kissed her on the cheek.

'I brought you some flowers, but I see you're surrounded with them.'

It was a pretty trite remark, but that didn't explain Joan's reaction. To my horror tears welled in her eyes and trickled, one on either side of her nose, past her mouth and down her chin. She made no sound but when I stretched out a hand to ring the bell for the nurse, her fingers closed over my wrist and her nails dug into me until I winced. She wiped away her tears with the back of her arm, leaving a smear of lipstick on the sleeve of her bed-jacket, and said hoarsely:

'Oh, Sterling, thank God they didn't kill you!'

'Why, Joan dear, I never knew you cared.'

'Don't mock me! And don't give me any guff about being

mugged either. I know what happened. I put some stuff in your drink at The Toothless Dragon. It made you feel sick, didn't it? You had to go to the loo and they grabbed you, and when you wouldn't answer the *taipan*'s questions they beat you up. They could have killed you.'

It was so near the truth that she couldn't be guessing. Perhaps too near. She had admitted doctoring my drink but she could still be trying to trick me into disobeying Teng's orders. I decided to play it safe. I pulled up a chair beside the bed, sat down and took her hand.

'Sweetie, you've been having nightmares. Don't you remember? Your baby started and you were whisked away. I didn't leave The Toothless Dragon for ages after that. You couldn't –'

'Listen!' It was a fierce hiss. 'I've very little energy and the nurse will be coming in soon. We've not got much time.' Joan closed her eyes tight and opened them again; there was perspiration on her upper lip. 'For more than a year I've been working for a Mr Jones. That's what he told me to call him, but the name means nothing. He's Chinese, I'm sure, though I've never seen him. He phones his orders. Keith, believe me, I never meant it to be this way, but I like good clothes, jewellery, expensive scent, all the luxuries. Ian has only his pay and he helps an invalid sister.' She stopped, momentarily exhausted.

'Why are you telling me this?' I asked gently.

'Because you can help me. You can, can't you, Keith?' She was biting her lower lip to keep herself from crying. 'Please, I want – out. I'm scared. I've got in too deep.'

'Joan!' I squeezed her hand in sympathy. 'You may regret this – this confession when you're really well again, you know. There'll still be beautiful things to tempt you. Supposing I forgot about it, until we can have dinner together. How would that be?'

'Oh, Christ! They've bent you too, have they?' She pulled her hand from mine and began to weep uncontrollably. 'What's going to happen to me – and poor, bloody Ian?'

There was a tap on the door. A nurse came in, gave one look at Joan and asked me to leave. I cursed beneath my breath. Joan had convinced me she wasn't putting on an act but I didn't believe she knew anything important. Yet I couldn't take the risk that I was wrong.

Somehow I managed to reassure her, and placate the nurse. I was awarded five minutes' grace. I tried to make the most of it but it was difficult to control Joan. Now that I had agreed to help she wanted promises, promises that even Crowne couldn't have kept. I could get her out, in the sense that I could arrange for Ian to be posted; in fact, this would happen automatically as soon as I made a report. But there was no hope of a cross-posting. Ian would be recalled to London, where Joan would be debriefed and the Hackards' future decided. Ian would have to know what she had done, and it was absurd to suggest it wouldn't affect his career; Celia Milment would have scorned such an idea. Joan, however, seemed to think all things were possible for me. And I promised; I wouldn't be around when she discovered what my promises were worth.

The other trouble was that she wanted to rid herself of the whole story. There could have been grains of interest for me in how the first approach was made to her, how she was told to bring certain people together, how she gave references for Chinese she had never seen, how she once housed an illegal immigrant . . . But I hadn't the time, and this really wasn't what I wanted.

What I really wanted were hard facts – definite pointers to the Chinese set-up and its purposes and the names of other Westerners who might be involved. I got neither, only a spew of suspicions. She even produced the one about Howard Farthingale living beyond his means. I didn't bother to shoot it down. She seemed to have it in for Howard; she swore that a few weeks after the illegal immigrant left her house she had seen him again – in Howard's kitchen.

All this was useless to me and I was glad when the nurse reappeared. Ignoring Joan's protests, I stood up, told her to trust me and not worry, kissed her goodbye. I was at the door before I remembered Ian. He had to have some explanation.

'Joan,' I said, 'I'm going to tell Ian that since it was you and your baby that broke up the party on Saturday night, you felt a bit responsible for my mugging and wanted to see for yourself that I was all right.'

It was weak but the best I could do, and Ian accepted it; he was prepared to accept anything that showed Joan in a good light. But as a penance for usurping the time she should have given to him I had to 'pay a visit to Baby', which meant more delay. By now I was running very late.

I had planned to be at Hua Bai a half-hour before the Exhibition of Contemporary Chinese Art had its Grand Opening. In the event it was almost eight o'clock when the taxi dropped me in Phai Lip Street. I hurried back towards the Temple of Hung Shing.

Phai Lip was busy, heavy with traffic and bustling with pedestrians. There were several parked cars, though parking was theoretically illegal. Progress along the thronging pavement was slow and it was impossible to walk in the gutter. I was hot and sticky with sweat, the virtues of a hasty shower already dissipated, and my attention was concentrated on getting to the arcade. If it hadn't been for the two boys I might have walked straight past Macfar and the Government House Rolls.

The boys were small. They looked about six. Probably their only crime was an excessive interest in the official car, but Macfar had taken umbrage. He stuck his head out of the window and emitted a roar of such sergeant-major proportions that it carried above the general noise level – which was saying a lot. The boys fled, dodging the arms of a sailor who pretended to catch them, running between a Chinese and his girl-friend, knocking against the cameras of a rotund tourist. In thirty second the boys had disappeared, leaving behind them a wake of amusement, unshared by Macfar.

From the shelter I had sought in a doorway, I watched Macfar close the car window and resettle himself in his seat. He started to read a newspaper. I waited until he seemed engrossed then, keeping to the far side of him, I attached myself to a European couple and walked boldly past the Rolls. Macfar never glanced in my direction.

Once in Temple Lane I hesitated. Since I had no idea what was likely to happen tonight, my plans were nebulous, but such as they were they had already gone awry. I had intended to get here early enough to study all the arrivals at the gallery; I was confident that Bill Rouge would be among them. But, from the presence of Macfar, it was clear that at least Bill had forestalled me – and God knew who else. Certainly, if Bill was alone, he wouldn't have come in the Government House Rolls with the number one driver.

Controlling my tension, I strolled down Temple Lane and turned into the arcade. It looked much the same as at lunchtime on Tuesday. One or two of the shops were shut but there were more people about and lights, not strictly necessary, were on in many places, giving the arcade a festive air.

I went into the bar, bought myself a gin, and took it to a table by the window. From here I had an excellent view of Temple Gallery and Mr Wang's apartment above it. Upstairs the curtains were drawn, which they hadn't been on Tuesday, and lines of light suggested that someone was at home. Downstairs the exhibition had opened. The door was standing wide and the gallery was brightly lit, but there wasn't a great deal of activity; the Grand Opening seemed to be something of a flop.

However, it was still early, not yet much past eight, and there was a whet of gin left in my glass when three Chinese youths paused in front of the gallery. They wore jeans and multi-coloured shirts and, as they turned to go in, they removed slips of cards from their shirt pockets with almost identical gestures. Evidently tickets of some kind were required. Unless they were available at the door this was a nuisance.

While I considered the point I ordered another gin. And one of the bar-girls detached herself from the British sergeant she had been sitting with, and came across to me.

'Hallo, you by yourself, Mr American?'

'However did you guess?' I said.

She giggled, showing a lot of gum. She wasn't the prettiest bar-girl I had ever seen. I wasn't surprised the soldier hadn't been responsive. The waiter brought my gin and hovered at the table. He knew the form.

'Bring the lady a drink,' I said.

'Champagne.' She sat herself down.

'No. It'll be pink water anyway, and I can't afford champagne prices.'

'But you're an American? You're not British?'

She pronounced it 'Blitish' and I didn't find the implication very flattering. However, after her disappointment with the sergeant, I could scarcely blame her.

'I'm a poor American,' I said absently.

Across the street a middle-aged couple – she with blue hair

and a scarlet trouser suit, he in a flowered shirt bulging over his waist-band – were studying the painting in the gallery window. The third-rate acrylic work I had seen on Tuesday had been removed from the easel and replaced by something that glowed with colour. It must have convinced them, for they went in – only to come out again, bristling with indignation. Tickets, it seemed, were not merely required; they were essential. I frowned. I might have trouble bluffing my way in and I didn't want trouble. I wanted to be as inconspicuous as possible.

The bar-girl was giggling to herself. 'No poor Americans,' she said.

I didn't bother to correct her. And, though she may have been full of misinformation, she wasn't stupid. She had perceived my interest in the gallery. When the waiter had brought her a green peppermint-smelling drink, for which I had to pay a silly number of HK dollars, she pulled her chair close to mine.

'You wanna go to Mr Wang's party?' she asked softly.

'I wouldn't mind,' I said, 'but I think it's by invitation. In other words, tickets are needed.'

Without speaking she dipped her hand into the cleft between her breasts and extracted two slips of card. She held them flat on the table so that I could see what they were but couldn't snatch them from her. She made her point directly.

'Fifty dollars – American.'

I roared with laughter. 'Don't be silly, hon.'

'Fifty dollars – American. We go to Mr Wang's. After I take you home with me and give you supper and good time. Fifty dollars.'

I could only beat her down to twenty British pounds, which was all I had on me. She had seen the gleam in my eyes when she produced the tickets, but she was shrewd enough to know I didn't fancy her and wasn't going to take her up on the supper and the good time. Anyway, the money would go on the expense account.

The bargain was struck at an opportune moment. A group of tourists – twenty to twenty-five of them – had erupted into the arcade and were being rounded up in front of Temple Gallery by a harassed Chinese. They looked like a bunch of middle-aged, middle prosperous, middle Americans, but two or three of them were younger. I would be acceptable. It was the bar-girl who would be exotic among the sturdy country flowers. Yet I had to take her. I didn't want her becoming too curious about me.

'Come along, hon. Let's go.'

As we crossed the street and joined the untidy queue slowly entering the gallery I noticed a letter-writer near the entrance to the incense shop. I hadn't been able to see her from my seat in the bar, but from where she was sitting, with an upturned keg for a table, she had an excellent view of the arrivals at Mr Wang's. And it seemed to me highly improbable that she was doing any letter-writing business.

'Tell me,' I said, 'that letter-writer over there, does she make a reasonable living? In the outlying villages I could understand it, but here in Kowloon where you have good schools – '

The girl shrugged. 'There are still lots of people who don't read or write, peasants who came from China in the fifties. But I not seen her here before.'

This was what I wanted to know, though it wasn't the answer I would have preferred. I could feel the letter-writer's eyes on my back. She was taking far too much interest in us.

'She's not a friend of yours like Mr Wang, then?'

'Mr Wang's an old man, not my friend.'

'But he gave you tickets for this exhibition.'

She shook her head. 'Mr Wang's in China, visiting his family. Everybody in the arcade knows that. So a girl comes round to explain why the gallery'll be open tonight. Mr Wang has kindly given permission for an exhibition. She offered tickets and I took two.'

'Which shows what a clever girl you are.'

Giggling, she said: 'Why you want to know all this?'

'Oh – curiosity. I'm an inquisitive sort of chap.'

'Curiosity killed the cat.'

Proud of the saying someone had taught her, the bar-girl emitted more giggles. But it was as if she had dropped an ice-cube down my back. My stomach muscles contracted. My mouth forced itself into a rictus. Out of the corner of my eye I saw the letter-writer abandon her keg and the rest of her paraphernalia and go into the bar. A seventh sense told me she was going to a telephone – to call Teng? The woman in front of me – I had put her down as a high-school teacher – turned round.

'Are you an American?'

Her voice implied that I was an impostor and an altogether undesirable character. It was my fault. I had let my accent slip and used an incredibly un-American turn of phrase. The bar-girl wouldn't have noticed but this woman was different. We were at the entrance to the gallery now and the Chinese youth taking the tickets had heard what she said. I produced my most charming smile.

'North American, yes. I'm Canadian actually, from British Columbia.'

Her face cleared. She had a cousin in Nanaimo. I shook my head regretfully; I was from Vancouver. But it was a bond. We were chatting about the beauties of the West Coast as she went ahead of me into the gallery. Somewhere a phone was ringing – the letter-writer? The youth at the door took my tickets, looked me up and down from rope-soled shoes through flowered shirt to tinted specs, and let me pass. To the bar-girl he murmured something in Cantonese, something obscene about having found a good prick tonight; and predictably she giggled, displaying her pink gums.

I glanced hurriedly round the gallery. It was larger than its frontage suggested, and the paintings were too widely spaced as if there were not enough of them on offer. A few metal sculptures stood about the floor. It wasn't much of an exhibition.

Nor was it much of a Grand Opening; before our influx the place must have been almost empty. Apart from the tour party, the bar-girl and myself, there were nine people in the room, all Chinese. They were the artists – I guessed they were students – and their friends, the three youths I had seen go in earlier; the staff, consisting of the ticket-collector and the girl I had met in the doorway of the gallery on Tuesday; and, surely superfluous, an official-looking photographer. There was no sign of Bill or anyone from Government House.

Either the girl had recognized me or she had been warned. She and the photographer were talking together, staring in my direction. Keeping well away from them, I began to circulate around the room, pretending to study the paintings. They were a poor collection, dull, derivative, muddy in colour.

Lui Chi-shung, who had painted that glorious canvas in the window, would have derided them. But there were red stars on two of the frames and on one of the pieces of sculpture to show they were already sold – to Mr Wang perhaps.

'We've been gypped!'

I had been right about the American; she was a teacher. She taught art at a college in the mid-West and her opinion of this show was as low as mine. Her companions were less well informed, but I overheard rumbles of discontent. It seemed the guide had promised them both high-class culture and a buffet supper with free drinks. Instead they were getting third-rate work, fruit punch and nuts.

'I suppose the wretched guide was bribed,' the American said, 'but why bother? None of us is going to buy anything and we're flying home tomorrow.'

Why bother indeed? I wished I could answer her question. And where the hell was Mr Rouge? I should have to try to get upstairs. There was a door between what looked like a piece of disused armour and the representation of a dartboard in browns and greens. I tried the handle of the door, but it was locked.

'You want to go somewhere, sir?'

'Er – yes. I'd like to use your washroom.'

'No washroom here, sir. You have to go across to the bar.'

'I guess I'll wait then.'

The youth who had collected the tickets nodded and left me. He had been drawing the blinds in the window. The front door was also shut now – locked? – the blind down. I was suddenly conscious of a change in the atmosphere. People were talking louder. The cameraman was in business. There was laughter, the sound of a glass breaking. Someone switched on a radio. The exhibition was turning into a party.

'You've not drunk the punch I brought you,' the bar-girl said.

'Nor I have,' I said. 'Tell you what. I'll drink it while you get me another. And bring one for this lady too.'

She went off obediently and I took a sip of the punch, smelling it. It tasted sweet and fruity, but there were going to be some hangovers in the morning. The stuff was spiked. Carelessly I bumped into the teacher and managed to spill my drink and what remained of hers.

Simultaneously the door I had found locked was opened from the other side. A Chinese, in his twenties, plump, prosperous, and wearing a beautifully-cut dove-grey suit, ushered Lord Reddington into the gallery.

Lord Reddington! Not Bill Rouge, whom I had expected, but Jacob Rouge, as he had once been called. John Milment had told me that Rouge was the family name, but it had never occurred to me . . .

The old boy stood blinking in the bright light. He looked shrunken, ill, quite unlike the autocratic figure he usually appeared. Obviously he was making a considerable effort. I saw him straighten his shoulders as he was led forward to be introduced to the artists. The cameraman began to take photographs.

He was then escorted on a circuit of the gallery, though the attention he gave the works was cursory. He either couldn't or wouldn't pretend to be interested. Passing close to me he stared straight into my face and I could have sworn he recognized me, but he gave no sign. More clicking of camera. But this time I was the subject, not Lord Reddington.

He completed the circuit, came to the door and was ushered out into Temple Arcade. The Chinese gentleman in the dove-grey natty went with him, presumably to show His Lordship to his car.

Five minutes later the Grand Opening was over. While interest had been centred on Lord Reddington, the punchbowl and much of the remaining food had been removed. Now the lights were dimmed. There were gasps of surprise, more laughter, a little grumbling. The guide was rounding up his tour. The artists and their friends were muttering together.

The whole spurious business was over.

ROUGE had played at 6 Hua Bai. What he had played I had no idea, but at least I now knew who ROUGE was. And, very dimly, I was beginning to see the outlines of a pattern.

Eleven

I never did see William Jacob George Rouge marry Sarah Elizabeth Milment, though later I did get to kiss the bride. And I was at the Cathedral – in an official capacity. In company with all but the most senior members of the Colonial Secretariat I had been co-opted as an usher and, because of my friend-of-the-family status, I found myself unanimously elected head boy.

It wasn't a very onerous task, not like being best man or father of the bride, and there were advantages. Indeed at one point I was walking down the aisle towards an altar massed with flowers, the organ singing its deep song, the whispering congregation in lines of bright colour and, by my side, Monica Cayton. Unfortunately, a minute later I was walking back, alone, to escort yet another guest to her pew, and in my heart I knew that in the unlikely event that I did marry it would never be like this. Still, why shouldn't I dream my dreams?

'I'd hate to know what you're thinking.'

I turned abruptly. It was Jake Dasser. I reassembled my expression and grinned at him, and at Ruth Cecil who was with him.

'I was thinking how beautiful life is.'

Ruth and I started up the aisle together and Jake followed us. This time my imagination was well under control.

'You okay again now, Keith?' Ruth said softly. 'Your bruises have faded.'

'I'm fine, thanks. We must make a date for next week, the dinner I promised you and Jake.'

'Great.' Suddenly I felt the pressure of her hand on my arm. 'Couldn't you put us –'

I had stopped beside Howard Farthingale and before I had realized she wasn't keen to sit with him it was too late. Howard was smiling at her and moving along the bench in a gesture of welcome. To hell with Ruth, I thought. These were better seats than she and Jake rated. And Jake seemed happy with the arrangement; he gave me a pat on the shoulder as he slid into the pew.

I returned to my ushering and very soon the Milment family began to appear; if Bill had relatives other than his father they hadn't come to Hong Kong for his wedding. H.E.'s two ancient aunts arrived first, then his brother and sister-in-law and Lady Milment's sisters, each with a husband and a grown-up daughter. There were late-comers among the rest of the guests too, including Ian Hackard who, breathless as if he had run from the hospital, almost found himself in a front pew with the relatives.

After that near-disaster there was a pause, long enough to be dramatic without being theatrical. Lord Reddington with Lady Milment on his arm – he looked much more in need of support than she did – stood for a moment at the rear of the nave. Behind them were John and Celia. I had been instructed to walk ahead, keeping well to the side of the aisle, and show them into their seats.

I gave a slight, formal bow and turned towards the altar. The organist, who had been meandering along in an idle voluntary fashion, decided that this was the moment for a paean of praise. The congregation hushed. Behind me I heard a heavy snore, a sort of shuffle, and my name urgently whispered. I swung round.

Lord Reddington had collapsed. He wasn't quite on his knees but he was hanging forward, held up on either side by Lady Milment and John, with Celia trying to take some of the weight from her mother-in-law. Fortunately his black-out was momentary. As I reached him and relieved Lady Milment of the burden he regained a degree of consciousness, enough to help himself. But his face was a greyish-green colour, sheened with sweat, his chest heaved and he was fighting for breath. It was obvious he couldn't go on. And he was furious, aware that he could scarcely have chosen a worse time and place.

Lady M was superb. I don't know how she did it, but she sized up the situation and instantly decided on her priorities. As far as I can remember the only thing she said was: 'Celia!', but everyone seemed to react to her unspoken thoughts.

While Lady M and Celia, each with an usher, walked proudly up the aisle to the triumphal music of the organ, faces that had been peering anxiously at the back of the Cathedral turned to smile up at them. Someone went for a doctor – most of the more senior members of the profession in the Colony were at hand. Someone else picked up Lord Reddington's top hat. A deacon appeared to show John and me where to take the old man. And, as we half supported and half carried him to a side chapel, I caught a glimpse of the choristers filing into the choir stalls and Bill Rouge coming from the sacristy to stand with his best man beside the altar-rail. That was the last I saw of the Milment wedding.

In the side chapel the deacon unlocked a door and led us through the cloisters to a room of indeterminate usefulness. It was furnished with a desk, a few upright chairs, a prie-dieu and – I was glad to see – a couch. Lord Reddington wasn't a big man but he was heavy and almost a dead weight; it had been a long haul for John and me.

We propped him up on the couch, undid his collar and tie and opened a window. It was hot outside but there was a slight breeze, and the room was airless. The deacon, muttering something about a glass of water, left us. There was nothing we could do but wait.

'John, you go back,' I said. 'The doctor'll be here in a minute.'

John hesitated. 'Do you think he's going to be all right?'

'Probably. His breathing's easier and his colour's improved.' I tried to sound encouraging. 'Go on, John. Sally'll notice if you're not there. And you want to see her married, don't you?'

'Yes, of course, but – Keith, are you sure?'

'Positive!' I was propelling him towards the door, praying he would go before the doctor came. 'Besides, someone ought to reassure your mother and Celia.'

'Okay.'

He was gone, and in two strides I was by the couch, sliding my hand into Lord Reddington's inside pocket and extracting his wallet. It was surprisingly slim and uncluttered. It contained a little money, a letter and two photographs, one a slightly faded print of a gaunt but still beautiful woman and the other of Bill; that they were of mother and son was self-evident.

But the letter was what interested me. It was on the letterhead of a highly reputable Bond Street art dealer and assured Lord Reddington that he could have complete trust in the integrity and judgement of Mr S. Wang of Temple Gallery, Temple Arcade, Kowloon. It was dated a week before Lord R had flown out to Hong Kong.

There was a sound in the corridor outside. Hurriedly I thrust letter into wallet and wallet into pocket. I was bending solicitously over Lord R when the deacon came back with a glass of water. He was followed at once by the doctor, a large florid man whom I remembered meeting at the Milments' dinner party last Monday. From his morning clothes and the flower in his button-hole it was clear he was a wedding guest.

He nodded to me, waved away the glass of water and pulled up a chair beside the couch. He hadn't bothered to shut the door behind him and in the distance, very faintly, I heard the choristers singing. I pictured Sally walking up the aisle on H.E.'s arm and Bill waiting for her by the altar-rail. I thought of Monica. For a moment I felt quite sentimental.

'I'll keep my word. I've got no choice. So bugger off!'

The doctor couldn't have been more startled than I was. Lord Reddington had opened his eyes – large, brown, tired eyes – and was staring straight at me. He struggled to sit more upright, but the doctor pushed him back, and anyway it was too much for him. His eyes closed.

The doctor turned to look at me. 'Don't worry,' he said in a deep, plummy voice. 'His Lordship didn't know what he was saying or, if he did, he didn't mean it for you.'

Myself, I wasn't so certain.

Although the doctor wasn't a type I particularly liked, I had to give him full marks for efficiency. His examination was short; the rest could wait until he got the patient to hospital. But the patient refused to go to hospital. Lord Reddington, briefly lucid, was adamant. The doctor settled for complete bed-rest and twenty-four-hour nursing at Government House.

'Not Orientals,' I said in the ambulance.

'What?'

'The nurses. They must be European, American, Australian – not Chinese.'

'If you say so.' The doctor was pleasantly sarcastic; he

wasn't quite sure who I was or how much clout I carried. 'Of course, it won't be easy to find private nurses at such short notice and if they must be –'

'They must. Lord Reddington would wish it.'

He raised a supercilious eyebrow but he didn't try to argue. I was glad. I had been prepared to insist because I had meant what I said – I didn't think that after Thursday night the old boy would want to be surrounded by Chinese faces. There were also security reasons. I didn't really believe that Lord R was in any danger but if his illness were to upset whatever plans the *taipan* had for him, he might be at risk. I didn't intend to be sorry after the event.

The doctor left me in Lord R's bedroom. I had agreed to wait there until a nurse arrived or Lady Milment made other arrangements when she returned from the Cathedral. I calculated that I wouldn't have a long wait. Even though I had irritated him the doctor wouldn't take it out on his patient; he would do his best to find a nurse. And the wedding ceremony must be already over. I could expect to be interrupted at any time.

I took a hurried look at Lord Reddington. He was fast asleep, his breathing deep and even. In spite of Lord R's protests the doctor had given him a shot of something and he was unlikely to wake for a while. I began to search the room.

I searched quickly but thoroughly, and found nothing. Since I didn't know what I was looking for, this wasn't altogether surprising. But, given such an opportunity, I couldn't let it go by default. More to complete the job than for any other reason, I finally climbed up on a chair and felt on top of the wardrobe. My fingers closed on the edge of a brown paper parcel.

I pulled it down. The paper came off easily and I was staring at the Lui Chi-shung that had been in the window of Mr Wang's gallery on Thursday evening. It was a lovely work, an abstract, glowing with rich colours, and I wasn't surprised that Lord Reddington had bought it. What I would have liked to know – and I intended to find out – was how much he was paying for it.

'Keith!'

'What on earth are you doing?'

It was, as they say in some circles, a fair cop. Here I was, standing on the chair in front of the wardrobe, the painting in my hands. In the doorway were Lady Milment and Bill. The doctor hovered behind them.

'Hush!' I said fiercely, and pointed to Lord Reddington, propped up on his pillows.

As if I had pulled strings they went at once to his bedside. For the moment at least I was safe from awkward questions. I wrapped the painting in its paper, put it back on top of the wardrobe, replaced the chair and joined them. The doctor was nodding his head with satisfaction.

'I don't believe there's any immediate need for worry. But we'll get some tests done tomorrow. Then we'll see.' He glanced at his watch. 'The nurse should be here in fifteen minutes or so. An American woman.' He glanced at me. 'Very competent.'

'That's splendid,' Lady Milment said. 'Thank you, Doctor. Bill, dear, we must go. Our guests – '

'I'll have to tell Sally we won't be able to leave today,' Bill said abruptly. 'She won't mind. She'll know I can't walk out on Father, not when he's – he's like this.'

It was obvious Bill didn't care a damn about the guests or the reception or the demands of protocol. He was much too upset. I saw one of Lady M's hands clench. She took him by the arm and propelled him towards the door. Her bright smile included me.

'It will all work out.' She spoke with determination rather than faith. 'Keith, I'll send Celia to relieve you until the nurse comes.'

'Whatever's convenient, Lady Milment.'

Her smile warmed but her eyes strayed to the top of the wardrobe. She hadn't forgotten about the picture. She sensed that it presented another problem – one she didn't understand.

I waited for Celia.

She came very soon. She only knew that Lord Reddington had collapsed in the Cathedral and I had to fill her in. She was quick with compassion. And, because I now more than ever seemed a friend of the family, she was happy to gossip.

She had noticed that Lord Reddington was looking unwell yesterday morning, and had urged him to take a rest after lunch. To her surprise he had agreed, but 'a wretched Chinese from some art gallery' had telephoned for an appointment and had taken up a large part of Lord Reddington's afternoon. At dinner Lord R said he had bought a painting.

'That should have made him feel better.'

'It didn't. He looked ghastly and he was bad-tempered too. Sir David made a joke about him being able to afford to buy paintings since he wasn't marrying off a daughter, and Lord Reddington was quite rude. He said sons could be as expensive as daughters if one loved them, and the painting had cost more than Sir David would probably have been prepared to pay at any time.' Celia was half laughing. 'It was all rather embarrassing.'

I didn't share her amusement, but I was grateful for the information and I laughed in sympathy. Then I said I had better go.

Downstairs the house seemed full of people, queueing up to sign the Book and pass along the receiving line. I had no intention of doing either.

The reception took the form of a garden party, and I decided that the outdoors was my best bet for a drink. However, in spite of the heat, I found everyone drinking tea as they walked and talked and listened to the band. I made for the shade of the marquee, and the first thing I saw was Teng offering Monica a tray of sandwiches.

I stopped in my tracks. So far there had been no repercussions from my expedition to Mr Wang's establishment, but since Thursday night I had been looking over my shoulder constantly and taking what reasonable precautions I could. If the *taipan* gave orders that I was to be done, then I would be done, but it was only sensible to load the chances in my favour.

Teng's presence at Government House, where I felt safer than in my own apartment, was a blow to my morale. And if he hadn't been with Monica I would have gone in the opposite direction. Monica, however, had seen me. She waved. I couldn't ignore her. I saw her speak to Teng, who bowed and moved off with his sandwiches.

'Keith, how is Lord Reddington? John Milment told me he had a sort of heart attack in the Cathedral and you'd helped cope. Is it serious?'

'No, I don't think so. According to the doctor, it's more a warning than anything else. He should be all right.'

'I am glad. He'll be able to go home next week then as he planned.'

'I really don't know.'

I had lost interest in Lord Reddington. Someone had gone by with a tall glass tinkling with ice cubes. It was probably fruit juice but my mouth was dry.

'What I need is a drink – and I don't mean tea.'

Monica laughed. 'There'll be champagne soon, but if you can't wait why not ask Teng?'

'Who's Teng?'

Howard had joined us. He gave Monica an avuncular kiss and turned to smile at me. Seeing them standing side by side I was once again amazed at the resemblance between them.

'Teng is Keith's houseboy. He's also an ex-pupil of mine – one of the brightest I've had.' My mouth must have dropped because she added: 'Didn't you know?'

'I had no idea,' I said truthfully.

'What's he doing as Keith's houseboy if he's a graduate?' Howard sounded mildly bored.

'It's a vacation job for him. He's intending to take a post-graduate degree and he needs the money. Keith – if you want that drink –'

Monica gestured towards Teng who was moving away from us. At the same moment one of the guests spoke to him. He turned, inclined his head and said something in reply. We had a clear view of his pale, composed, arrogant features. Beside me I heard Howard's quick intake of breath. It was involuntary, the sort of sound one makes at a sudden, sharp pain; but Howard's reaction didn't result from pain. He had recognized Teng, though the name had meant nothing to him, and recognized him as someone whom he had cause to hate or fear.

'. . . for tomorrow, Keith? Nine-thirty at the Yacht Club?' Monica was leaving us.

'Of course,' I said, hastily rearranging my thoughts. 'I'll be there. Nothing could keep me away.'

'If you and Monica are sailing tomorrow,' Howard said, his

voice so normal that I almost believed Teng had meant nothing to him, 'you may not get much of a day. The weather's building up. We're lucky it's held for the wedding.'

'And what a wedding!'

It was the wife of the Colonial Secretary. Howard introduced me. I found her a rather stupid woman and made my escape as soon as possible, but she had expressed my sentiments exactly. What a wedding! And it wasn't over yet.

Later, before Bill and Sally went out to Kai Tak to catch their flight to England, H.E.'s aide summoned me to the room I thought of as the sanctum, to say goodbye to them.

'Keith, we couldn't go without thanking you – for everything.' Sally kissed me on the mouth.

'I couldn't be more grateful, Keith. I hope –'

'You're leaving as arranged, then?' If my question was abrupt it was because they made me feel embarrassed; I didn't want their thanks.

'Yes. I managed a word or two with Father. He urged me to go and – and for once I'm doing what he wants.' Bill sounded rueful.

'That's fine,' I said. 'I must admit the last time I was in this room I saw you and him having one hell of a row out there in the garden.'

'It was my fault,' Sally said quickly. 'I wanted Bill to have a last try.'

'A last try?'

They told me; it didn't seem to occur to them that it might be none of my business, and it was certainly more grist to my mill. Bill was determined to be a teacher and a chance was coming up for him to buy a third share in a prep school, but he had no money – only debts. And his father – the man who had started life in some ghetto in the Middle East – thought school-mastering beneath his son, and refused to help.

'He's always tried to run my life,' Bill said sadly. 'Oh, I know I've been a fool. I got into the drug scene at Cambridge, deeper than I should, but if I hadn't –' He stopped, put an arm around Sally and grinned at me. 'If I hadn't I'd never have met Sally at Dolly Bell-Pauson's.'

'Anyway, that's all over,' Sally said. 'We're going to have our school – one of these days. You'll see, Keith!'

I wished them luck. I hoped they wouldn't need it; but I had learned a lot today and I had my doubts. In spite of Peter Krail's efforts and – such as they were – my own, ROUGE had been played. Lord Reddington, if I was right, was the latest victim and, as Celia Milment had impressed on me, the ripples could spread wide.

Twelve

Sunday came in very hot and humid; there was little breeze to stir the air. Howard had been right. The weather was going to break but, with any luck, not today. I had been scared of waking to solid rain and Monica on the phone to say that sailing was out, so I was more than content.

We met at the Yacht Club as arranged, and tipped a small boy to take us in his sampan to the mooring where our boat was waiting. To get clear of Victoria Harbour and its heavy traffic we used the engine. Then, under Monica's orders, I helped set the sails and we moved slowly, gently, over the deep blue, languid waters of the South China Sea.

Once or twice we altered course to avoid the jagged rocks of one of the myriad green islands on which surf broke in a dazzling spray, but mostly the boat sailed itself with an occasional hand on the tiller. This suited us perfectly. We were both feeling lazy, and I at any rate was surfeited with champagne and emotion after yesterday's wedding. It was idyllic to do nothing, to forget all my problems, to be alone with a desirable girl – especially when the girl was Monica and I was half in love with her.

The boat was small, made for intimacy, and as the sea shifted beneath us I became more and more aware of Monica's long brown thigh pressing against me. I propped myself on an elbow and looked down at her. She was wearing the shortest of shorts and a white shirt, mounded by her breasts. Her body was beautiful but, seen so close, the defects of her features – the broadness of her cheekbones, the too-short nose – were exaggerated. I loved her for them.

I slid my hand under her shirt, caressing her nipples. My mouth opened on hers. I came down hard on her. For a moment she responded, small breasts thrusting themselves at me, tongue probing, legs spread. Then she pushed me away. She sat up.

144

'No, Keith!'

'Sorry.'

I rolled on to my front so that she wouldn't see how much she had affected me, and pillowed my head on my arms. I felt her long hair sweep my back as she stood up. Then, gently, she pressed one foot between my shoulders. For a moment I thought she was going to stand on me, but she didn't. She laughed aloud.

'I'll take in the sails and we can have a swim before lunch. There's no need for an anchor. We won't drift much.'

'Okay.'

I didn't volunteer to help. I had simmered down by now but I was angry with myself. I hoped I hadn't spoilt what promised to be a perfect day.

The boat rocked violently. I looked up just in time to see Monica dive over the side. Broad shoulders, narrow hips, small buttocks – from behind she had the figure of a boy; a nude boy. A jet of water droplets shot in the air as her body cleft the sea. The boat continued to rock, waves slapping against the wood. I began to pull off my clothes.

I belly-flopped into the sea. After the heat of the sun it shocked me by its coldness. I came up gasping. But when my body temperature adjusted, the water felt pleasant, invigorating. I swam slowly around the boat, neither seeking nor avoiding Monica.

She was doing somersaults under water, like a dolphin, her long fair hair streaming behind her. I rounded the stern with my careful crawl and lost sight of her. A minute later, having swum beneath the boat, she came up in front of me, put her arms around my neck and drew me to her. Together, the length of her lovely naked body pressed against mine, we went down, down, down into the depths of the China Sea. God – but it was the most wonderful sensation!

I wished it could have gone on for ever. But Monica had taken me by surprise. I had only snatched a breath before the waters closed over us. Now I needed air. Reluctantly I took my lips from hers and gestured with my head. She understood at once. I felt the resistance of the sea as she trod water, then the thrust of her legs as she kicked upwards, carrying me with her. We broke the surface simultaneously.

Monica was breathing deeply, but not gasping for breath

like a stranded fish as I was. She watched me, laughing. When I had recovered a little, she swam off, calling over her shoulder that she needed some exercise. I turned on my back and floated. I savoured my pleasure – and the pleasure that I hoped was to come.

After a while I had had enough. I paddled to the boat and pulled myself up by the rope hanging over the side. I looked for Monica and saw her pale head bobbing what seemed like half a mile away. I waved but she paid no attention.

The sun was already evaporating the beads of water on my body and there was no need to dry myself. I put on my slacks and shirt. I didn't want to get too sunburnt. Even here on the open sea, where it's always cooler than on land, it was hot – unreasonably so for mid-September. I thought about Monica . . .

When eventually she climbed back into the boat, I had laid out our food and was busy easing the cork from a bottle of champagne, already sweating two minutes out of the Thermos bag. I threw her a towel.

'Thanks, Keith. That looks terrific.' She gestured towards the lunch and spattered me with drops of water. 'I'm sorry.'

Entranced by her – careless – I answered with a Cantonese phrase that, roughly translated, said an apology was uncalled for because any pain she might have given was to me an infinite pleasure.

Immediately I sensed her shock of surprise, and I cursed my stupidity. If Crowne got to hear of this he would slay me. Somehow I had to cover my gaffe.

'How do you like my Chinese – all in two easy lessons?'

'I'm impressed.' Her voice was cold.

'That's what I hoped.' I laughed. 'But to tell you the truth, Monica, I've a very good ear and all I've done is learn a few phrases by heart. The trouble is to remember which is which.'

She didn't bother to comment. She stood, her legs apart to keep her balance, and seemingly unconscious of her nakedness continued to rough-dry her hair on the towel. She was so close that if I had leant forward I could have touched the beard which hung, damp, like pale sea-weed, between her thighs. I averted my gaze. I had been rebuffed once and, although in the sea she had all but ravished me, this wasn't

146

the moment to try my luck again.

I had made a mistake and had covered it badly. Monica had realized this. She was an intelligent girl, a language teacher of all things, and she must be wondering why I had deceived everyone by pretending ignorance of Cantonese. My thoughts were bitter.

Suddenly we were both distracted. A light aircraft that had been circling high above us for the last couple of minutes had dived and come in on our port side. It was so low I could read the name painted on the fuselage – *Little Annie*. It roared over the boat and Monica shook her fist at it. In reply the pilot waggled his wings and almost skimmed the water before he began to gain height.

'Bloody fool!' Monica said; she sounded disproportionately angry.

'Someone from the Flying Club?'

'Yes. They're always doing that sort of thing. It's supposed to show how clever they are.' She was pulling on her shorts and shirt. 'I'm waiting for the one I have to rescue after he's tried a stunt like that and gone into the sea.'

I smiled my sympathy. But I said a silent thank you to the pilot. He had got us out of a difficulty. If my Cantonese gaffe wasn't forgotten, at any rate the awkwardness it had caused could now be ignored.

'Come and have some champagne before it gets luke-warm,' I said, holding out a glass to her. 'After all, you must admit we've not been bothered with much company this morning.'

In fact, once we had cleared Victoria Harbour and were away from the ferry routes, we had met very little traffic. We had seen one or two junks, a few small pleasure boats and in the distance a Hong Kong Marine Police launch. Apart from these – and the inquisitive aircraft – we seemed to have the South China Sea to ourselves.

For the next half-hour we drank champagne and ate chicken, salad, cheese, fruit. We talked in a desultory fashion, mostly about yesterday's wedding and Lord Reddington's illness and Bill's prospects as a schoolmaster. When I asked her questions about herself Monica answered, but briefly, and she wasn't sufficiently interested in me to ask questions in return. Twice during this time she looked at her watch, so that at last, reluctantly, I was forced to realize that the promise of that long, sensual glide down into the water together wasn't going to be fulfilled.

Somehow the day had lost its magic, and the chugging of an approaching boat suited my mood. The junk, its hull black against the sky, was still some distance away – sound carries over water – but I estimated that if it continued on its present course it would pass nearer to us than any other vessel we had met. Monica was staring towards it, her eyes narrowed. I wondered if she would object to its intrusion as much as she had to *Little Annie*'s.

'They're more picturesque under sail, aren't they?'

'Like the peasant tilling his land without the help of machinery?' There was acid in her response. 'If Westerners admire the picturesque so much, why do they always sacrifice it to progress in their own countries?'

I didn't reply. I wasn't prepared to have a philosophical discussion. And we watched in a not altogether compatible silence as the junk drew closer. It was a big boat, diesel-powered like more than half the junks out of Hong Kong, and it had a fair turn of speed. The distance between us was narrowing fast. I could see one of the crew standing on the prow. He was wearing a white singlet and trousers turned up to the knees, a straw hat on the back of his head.

I could see this with the naked eye. The crewman, one arm around the foremast to balance himself, was studying us with equal interest, but through a pair of binoculars. Binoculars. Crewman. Fishing junk. The words clicked over in my brain; it produced the right answer, but much too slowly. Not that there was anything I could have done.

The junk, its engines at full throttle, was coming up very fast. It could still avoid us but that, I knew, was not the intention. We were a sitting duck, and it was about to ram us, to sink us.

Monica scrambled aft and stood up, semaphoring wildly with both arms. She had realized the danger before I had, but misinterpreted it. This wasn't going to be any freak accident.

'They're mad! They're mad!' Her movements were making our boat – a frail thing compared with the junk, and no protection – rock alarmingly, as if that mattered. 'They must have seen us. They're as stupid as that plane.'

Her words came to me over the thud of the diesel. The junk was now less than two hundred yards away. It wasn't going to swerve at the last moment and overwhelm us in its wash, as Monica probably thought. It was going to slice right through us.

There was one chance. If we were under power we might slip beneath its bows and get away. We didn't have speed, but we were far more manœuvrable than the big boat, and I didn't think they would chase us. We were low in the water and, when they got back to Hong Kong, an accident could be blamed on a sleepy helmsman – or not reported at all. But if they tried to play tag with us someone might spot their odd behaviour; there must be other boats in the area.

These thoughts stormed my mind, and I was moving a split second after Monica, though not to make any appeal, any protest. I was already pushing the starter button.

The pause before the engine caught seemed endless. I was half expecting it to fail, but it didn't. The junk was almost on us now, its dark, shining hull about to crush us. I opened the throttle wide.

Monica screamed. 'Jump, Keith! Jump!'

Distracted, I turned to see her dive off the stern of the boat. I swore. And the engine coughed, spluttered, died. Time had run out on me. But somehow, fractionally before the junk tore through the little sailing boat, I managed to launch myself over the side.

To be truthful I don't really remember going into the water, only being in it. It was cold and dark and full of flying débris, bits of wood and metal, and a soft object that hit me in the face. As I realized that it was one of the boat's cushions something hard crushed into my shoulder. I scarcely felt the pain, just a sensation of warmth, of stickiness. Involuntarily I kicked with my feet, driving my body up and out of the water.

Sun and sky! The shadow of the junk had passed over me. Wallowing in its wake I gave thanks. I was alive and whole. Only then did I think of Monica. I lifted myself out of the water and looked around for her.

The débris – all that remained of our boat – was coming to the surface, but there was no sign of a pale head bobbing in the swell. Yet she had dived overboard several seconds before me, and she was a far better swimmer. Frantically I trod water, refusing to think of the junk's propeller, refusing to think that stunned by a piece of wreckage she might at this very moment be floating under the sea.

I was getting exhausted. I had to let myself sink back into the water. There was nothing I could do for her. The realization was gall, and I was filled with an overpowering hatred for the *taipan*. He could so easily have devised some other 'accident' to get rid of me without squandering Monica's life too. Or had it amused him, since she had been linked with Peter Krail's death, to link her also with mine?

Hatred renewed my energy. Once again I trod water and searched for her. The junk had slowed and was coming around in a semi-circle, presumably to make sure we hadn't escaped. I would have to dive, but not yet – at the last possible second. Then I saw Monica.

She was farther away than I had expected, and in the opposite direction. I shaded my eyes against the sun. She seemed to be lying on her front just below the surface, her hair streaming about her. It was the long pale hair that had caught my eye.

The junk was now very near to her and almost stationary. Regardless of whether the Chinese spotted me, I kept myself upright, pumping my aching legs. I couldn't help her but I had to know what was to happen.

There was considerable activity on the junk. Men in singlets and trousers rolled up to the knee – like the chap with the binoculars – were running about the deck, gesticulating, calling to each other. Obviously they had seen Monica. Two of them leapt over the side and started to swim towards her. In fear for her, I groaned aloud and sank, swallowing a mouthful of sea.

I came up, choking and spluttering, and once more forced myself to tread water. They had towed Monica to the junk, and were lifting her gently into the boat. I got the distinct impression that she was hurt, but that they were doing their best to care for her.

My relief was overwhelming. Since they had picked up Monica they would have to pick me up. Otherwise, as soon as they got back to Hong Kong they would have some tricky questions to answer. There was no way they could keep Monica quiet. I didn't understand but, unutterably thankful that I wouldn't have to dodge the junk again, I began to wave and shout.

It was only when I heard the note of the junk's engine change that the other possibility occurred to me. I let my arm drop. I bit my tongue in mid-shout. I'm not without courage but to drown has always been one of my nightmares. And the sound of the diesel was growing fainter and fainter. The junk, instead of completing its turn, was heading away from me. Unbelieving, I watched it recede into the distance. They had gone. Monica had gone. She had left me to die, alone.

I got over the shock fast. I had already wasted too much energy and I wasn't a strong swimmer. How far could I get, if I took it easy? I might manage a quarter of a mile, even half a mile since my life depended on it, and there were innumerable islands. The trouble was I had no idea in which direction the nearest one lay.

Envying Peter Krail who had died quickly and without time for recrimination, I started to swim. A half-dozen crawl strokes later, I knew I was not going to make it – not to any island, not to anywhere. My left shoulder was worse than I had realized. Whenever I lifted my arm over my head an excruciating pain shot up my neck, paralysing me. A crawl was impossible. Breast stroke wasn't much better. I could turn on my side, crab-wise, or I could dog-paddle. It didn't seem worth the effort.

Hopelessly I looked about me. Apart from sea and sky there was nothing. The junk had sheared our little sailing boat in two and it had sunk almost immediately. Such débris as had stayed on the surface was useless to me. None of the bits of wood was big enough to bear my weight. Then I remembered the cushions. They were kapok. They would float.

I saw one at last. It had drifted away and the swell of the sea had hidden it from me. I paddled after it. And when I reached it – the fifty yards seemed like five hundred – I was elated.

I managed to clutch the cushion under my good shoulder. At least it kept my head above water. All I had to do was hang on. There was a limit to the amount of time I should be able to do so, but for the moment this was irrelevant.

Absorbed by my triumph with the cushion, I didn't notice the far murmur of the aircraft's engine until it became a steady buzz. I searched the sky and found the plane. It was low over the water, but its path was half a mile distant. There wasn't a chance the pilot would spot me. Even while I watched he gained height and flew off. It was worse than if he had never been.

Five minutes later he was back, much higher but almost directly above me. I couldn't wave without letting the cushion go, but I shouted, though I knew it was a waste of time.

The aircraft roared over me and then – thank God – swooped down, banked and turned, waggling its wings as it came towards me. It was *Little Annie* again, and *Little Annie* would be in touch with its airfield. In spite of the pain I forced my left arm high, and gave a thumbs-up signal. The pilot leaned out of his window and waved, pointing downwards.

It was Ruth Cecil flying the plane!

The next time she came round the aircraft was higher and to one side of me. The door was open. A rectangular, orange-coloured package tumbled out and inflated as it fell, blossoming into a one-man life-raft. At that moment I loved Ruth Cecil more than anyone in the world.

The life-raft landed in the sea about thirty yards away and, mindful of how long my last swim had seemed, I didn't abandon the cushion. Instead, kicking with my legs, I propelled it in front of me until it was nuzzling the raft. Only then, when I could swap one security for another, did I let it go.

Fortunately the raft had landed right side up, and with some difficulty I climbed into it. In comparison with my cushion it felt incredibly solid and safe. Ruth was circling above me. When she saw I had made it, she gave a last wiggle of her wings and flew off. Suddenly I was very lonely.

It was more than half an hour before the Marine District patrol launch picked me up. They looked at my shoulder; it was very badly bruised and the skin broken, but there was no lasting damage. Otherwise, apart from a little sunburn, I was fine. And the police weren't interested in asking questions. It seemed they already knew about the junk and Monica, and their account of what had happened answered a lot of questions. Monica had apparently been saved in the nick of time; she was unconscious when she was taken from the water. The junk's captain had seen the point: the rescue of a Monica clearly unable to tell him of my plight could only add conviction to his tale of accidental woe.

Thirteen

The Marine Police Commander was a Chinese, very smart in his uniform and very correct. He rose to his feet as I was ushered into his office. He would have shaken hands but, to his annoyance, my unofficial reception committee forestalled him.

'Keith! My dear chap, I'm so thankful – so thankful.' Howard Farthingale was positively effusive. 'Monica would never have forgiven herself if anything had happened to you. Never.' He grasped my damaged shoulder and I gave a shout of pain.

'Howard, be careful. He's hurt.' Ruth Cecil pushed Howard away. 'Get him a chair, Jake.'

Jake Dasser produced a chair. Ruth put me carefully into it and kissed me on the cheek. Jake gave the top of my head a friendly pat. Howard watched me anxiously.

'I'm sorry about your shoulder, Keith. Are you all right?'

'I'm fine.'

This wasn't strictly true and, if I sounded irritable, it was how I felt. In spite of the air-conditioning I was hot and clammy. The police blanket, which alone covered my nakedness, was uncomfortable and kept slipping. My shoulder ached. I was grateful for the kindness everyone was showing me, but what I really wanted was a shower and some dry, clean clothes.

'That's great,' Jake said. 'Then we'll be able to eat together as arranged.'

I gave him a long, hard look. My date with him and Ruth was for next Wednesday. After all, tonight I had hoped that Monica and I might –

'But Keith has to come and see Monica.'

For a split second Howard reminded me of Ian Hackard. I nearly groaned. Only the set line of the Commander's mouth deterred me. He didn't like the way his office was being taken over. I said:

'Of course, Howard, when I know what the Commander wants.'

'Thank you, Mr Sterling.' Like all Chinese the Commander had trouble with my name. 'We have arrested the helmsman of the junk and charged him with criminal negligence. I should like you to see him so that you will understand how the accident occurred. Whether or not we make other charges will depend on you.'

'He deserves to be drowned inch by inch in a barrel of water,' Howard said viciously before I could speak. 'No thanks to him that Mr Sterling and my niece aren't both dead.'

The Commander ignored this remark. He pressed a concealed button – I heard the buzzer in the next room – and immediately two policemen came in, dragging the 'negligent criminal' between them.

'Oh, the poor wretch!' Ruth said involuntarily.

I understood her feelings. The Chinese seaman was just a boy, and he had been well worked over. He had a swollen face, one eye fast shutting, and a split lip. I assumed he had 'resisted arrest', but it seemed I was wrong.

As if he had read my thoughts, the Commander said: 'The skipper of the junk says that the crew was so angry when they realized what the young lady had suffered – they didn't know then that Mr Sterling had also been on the boat – that they beat him up before they could be stopped.' He nodded to the policemen, who hauled away the sagging youth. 'Perhaps the skipper didn't try very hard. But he knows it's his job to make sure there are no narcotics aboard.'

'I thought so,' Jake said. 'The boy was as high as a kite.'

'Drugs?' I tried to sound mildly surprised. 'Well, at least that explains how he managed to run us down on the open sea, doesn't it?'

'To hell with that,' Howard said. 'If he wasn't responsible, the skipper was. They ought both to go to prison for endangering your lives. And what about the boat? It belonged to the Yacht Club. Who's going to pay to replace it?'

'Mr Farthingale, please,' the Commander said. 'I can understand your anger but it doesn't help. The skipper is also the owner of the junk. He's a trader, not a fisherman, and he

155

promises to pay for the boat himself. As for the rest, he's not a rich man, but he would offer what compensation he can.'

'I suppose he's not still around?'

'Yes, Mr Sterling. Would you like to see him?'

I nodded. The youth on his high was unimportant, a scapegoat, but it might be useful to recognize the skipper if we met again. The Commander gave orders and we waited.

'How is Monica?' I asked. 'She isn't seriously hurt, is she?'

'No-o, but she could have been killed!' Howard said. 'As it is she may be left with a scar on her forehead. She got a nasty blow – from some bit of the wreckage, I suppose. She doesn't remember. She's suffering from concussion and shock. But it's you she was so upset about, Keith. As the Commander said, those bloody men didn't realize there was anyone with her, and they were coming into Victoria Harbour before Monica discovered you weren't aboard. Poor girl, she was nearly hysterical when I – I – '

Howard's voice trailed away and an extraordinary expression flickered across his face. It was an expression I had observed before – when he caught sight of Teng at the wedding reception. It seemed that the skipper of the junk had the same effect on him.

I recognized the skipper too, in spite of his grubby clothes and hang-dog look. The last time I'd seen him was at 6 Hua Bai; he had been showing Lord Reddington around the Exhibition of Contemporary Chinese Art at Temple Gallery. And before that, I suspected, we had met at The Toothless Dragon, though on that occasion, when he had subjected me to such pain and indignity, he had been wearing a hood.

I now had a moment of revenge. He had been keeping his eyes modestly on the floor but, as the Commander addressed him, he lifted his head. He found himself gazing straight at me. It was an unexpected blow; no one had told him I had been rescued. His nostrils flared and his chest muscles tightened, but I had to admire his control. He gave me a deep bow and spoke very rapidly in Cantonese. The Commander translated.

'He says Tin Hau, goddess of the sea, is to be praised because she has offered you her protection. He himself had believed you were under the waves and he was very sad. So now he rejoices. He will make Tin Hau due payment for your life.'

'Tell him he owes me that and more,' I said. 'Tell him he's going to pay, sooner or later.' I stood up. It isn't easy to be authoritative when wearing a blanket, but by treating it as a toga I was moderately successful. 'And now, Commander, I'm most grateful to you and the Marine Police – not to mention Tin Hau – for saving me, as it were, to fight another day. I'm not making any charges against anyone, I'm leaving everything in your capable hands, and I'm going home.'

Somewhat to my surprise, there were no objections. Within five minutes I was sitting in the back of Jake's automobile, heading towards Mid-Levels and my apartment.

'I don't know how to thank you two,' I said. 'This is the second time you've come to the rescue.'

'Well, don't count on us a third time,' Jake said ominously. 'We've been doing our best to keep you alive, frankly because we hope you may be useful – and luck's been on our side so far. But you could easily have drowned today, and the other night when Ruth called me from the hospital, I was very lucky to spot what looked like a drunken Sterling being taken out of the back door of The Toothless Dragon. Even then I couldn't have helped if they hadn't decided to leave you in a gutter for the scavengers. Why do you take these risks, Keith? Night-clubbing with that odd bunch wasn't exactly sensible, and as for going out in a sail-boat – surely you know how vulnerable you are?'

I ignored the implications. I wasn't quite ready to co-operate with the CIA yet, though I guessed I was going to. It was open war now between the *taipan* and me, and I needed all the allies I could get.

'Jake, what man could refuse when Monica Cayman asks him to go sailing?'

'Peter Krail couldn't refuse her either, and he's dead!' Ruth was bitter.

'Are you implying Monica's involved –' I began.

'Yes.'

Seldom had I heard a more definite monosyllable. I winced. Ruth turned around in her seat and grinned at me.

'Cheer up, Keith. There are a lot of people involved in this operation, some willingly, some unwillingly, some without even knowing it.'

'I'll give you an example: an extremely powerful United States Senator, who died a week or two ago in an automobile accident.' Jake hooted viciously as a rickshaw stopped unexpectedly in front of us. 'So what do you say, Keith? Are you prepared to contribute? Or shall we agree to forget this conversation?'

I made up my mind. 'How do you like a British lord, at present staying at Government House, Hong Kong?'

'Brother, I love him dearly!'

Jake took his right hand off the wheel and reached behind him. I leaned forward and shook it. Ruth was beaming. I didn't know if Lord Reddington's involvement had really been news to them, but they seemed delighted. As for me, though Charles Crowne might raise hell at not having been consulted, I had an idea this might be one of the best things I had done for a long time.

'When can we talk?' Jake drew up in front of my apartment block. 'Now?'

'No, definitely not. Teng, my houseboy, was planted on me. He's a menace and the place is almost certainly bugged.'

'Okay. After we've been to Farthingale's and seen Monica.'

In the apartment I showed them into the living-room and went to find Teng. He was in the kitchen, admiring a plastic bag three-quarters full of water, in which swam a small fish, probably destined for his supper.

'Mr Sterling, sir. You are ill?'

'Ill? Oh, you mean the blanket. No, Teng, I just had a slight accident.' I couldn't keep my eyes off the unfortunate fish, swimming round and round. 'Will you bring tea, please, for three.'

I went along to the bathroom. I showered – hot as I could bear, cold as I could bear – and felt a new man. I part dressed and shouted for Ruth, who wanted to inspect my shoulder. The bruise was already discolouring. The shoulder would be stiff tomorrow. Nevertheless, after she had put on a fresh dressing I scarcely noticed the discomfort. I was all for setting out at once, but Jake insisted there was no hurry, so we sat and talked about the weather. We agreed it was hotter than ever – a storm must be on its way. And Teng, bringing some

158

little iced cakes, volunteered that the radio had reported a typhoon east-south-east over the South China Sea, heading in our direction.

Personally I found these tea-table politenesses irritating in the extreme. I was glad when we got to Howard's house. He was watching for us and if Jake's delaying tactics had been intended to make him jittery it was clear they had succeeded. He fussed us into his splendid drawing-room and called to Cheung, his houseboy, to bring refreshments. He looked reproachful when we said we had already had tea.

'Then, if it's not too early for you, Cheung will bring you drinks,' he said to Jake and Ruth. 'You come with me, Keith. The doctor left Monica a sedative, but she won't take it till she's seen you.'

He led me upstairs to the bedroom I had used when I had arrived, soaking wet, for his party. Instinctively I looked at the chest on which the photographs of young Howard and his sister had stood. The photographs were no longer there.

While an infinitesimal part of me registered this, all the rest of my attention was focused on Monica. And what I saw horrified me. She had a wound reaching from the centre of her skull to a point about two inches above her left eyebrow. It had been stitched and covered with a protective plastic film. Superficially it was a revolting sight and I remembered what Howard had said about a permanent scar. But what really got me, what really made me sick, was the sight of Monica's hair. In order to treat the injury almost half of her head had been shaved, and she had a rough triangle of baldness where once long pale beautiful hair had grown.

'Monica darling, here's Keith.' Howard pushed me forward. 'She wouldn't believe me when I told her you were all right.'

'Keith! Oh, Keith! My dear, I'm so sorry. So terribly sorry.' She held out both hands to me. 'When I came round I was on the junk and I thought you were too. I asked for you but they didn't understand. And when we got back to Victoria Harbour – God, it was awful. To have left you to drown. Can you forgive me?'

I was sitting on the side of the bed, holding her hands, and I kissed her on the mouth. It was the easiest way to stop her talking.

'Forget it! There's nothing to forgive. I'm here. I'm fine.

You're the one who was hurt. Your – your poor hair.'

'Yes. If you're truly all right, I – I have to admit – it's what I hate most.'

'Monica, you must rest.' Howard interrupted. 'Come along, take the pills the doctor gave you and you'll have a good sleep.'

'Stop fussing, Howard.' Monica smiled at me. 'He still treats me like a little girl sometimes.'

'May I come in?'

Howard turned angrily but, short of pushing her out of the room, there was nothing he could do. Ruth was already by the bed, regarding Monica with compassion and, I knew, clinical interest. I suppressed my distaste; I wasn't such a fool that I hadn't done the same thing myself.

'Monica, when I spotted that wreckage and flew down and saw Keith hanging on a cushion, I thought we'd lost you.' Ruth bent over the bed. 'My dear, I'm just so happy you're safe.'

'Thank you, Ruth.' Monica was tiring. 'If you'd not been there – I hate to think . . .'

This was as much as Howard could bear. He exerted his authority. Monica had to rest, doctor's orders. We must leave her to sleep now.

Ruth and I didn't resist. We allowed ourselves to be shown down to the drawing-room where Jake, highball in hand, was studying a wall scroll. Everyone would have been pleased to say goodbye, but the decencies had to be preserved. Howard had to offer me a drink, and I had to accept one. We chatted pointlessly.

'What do you suppose will happen to those guys from the junk, Howard?' Ruth asked.

'My dear girl, how should I know?'

'They'll get bail and they'll skip,' Jake said decisively.

'That's what you – you –'

Without warning Howard began to shake. The ice cubes chattering in his Collins betrayed him first. He put the glass down quickly and tried to make a joke of it. Then, realizing this was impossible, he looked slightly desperate.

'I'm sorry. You must excuse me. This afternoon has been horrible. Horrible! When the police phoned I got it wrong. I thought Monica was dead – drowned. And when I saw her –

they'd bandaged her head and the blood was seeping through – I can't tell you what I felt.' He gave a feeble laugh. 'I suppose I must be suffering from some sort of delayed shock.'

Ruth was full of sympathy. But she made his agitation an excuse for us to leave, and the car was scarcely moving when she said: 'Howard Farthingale is on the edge. He could break any time.'

I accepted the implications of Ruth's comment readily. Last week I might have been surprised – not stunned, perhaps, but surprised. Now, Howard's reactions to Teng and to the junk's so-called skipper left little room for doubt.

'What about Monica?' Jake asked.

'Her injury looks genuine enough. She's got a horrible gash that could easily have knocked her out and been the end of her. And that convinces me it wasn't Howard who organized the "accident". He wasn't faking. He really is devoted to Monica. Of course he knows she's being used, and I'd say he hates it but can't do anything about it. That may be what's breaking him.'

'Okay, Ruth. Let's leave it for the moment. Priority One is to swap info with Keith here. I suggest we go to my apartment. I'll guarantee we can talk as safely there as anywhere. Besides, there's free liquor in the cabinet and steaks in the freezer. What more do you want?'

'Extra pay for being cook,' Ruth said, and the laugh broke the tension.

Fifteen minutes later we were sitting, drinks beside us, in Jake's living-room. Progressive jazz served to shield our words. We had started what was to be a long session.

'The operation – we'll call it Operation Dragon – originates in Peking and it's controlled from Peking; at least we know that,' Jake said. 'Its ultimate object is anyone's guess, but the immediate aim is to get in position to blackmail certain men who are important in their own countries. We don't know why, but for some reason they always choose targets who are visiting Hong Kong, and the set-ups always take place here.'

'Yes. I agree. Rouge played at 6 Hua Bai last Thursday. In other words, Lord Reddington was set up for blackmail in an apartment over a spurious Chinese art exhibition in what's now called Temple Arcade, Kowloon. Afterwards, he was persuaded to buy a very fine painting. I don't know how he's going to pay for it, but I'm sure it'll be in some way he won't like.'

Of course I had to amplify. I told them about the scratches on the box I had found under Peter Krail's car and the torn end of paper that Peter had sent to Charles Crowne. I told them of my two visits to Mr Wang's gallery, and I exonerated Howard of any prior knowledge of Hua Bai.

'Okay!' Ruth said. 'So I was wrong. Howard isn't the Hong Kong *taipan*, though there must be one. I still don't like the man. He gives me the creeps.'

Jake grinned at me. 'Women's intuition. The odd thing is she's often right.' He stood up to pour fresh drinks. 'Ruth, why don't you go and cook the steaks while I tell Keith about the Senator.'

The Senator's experience appeared to parallel Lord Reddington's. His interest was jade, not paintings, but during a fact-finding mission to the Far East he had received a series of introductions that had eventually led him to 10 Chou Nol Street. There he had been promised the sight of one of the finest private collections of jade anywhere, and the opportunity of acquiring a superb piece. The owner was said to be a recluse, and the Senator had gone to his appointment without an aide. He had a black-out, felt ill and was escorted to his official car. The next day he was offered a beautiful jade bird at a fair price. He was also shown obscene photographs of himself and told what he was to do.

'So you do know the purpose of the blackmail. But you said it was anyone's guess.'

Jake shook his head. 'I do not know. Look, the Senator had had this automobile accident. He was dying and he knew it, and he wanted to die with a clear conscience. I was with him for hours, but much of the time he was rambling. I've had to piece the story together.'

'But you asked him?'

'Goddamit! Of course I asked him. His answer was, and I quote: "It was a terrible thing to do, but others have done the same. Before me there was a German prince, keen on horses – " '

'Horses! Then it's not some sort of art swindle.'

'No. They just use the guy's particular interest to hook

him. And I don't think it's narcotics, either. I asked the Senator and he managed to shake his head, though what he said was either "Red China" or "Red Chinese".'

'Dope's out, Jake. I'm sure of that. It's one thing Lord Reddington wouldn't go for.'

I told him about Lord R's wife and his abhorrence of drugs. We mulled over other possibilities. They didn't get us anywhere. All we knew was that certain Americans and Europeans – powerful, politically influential, intelligent, aware men, if they were all like the Senator and Lord Reddington – had been set up for blackmail in Hong Kong. Such men were not easy to trap, so the set-ups were elaborate, involving a lot of money and a lot of people, of whom some at least were acting under duress. But why Peking should take this trouble, we had no idea.

Ruth brought in the steaks and we had supper. It was a satisfactory interlude in a far from satisfactory day.

Fourteen

At midnight Ruth went to make us another pot of coffee. Since supper we had done nothing but drink coffee – and talk. Jake turned on the radio, and we half listened to the latest report on Typhoon Tessie. She was still a long way away, but she was travelling fast and she was no mean typhoon – almost a thousand miles wide, with winds over eighty knots. She deserved far more attention than we were prepared to give her.

Ruth returned with the coffee. Jake switched off the radio. And once more we talked, shaking and picking at everything we knew or surmised, as a woman shakes and picks at a tangle of wool in the hope of finding a loose end that will enable her to wind the skein into a satisfactory ball. We talked of Dolly Bell-Pauson and her parties and Peter Krail's death. We discussed Bill Rouge and his love-hate relationship with his father and dismissed the small likelihood that he would deliberately cause the old man harm. The Hackards were relevant, too – her expensive tastes, and the fact that 'Baby' was probably fathered by a former American Vice-Consul. We considered the Chinese element – Ling, Teng, the phoney skipper of the junk and, above all, the Hong Kong *taipan*. Maybe some of the Chinese teachers at Hong Kong University had involved Monica, but it seemed unlikely that Howard Farthingale would allow himself to be blackmailed merely to keep secret his dead sister's age when her daughter was born. Finally we reviewed the cases of blackmail: the minor characters, probably the Vice-Consul and Howard and undoubtedly others; and the main players, Lord Reddington, the Senator, the German Prince and whoever else had been listed 'to play'.

At two in the morning, exhausted, we called it a day. We had had some success. Between us we had filled out the overall picture. Yet, though I had held nothing back except for

John Milment's slight involvement, and I was ready to bet that Jake had been equally forthcoming, the central explanation was still missing. We were no nearer knowing why some Peking *taipan* had set up what was obviously a very elaborate and expensive operation.

We had two options. Either we could try to break Howard, which might not be difficult, but probably wouldn't get us any further. Or we could approach Lord Reddington. In the latter case 'we' meant 'me', because he certainly wouldn't open up to the Americans. And I didn't relish the idea. I thought my chances of persuading him to talk were infinitesimal. It was more likely he would order me hanged, drawn and quartered for my impudence.

'Sleep on it,' Jake said, 'and see what you feel about it in the morning.'

'No.' I knew pride had already committed me. 'I'll do it. I'll have to tell him who I am and try to shake him. But don't count on anything. Lord R isn't exactly the shakable type.'

Sighing, I pushed myself out of the armchair. I was surprised how much effort it required. Things had finally caught up with me and I was asleep on my feet.

There was no question of my going home. My car was still at the Yacht Club and, though Jake or Ruth could drive me, we agreed it wasn't safe. Lord Reddington's name had been the last on that list, and Operation Dragon seemed to be coming to some sort of climax – perhaps a temporary pause, perhaps an end. If the enemy were rattled by the situation, risks could be high. Certainly I should be most vulnerable alone in my apartment.

So once again I slept in Jake's spare room, in a pair of Jake's pyjamas – these had green and white stripes – and I woke to find Ruth, fully dressed, sitting on the end of the bed and obstructing my view of the nude on the wall.

The first thing she said was: 'The typhoon's steaming towards us and it's as hot as hell outside, too hot to have breakfast on the balcony.'

I groaned. 'What a welcome to a new day. I've scarcely got my eyes open. What's the time?'

'Quarter after nine.'

'Quarter past nine!' I sat up with a jerk and winced as my shoulder hurt. 'Christ! I should be at the office.'

'No need for you to panic, Keith. I called them. Howard wasn't in yet, but I spoke to Ian Hackard. I told him you nearly drowned yesterday and had swallowed such gallons of the South China Sea you were sick to your stomach and wouldn't be in today.'

'Well, I'm damned!' I had to laugh. 'Ruth, if you were as beautiful as that charcoal nude behind you, you'd have everything.'

'Thanks.' She pointed at the bedside table. 'Drink your orange juice and get dressed while I make you breakfast, English style. There's lots to be done this morning.'

I did as ordered. Soon I was sitting at the kitchen table, eating a meal that would make lunch unnecessary; Ruth had an enormous idea of what constituted an English breakfast. When I was on my third cup of tea and my fourth piece of toast, I said, my mouth full:

'Ruth, my first job must be to send a telegram to my boss in London. Given some paper I can encypher it here, but it's bound to take some time.'

'Okay.' She began to stack the dishwasher. 'You cypher your telegram and fix to see Lord Reddington. I'll take a taxi to the Yacht Club, pick up your car and get some clothes from your apartment. You remember, we agreed you're to stay here for a few days.'

I gave her my keys. 'That was a wonderful breakfast. Ruth – watch out for Teng!'

'Don't worry. I expect he's been to the Luk Chi Fu School of Martial Arts, but you should see my *kung fu*.' She grinned at me and I laughed.

Ensconced at a desk with all I needed, I got down to work. It was one of those times when everything goes right; I had had a good sleep and my brain was clear. Ruth put her head round the door to say she was going and would be back in an hour. I reminded her to bring my electric razor – Jake's spare model didn't suit my light beard – and wished her luck. I heard the front door slam.

I gave her five minutes in case she returned for anything. Then I went to the telephone. Howard's number was engaged. I dialled Government House and got on to John Milment. He didn't sound as friendly as usual, but when I invited myself to a pre-lunch drink he didn't demur. I tried Howard again. This time Cheung answered; Miss Monica was sleeping and couldn't be disturbed. I sent her my love and phoned a florist to deliver two dozen pale yellow roses. As an afterthought I added a dozen, pink ones, for Joan Hackard. I had put down the receiver before I remembered Ruth.

Back at my desk things went well and by half past eleven I had finished a long report to Crowne. Expecting Ruth any minute, I hurriedly burned the superfluous paper and flushed it down the lavatory pan. I wished she would come. If the traffic was bad it could take me half an hour to get to Government House, and I had promised to be there soon after twelve.

At a quarter to twelve I was getting impatient. For something to do I went out on to the balcony. The sun was beating down out of a copper-coloured sky and the humidity must have been breaking records. Everything was very still. The cotton shirt I had worn yesterday evening was already sticking to my skin like a damp rag, and the heat-haze, distorting the high view from The Peak, made me momentarily dizzy. I retreated to the air-conditioned apartment.

At three minutes to twelve, when I was biting my nails, Ruth appeared. I was so relieved that I was angry. I swore at her.

'Calm down, Keith. I'm sorry I'm late but I've not spent the morning at the Laichicok Amusement Park, you know.'

I apologized. I grabbed the bag she had brought, extracted a suitable shirt and raced to the bathroom, where I had a quick wash and made myself presentable for Lord Reddington. Ruth lounged in the doorway, telling me what she had done.

'. . . your automobile's outside. Here are the keys. Incidentally, the traffic's very heavy and everyone's bad-tempered. It must be the weather. The other thing that held me up was searching your apartment. Teng wasn't there and it seemed a good chance.'

'Find anything?'

'No-o. But I think Teng's gone. Except for the furniture, his room's bare. Not even a toothbrush. It could be a pointer. Jake may be right. Perhaps the Hong Kong *taipan* is closing down his operation.'

I thought about this as, thumb on the horn, I drove

furiously to Government House. A lot was going to depend on Lord Reddington – and on my persuasive ability. I wasn't hopeful.

The butler showed me into the usual book-lined room and I waited for John Milment. Through the window I saw a sudden gust of dusty wind shake the garden. Then everything was still again. John came in.

'Another telegram for Dad to send? What will you do when I've gone home, Keith?' He was amused.

'I might be there ahead of you.'

'Really. Success?'

'Failure. By the way, how's Lord Reddington?'

'Much improved. He's up and about. It was a very slight attack apparently. But the doctors say he should take it as a warning. Not that he'll heed their advice. He's already arranging to fly back to London.'

'Immediately?'

John shrugged. 'He'd like to go at the end of the week. He doesn't believe in holidays. Personally I do, and I was scared Celia and I might have to go with him. It's obvious he can't travel alone. However, that problem's solved itself.'

'Splendid. I thought you were going to ask me to volunteer.'

My mind wasn't on what we were saying. I was considering how – without a direct request – I could get to talk to Lord Reddington. I had been stupid to hope that John might suggest it.

'I'll take Dad your telegram. Shan't be a minute.'

In fact, it was more like ten before he returned, and I had become restless.

'Keith, why didn't you tell me you were nearly drowned yesterday?' John was visibly upset. 'We had no idea, not until the Colonial Secretary mentioned it when he was talking to Dad on the phone just now.'

I made a dismissive gesture that hurt my shoulder. 'No damage done, except to poor Monica who –'

He gave me a hard look. 'All right. You'd better wait until Dad's free. That way you'll only have to tell your story once. Meanwhile, come and have a drink with the family. I told Mother you were here.'

And Lord Reddington? Hopefully I followed John into the drawing-room. Lord Reddington was seated in an armchair, with Lady Milment and Celia standing one on either side of him. They were all three studying a painting that was propped against a table some distance away. It was the picture that Lord Reddington had been keeping on top of his wardrobe. Indeed, Celia was still holding the brown paper in which it had been wrapped.

'. . . not only is it a superb painting, but it has a scarcity value. The artist is such a perfectionist that he destroys ninety per cent of his work. I was most fortunate –' He broke off as if he had just noticed John and me.

I greeted Lady Milment and Celia. And John said: 'Sir, do you remember Keith Sterling?'

'But of course. This is our – fourth meeting, isn't it, Mr Sterling?'

Lord Reddington smiled at me benignly. I smiled back, taking the dry, papery hand he offered me. I had the resentful impression that he had laid on the whole scene for my benefit. I was about to be out-manœuvred.

'Fourth?' Celia had been doing her arithmetic.

'Fourth,' Lord Reddington repeated. 'The last time was at the wedding when I was taken ill. I must admit I don't remember much about that particular occasion. But I'm extremely grateful for the help I'm told you gave me then, Mr Sterling.'

'Not at all, sir.'

Ignoring my murmur, he swept on. 'Prior to that we met at dinner here – and at the Exhibition of Contemporary Chinese Art at Temple Gallery. Dreadful exhibition it was too, but I gather Mr Wang likes to encourage students occasionally. Anyway I couldn't grudge a few minutes spent on it – giving it my blessing, as it were – since in return he was prepared to sell me that beautiful object. What do you think of my Lui Chi-shung, Mr Sterling?'

'It's an exceptionally fine painting, sir.'

'Yes. Glad you agree with me. Of course you've seen it before, haven't you?'

'It was on display in the window of Temple Gallery during the exhibition.'

'So it was. I'd forgotten that. But Rose – Lady Milment – told me she saw you having a peep at it in my bedroom on Saturday.'

The old man beamed benevolence at me and I managed a thin smile in return. Lady Milment was trying to look unconcerned. I glanced at John and Celia. It was clear from their expressions that they had already heard about my odd behaviour. Probably it accounted for John's slightly cool reception when I telephoned.

'Lord Reddington, you must forgive me.' I laughed sheepishly. 'I was overcome by curiosity to know what you'd bought from Temple Gallery.'

'You were sure I'd bought something?'

'Why, yes.' Two could play at this verbal game, I thought. 'I had no doubt you'd bought, sir, none whatsoever, not after I saw you come down to the exhibition with that very persuasive chap – what is his name? I know he's not Mr Wang because Mr Wang's visiting his family in China.'

The heavy lids drooped over the eyes, but not before I had caught a glint of anger in them. Lord R had been startled, either by the extent of the information at which I had hinted, or because he himself hadn't known about Wang – possibly for both reasons. And he hadn't liked being challenged.

'That was the young Mr Wang. He's a part owner, but I'm not sure what the relationship is. He could be either a son or a nephew of the head of the firm.'

He spoke with indifference and, turning to Lady Milment, asked if he might have some iced soda-water. I gathered our conversation was at an end. Lord Reddington had made his position clear. He had given an innocent explanation of his behaviour and he had forestalled all the questions I might have put to him. If, after this, I had the temerity to make any accusations, he would deny them bluntly. He was prepared to bet I had no evidence against him.

Thoughtfully I sipped the gin John had given me. It was interesting that Lord Reddington had answered a case that hadn't yet been brought. When he had regained consciousness in that depressing room at the Cathedral and had told me to 'bugger off' he must have believed me his enemy, involved in blackmailing him. He still thought of me as an enemy, but in a different sense. I supposed he had made some casual enquiries and had learned what I was. I could imagine H.E. saying: 'Oh, he's one of Charles Crowne's boys, out here on a special job.' And why not? Lord Reddington was the repository of so many vital secrets it would have seemed ludicrous to deceive him about me. In the event, however, it had fore-warned him. I would never break his story now.

The Governor came bustling in with his aide. 'Good morning, everyone. Jacob, how are you?' He scarcely waited for Lord R to answer. 'What's this I hear from the Colonial Secretary, Keith? He tells me you nearly drowned yourself and Monica Cayton yesterday.'

'Well, I wouldn't have put it exactly like that, sir.'

'How would you put it, then?'

I gave them an abridged account of what had happened, and they were duly sympathetic – though seemingly more with Monica than with me. There was an awkward silence when Celia said I was accident-prone and we each thought our own thoughts. John offered me another drink, but no one suggested I should stay to lunch. Silently cursing the lot of them, I refused the drink and said my goodbyes.

John saw me to my car. I had told him not to bother but he insisted, in spite of the heat. Yet he appeared to have nothing to say or, alternatively, he was steeling himself to say something important. Disgusted with my failure to get any help from Lord Reddington, I let my preoccupation show and I was settling myself into the driving seat before John brought himself to ask:

'Keith – is Bill Rouge in trouble?'

I was tempted to take out my frustrations on him, to pretend not to understand, but John had always done his best to co-operate. I said:

'Not as far as I'm concerned, John.'

'Thank God for that! I was afraid – for Sally.' His smile widened with relief. 'For all of us,' he added honestly.

I didn't bother to enquire why he thought Bill might be in trouble; he must have sensed that Lord Reddington and I had been talking cat and mouse. I wanted to go. Until I could turn on the car's air-conditioning I was like a loaf in an oven.

'Goodbye, John. I hope you and Celia will enjoy the rest of your holiday here.'

'Thanks, Keith – and thanks for answering that question. I'm grateful to you –' He didn't want to sound too serious. 'Almost as grateful as I am to the Colonial Secretary's daughter.'

I put out my hand to shut the door. 'Good heavens, what has she done for you?'

'It's a Chinese friend of hers from the University who's flying to London with Lord Reddington. He was going anyway, so he's happy to have his fare paid, first class, and if I know the old man a handsome present too.'

'How – how very convenient.'

The words stuck in my throat. Why on earth hadn't I pursued the matter of Lord Reddington's travelling companion when John first mentioned him? I had just assumed it was someone from the European community going home on leave. But a Chinese friend of the daughter of the Colonial Secretary – the same girl who had introduced Sally and Bill at a party of Dolly Bell-Pauson's – this smelt.

'It's a life-saver for Celia and me.'

John slammed my car door. Hurriedly I wound down the window. I no longer cared about the heat or a sudden swirl of grit and dust around us. My wish to be gone had evaporated.

'John, it's not my business, but hasn't everything been arranged very rapidly? What do you know about this Chinese? Has he got a passport, papers, whatever he needs? I mean – it would be awful if he let you down at the last minute, wouldn't it?'

'Oh, there's no fear of that. He was all set to go, as I said, and everything's in order. He's a pleasant chap.'

'You've met him – ?'

'Yes. Lord Reddington remembered him from the Colonial Secretary's party last week, Mother made some phone calls, and he came to see us this morning. It was as simple as that.'

I didn't contradict him. I wound up the window, started the engine and waved goodbye. What was it Joan Hackard had said? She had been forced to house a Chinese, an illegal immigrant from the People's Republic, and later she had seen him at Howard Farthingale's. I was shaking with excitement. My every instinct told me I had hit the jackpot.

Fifteen

It wasn't until the evening of the next day that Jake and I set out to visit Howard. The typhoon signal had gone up at noon and the radio was reporting on Tessie's progress every half-hour. She wasn't expected to score a direct hit on Hong Kong, but her skirts were wide and even a flick from them could cause disaster.

Office workers had been sent home early. Shopkeepers had boarded up their windows. Junks were putting back from sea; the typhoon shelters were already forests of masts. The aircraft at Kai Tak had been lashed to the tarmac. Everyone – from those who lived in rich houses on The Peak to the squatters in their shacks on the mountainsides – had tied down everything that could be tied down, and had barricaded their homes. Now the streets, which had seethed with people ever since the Number Three warning had gone up, were almost empty, the bars shut. Everyone was waiting, sweating it out – at prayer or at party according to their inclinations.

It was no night to be paying a social call and we weren't welcome. Howard's house was blind with shutters and there was no answer when we rang. Jake leaned on the bell. After a full five minutes, while we suffered in a blanket bath of humid heat, the door was opened and Howard stood blinking at us.

'Sorry,' he said. 'I was asleep.'

'What's happened to your houseboys?' I asked.

'The two young ones have gone to their families and I sent Cheung to make sure that Monica was all right. She insisted on going back to her own house yesterday. She said there was nothing wrong with her except a headache.' He sighed resignedly. 'Jake, you had better put your car in the garage. The winds may come any time.'

While Howard opened the garage for Jake, I waited in the hall. The yellow roses I had sent to Monica stood in two vases on the top of the chest; either they had arrived after she had gone or she hadn't bothered to take them with her. I sighed. They had certainly brought her no pleasure.

'Well, what do you want? Why did you have to see me tonight?' Howard said. 'Have a drink, anyway. Gin?'

We nodded and Jake said: 'We wanted to see you yesterday, but you weren't available.'

Howard stared at him blankly. 'Yesterday I had to take Monica home and settle her in, and we were busy at the office. The CS kept me very late. For that matter I've spent most of today with him – when I wasn't trying to make my junk as typhoon-proof as possible. You never said it was urgent and I've been bloody occupied.'

'Sure,' Jake said sympathetically. 'There's no need to explain yourself.'

We had been occupied too. Communications between Hong Kong, London and Washington had been throbbing. Everyone accepted that I had discovered the purpose of Operation Dragon – to place communist Chinese agents in the homes and offices of powerful and influential men in the West. The next thing was to get leads on all these men, so that we could protect them and dispose of the dragons on their backs. More information was vital; our main source had to be Howard and we hadn't dared to press him hard unless he panicked and ran.

'What can I do for you now you're here?' he said again. He handed us drinks and sat down.

'Give us some information if you can – and we're sure you can. After all, Howard, you're an expert on the People's Republic of China.' Jake paused to sample his drink. 'The position's this. Everyone knows there's a steady trickle of illegal immigrants into Hong Kong. It's inevitable, whatever the authorities try to do to stop it. But these people are peasants, simple folk, and when they get here they stay. We're interested in a different kind of Chinese – educated, city-bred guys, who use Hong Kong as a stepping-stone to the West.' He laughed. 'For some reason they've decided our great gay capitals are more attractive than Peking. At any rate, they go to immense trouble and expense to get to them.'

Howard frowned. 'I don't understand, Jake. It's interesting, as you say, but if – if you're sure of your facts, why come to me? What information can I give you?'

'Oh, we're sure of our facts. We want your – estimate of them, Howard. We want to know more about these people.'

I had been watching Howard while Jake talked, the nervous tic in his right cheek, the way he swirled the ice cubes round and round in his drink, the constant shifting of his body as if he couldn't get comfortable in the chair. He was as tense as a tightrope, and he was an indifferent actor. It wasn't difficult to read him. Ruth had been right when she said he was on the edge of breaking. Nevertheless, he was making a desperate effort.

'I suppose it's possible,' he said slowly, 'but I wouldn't have thought there would be many Chinese yearning to get to the fleshpots of Europe and the United States.'

'Aw – it's not the fleshpots that interest them,' Jake said. 'Their aim is to get into nice, influential positions. For instance, I was on the phone to Washington today, and they confirmed that one of our more powerful Senators came here on a visit and was – shall we say – persuaded to take a new Chinese secretary back to the States with him.'

'And there was that London friend of Monica's,' I said.

Howard's concentration had been fixed on Jake. He had scarcely been aware of me, sitting to the side of him. But at the mention of Monica he swung round to face me as if he had been stung by a poisoned dart.

'What London friend of Monica's? Monica knows nothing about – about any of this. How could she?'

His voice trailed away. He knew he had made a mistake. In exonerating Monica he had as good as pleaded his own guilt. Nor was it his first mistake. Perhaps it wasn't unreasonable for him to accept Jake in the role of inquisitor, though he was certainly under no compulsion to do so, but it was ludicrous that he hadn't questioned my presence. I was his new PA, very much his junior, and he should have asked me what the hell I thought I was doing with Jake. It didn't seem to have occurred to him.

'The butterfly expert who lives in South Ken,' I said. 'Monica stayed at his house when she was in the UK. He had a factotum from Hong Kong too, though his chap disappeared when Special Branch showed an interest in him.'

'Obviously you know more than I do. I'd no idea. If I had, I'd never have let Monica go near the place. I've always done my best to keep her out of my – my affairs.' He looked from me to Jake and back again. 'What are you two after? Do you want me to admit I've brought illegal immigrants into Hong Kong? Is that it? All right! I have – and I'm not particularly ashamed of it. Is it – is it such a terrible crime to give a young man a chance of a decent life?'

Howard stood up. For no apparent reason his confession seemed to have restored some of his confidence. He went and poured himself another drink.

'Help yourselves when you want to,' he said as he returned to his chair, rather overdoing the show of bravado. 'You may be right. Some of the wretched Chinese could have gone on to the States or to Europe. But if they have I've had nothing to do with it. I'm just a staging post. I collect them at sea, bring them into Hong Kong, give them a bed and food and clothes. Within a week I'm rid of them.' He smiled wryly. 'You know, when Keith arrived soaking wet for my party the other night I lent him some of the gear that was waiting for one of them.'

'When did you bring in that particular man?' I was suddenly interested.

He looked his surprise. 'Let me see. It must have been Wednesday – the day I met you and Hackard going to the Yacht Club. Is it important? He should have come earlier, but he didn't, and it was an awful trip. Everything went wrong. In fact, we were nearly caught.'

My eyes met Jake's. We were both thinking the same thing. Howard's latest illegal immigrant, probably wearing the clothes I had borrowed temporarily, would soon be accompanying Lord Reddington to England. God knows what excuse the old man had originally intended to make, but his need for a companion was excellent cover. I wondered how much Howard really knew.

'What else do you want?' Howard said.

'Quite a lot,' I said coldly.

'Of course, we appreciate you were being blackmailed. They found out about your sister, didn't they?' Jake said, probing with seeming sympathy. 'For Monica's sake, you couldn't let that be made public, so—'

Howard gestured wildly with his glass and slopped gin over his slacks, but he didn't seem to notice. He made a sort of strangled noise in his throat. I wasn't sure if it was anger or despair. At last he managed to speak.

'Christ! Oh, Christ!' Howard whispered.

It was a prayer rather than a blasphemy. Slowly he got to his feet and just stood. All his fragile confidence had flaked away. He was a fat, middle-aged, pitiable man, stunned by an incomprehensible disaster.

Our guess had been correct, but it didn't make sense. Monica had been born when her mother was below the age of consent and was probably not Joshua Cayton's daughter. So what? It was ludicrous that Howard should be unmanned by the disclosure of this pathetic secret.

Irritated, I opened my mouth to ask more questions when suddenly the lights grew very bright, flickered and went out. Jake shouted a warning, which had to be unnecessary; Howard wasn't going to attack us. It was just Typhoon Tessie choosing a poor moment to hit us with her first squall.

The wind hammered at the house, shaking the shutters, tearing at the roof tiles. Then the rains came, sluicing us down like a hose. As the wind passed I could hear the water rushing in the drainpipes and the overloaded gutters. I thought of the squatters, and was thankful for the shelter of a solid house. Apart from the rain, it was all over in a minute.

The lights came on again. I hadn't moved. Howard had collapsed in his chair and was sitting with his face in his hands. Jake, acting on his own advice, had taken up a defensive position against the wall. It didn't do him any good. Smiling in the doorway stood the two Chinese I knew as Cheung and Teng. There was nothing to reassure us about their smiles. They were holding business-like guns.

'Good evening, gentlemen.'

'Cheung! I thought you—' Howard stopped in abrupt amazement. 'What the hell are you doing, Cheung, with—with him?' He gestured towards Teng.

Cheung shrugged delicately. 'He's a colleague of ours, Mr Farthingale. You must have realized that. The *taipan* said we were to tell you that other colleagues are with Miss Monica.

They include Yo Chan, who so lamentably failed to drown Mr Sterling on Sunday afternoon, but who is no longer a guest of the Marine Police.'

'They've got Monica? My God! If they hurt her, I'll – I'll kill them,' Howard said, but his voice broke; he couldn't have sounded convincing even to himself.

The Chinese laughed politely, as if Howard had made a joke they didn't understand. They came farther into the room, but they were careful to keep a safe distance from us, and their gun hands never wavered. I finished my drink, half wishing I had taken up Howard's offer to pour myself another. Out of the corner of my eye I saw Jake edging along the wall and drawing infinitesimally closer to the Chinese. I willed Howard to go on talking so that at least part of their attention would be on him.

Howard took a long, shuddering breath. 'What – what does the *taipan* want?'

'You're to come with us,' Cheung said, and added without any perceptible change of tone: 'Stand still, Mr Dasser, please.'

I shifted my weight in the chair as if to make myself more comfortable. The muzzle of Teng's gun moved fractionally upwards. It was a natural reaction but the wrong one. Neither he nor Cheung was in any danger from me. However good my aim and however heavy the tumbler in my right hand, I couldn't hope to hit both of them.

But near Howard was a pedestal table on which stood a vase, tall, linearly pure and duck-egg blue in colour. It was more beautiful than any woman could ever be. If it had been only Howard's life at stake, I'm not so sure – but there's nothing I value more than my own skin.

I glanced casually at Jake; he was watching me. I brought back my arm in an innocent gesture, and hurled the glass I had been clutching. I was already rolling out of my chair when the vase shattered. There was a cry from Howard and a spatter of shots. One of them broke a lamp beside me. Another went through the padding in the shoulder of my jacket. I crouched, momentarily safe, behind a love-seat.

'That was a very foolish thing to do, Mr Sterling,' Cheung said.

I sighed. Jake had been carrying a gun and I had hoped to give him a chance to use it. But my effort had been inadequate, or Jake had muffed the opportunity. At any rate, between us we had achieved nothing.

'Stand up, Mr Sterling, slowly, please, hands on your head. Don't try anything else or I shall kill Mr Dasser.'

'For God's sake do as he says, Keith. He means it.'

I was almost more resentful of Howard's remark than of Cheung's order, but I got carefully to my feet. The sight in front of me was chilling. Howard hadn't moved but his knuckles were white as he grasped the arms of his chair. Teng, blood flowing gently down his cheek from a nick on his ear, was yearning to use his gun on me. Cheung stood over Jake. And Jake lay on his face, a widening pool of blood staining the carpet by his head. There was no sign of his gun, and I guessed that Cheung had pocketed it.

'Mr Dasser isn't dead, Mr Sterling, but unless you do exactly as you are told I promise you that he will be. Do you understand?'

I nodded, weighing up the situation. It wasn't exactly hopeful. I couldn't tell how badly Jake was hurt, but he seemed to be unconscious. As for Howard, he was too scared of what the *taipan* might do to Monica to think of co-operating with me – and I didn't blame him for that, not one bit. Nevertheless, it meant that I was on my own. Cheung had realized this, of course. He knew I was desperate and he wasn't taking any risks.

'In the middle of the room, please, Mr Sterling, and lie down on the floor, ankles together, hands behind your back,' he said. 'Hurry! Every minute the typhoon's getting closer and we haven't time to waste.'

I didn't move. 'Haven't you? That's interesting.'

'Mr Sterling, the *taipan* ordered that we should bring you and Mr Dasser with us, alive if possible. But –'

'How did he know we were here?'

'Monica phoned. I –' Howard began.

Cheung interrupted him. 'Please stop wasting time. Mr Sterling, do as you are told. If you continue to be obstructive, I warn you I shan't hesitate to kill you and Mr Dasser.'

But he was hesitating, because the *taipan* wanted us alive.

This meant we had a reprieve – perhaps a bargaining point, however small.

'I'm not moving until you attend to Mr Dasser. He needs help.'

After a moment's pause Cheung nodded. 'Very well, Mr Sterling. Mr Farthingale, see what you can do for Mr Dasser.'

I waited while Howard carefully turned Jake on to his back. Jake was pale beneath his tan and breathing noisily. He appeared to have been hit twice, once in the head and once in the chest. I didn't like the look of him.

Howard knelt beside him. 'I need water, bandages. He's bleeding badly.'

'Get what you want, but no tricks, Mr Farthingale. Remember your – your niece.' Cheung gestured at me with his gun. 'Now, Mr Sterling, be quick.'

It was useless to quibble any more. I could hear the impatience in Cheung's voice and, as if to emphasize the need for haste, the wind buffeted the house again, lashing the rain against the shutters. I walked into the middle of the room and lay down, ankles touching, hands behind my back, as instructed. I could guess what was to happen to me.

Teng lashed my wrists and legs together. He wasn't gentle, he wanted to hurt, and the nylon cord was biting into my flesh before he had completed the job. Then he seized me under the arms and pulled me into the hall where he let me drop in an exquisitely uncomfortable heap by the front door.

Eventually Jake was laid beside me. His head and chest had been bandaged with more expertise than I would have expected of Howard, but he hadn't regained consciousness and, if anything, looked worse. There was a greyish tinge to his skin, and a smear of blood on his cheek made him appear discarded and forlorn. Fortunately for him, however, neither his hands nor his feet had been bound – a concession I didn't attribute to Cheung's kindness of heart but to his belief that Jake was no longer a threat. I didn't get any encouragement from it.

Teng opened the front door. Immediately it whipped back on its hinges and a hot wind howled into the hall, bringing with it a sheet of rain and mud-sodden leaves. Somewhere there was a rumble of tiles coming off a roof, the smack of breaking glass. Beneath me the ground shook; probably a heavy tree had been uprooted. Teng and Howard, doubled up against the violence of the weather, dashed outside. And the front door shut itself behind them with a shattering bang.

For a moment I abandoned the unequal struggle with my bonds. Except for Jake's rasping breath it was quiet in the hall, the sounds of the storm muted. We waited. When Teng and Howard returned, their clothes were plastered to their bodies and rivulets of water ran down their faces from their soaking hair. Without a word Teng seized my shoulders, Howard took my legs, and they ran me out and dumped me in the driveway, leaving me with my face in a pool of muddy water.

I twisted myself on to my side, partly to avoid drowning and partly to see what was happening. I was lying beside Howard's station-wagon, which afforded some shelter from the rain but threatened to blow over on me as a fresh swirl of wind hit The Peak. Jake's car had been driven out of the garage and parked in front of the station-wagon. Jake himself was being carried from the house. Cheung was struggling to close the front door.

When Jake had been laid in the back of the station-wagon, I was picked up, wet and muddy and sweating, and more or less thrown in beside him. I caught my breath. I had landed cruelly on my arms and an agonizing pain shot through my shoulders, up my neck and into my head. I had to bite my tongue to stop myself from crying out. Howard would have made me more comfortable, but Teng pulled him away and gestured towards Jake's car; speech was impossible in the battering wind. Howard went reluctantly, and the last thing I saw before Teng threw a couple of rough blankets over Jake and me was Cheung climbing behind the wheel of the station-wagon.

It was a terrifying ride. Under the dark weight of the blankets I rolled from side to side on bound wrists, unable to prevent myself from crushing Jake every time a bend in the mountain road threw me in his direction. I was scared, scared of doing him irreparable damage when I fell on him and scared of smothering him by pulling the blankets tight over his face when I fell away from him.

Forcing myself to disregard my rising panic and the outrages being done to my own body, I seized a piece of blanket in my teeth and tried to pull it off my face. It seemed to take forever, but at last I managed to get my head free. This was a major achievement. I could breathe properly. I could see what there was to see, which wasn't much. Rain obliterated almost everything. But in the headlights of the station-wagon I caught glimpses of water pouring over the embankment and flooding down the mountain, and of the road littered with mud, branches, rocks, even a shutter torn from a house. More important, I could dimly see the long mound beside me that was Jake. By working at it I succeeded in pulling the blanket from his face too. His eyes were open.

When the station-wagon went around the next bend and I was again swung towards him, he winked at me. It was a moment of pure joy. He couldn't be as bad as I supposed. I gave him a wide, thankful grin in return. Then I looked at Cheung.

Cheung had his difficulties. He was fighting the station-wagon every inch of the way. Sheets of water curtained his vision; débris and flood water menaced him; wind buffeted violently. The attention he could pay to his passengers was all but nil.

'Knife in left trouser-pocket,' I shouted at Jake, confident that the havoc outside would prevent Cheung hearing me.

'Okay! Try to keep still.'

I tried, with little success. Jake found the knife first go – the Chinese, knowing I hadn't a gun or I would have used it, hadn't bothered to search me – but to cut me free was another matter.

While the station-wagon swayed and slithered down The Peak, Jake seemed to me to be performing surgery on my wrists rather than ridding me of those damned bonds. But eventually I felt the cord give and, in a shock of pain, brought my arms around to their normal position. Seizing the knife from Jake I reached down to free my ankles.

I don't know exactly what happened next. I remember hanging desperately on to Jake so that he didn't shoot over the front seat as Cheung slammed on the brakes, and I remember the noise. It was a long, groaning, shuddering noise that drowned out the beating of the wind and the rain. It was the noise of tons of mud and rocks and trees surging down the mountainside and pouring across the road in front of us. Cheung's reactions were quick. Before we had slithered to a stop he was ramming the car into reverse, but he wasn't quick enough. I remember his scream as a boulder crashed through the roof of the station-wagon and killed him. I remember the thick, smothering darkness. I remember being terrified.

Sixteen

'Keith! Keith, are you okay?' There was an edge to Jake's voice.

'Yes. I'm all right.' I was thankful to sound as steady as I did. 'What about you?'

'Better than I look, chum.'

'As if I could see you. It's blacker than hell in here.'

'Wait. I've got a lighter.'

There was a pause, the rasp of a flint, a flame. Our conversation had given me – and, I suspected, Jake – an injection of courage. We needed it. The flickering light revealed a terrifying scene.

The station-wagon was buried under earth and rocks and branches. Cheung had been squashed like a beetle by the boulder that had crashed through the roof. It was a warning of what would happen to Jake and me if more of the mountainside collapsed or if the station-wagon failed to support the débris already pressing on it. And there was the question of air. We had to get out, quickly.

The windows on either side of the station-wagon were blocked to the roof, and it was obvious that we couldn't climb over or around Cheung's body and the boulder. But the darkness beyond the rear door was not impenetrable. There seemed to be a tree in the way but no insurmountable barrier of earth and rock. Thanks to Cheung's quick reactions, it looked as if we might be on the edge of the landslide and not completely buried by it.

'Jake, this may be tough. What shape are you in? Be honest.'

'I've a bullet under my collarbone and I've lost some blood, but I'll manage. I can walk, climb if I must.'

'What about your head?'

'Forget it. The bullet just grazed me. Keith, for Chrissakes, quit talking and get on with it. Somebody's got to get after those goddam Chinese – and Monica. You can always send back a search party for me.'

'Okay. Ready? Give me some light.'

Jake flicked on the lighter and I grasped the handle of the rear door, twisted it, pushed. Nothing happened. I tried again and again and again, throwing all my weight behind the effort. I was running with sweat but the door hadn't moved a centimetre. And I knew it was never going to move. The whole frame of the station-wagon had been distorted.

'Take cover,' I said roughly. 'I'll have to kick out the bloody glass.'

I lay on my back and kicked. It wasn't as easy as it sounds. I was past caring about getting cut, but the glass was tough and I was wearing my best kid slip-ons. They didn't make much impact. Suddenly I thought of my Dad's clumping old garden boots – and I wanted to cry. Instead I kicked out the fucking glass.

It was then, above the soughing of the wind and the rain, that we heard the sounds, the slithering, the rumbling, the pattering of earth. And, in the lighter's flame, I read in Jake's face what I knew was mirrored in my own, fear of being buried alive.

Together, blindly, regardless of the jagged edges of the door frame, we tore at the branches that blocked our way. Our progress was nil. We were sobbing for breath when suddenly the tree before us took on a life of its own. It heaved and shook and finally wrenched itself from our grasp. A brilliant light dazzled us. A voice, Howard's voice, said:

'Thank God I've found you.' He seized Jake by the arm and Jake shouted in pain. 'Come on! Where's Cheung?'

'Cheung's dead.'

Howard swore. Jake and I scrambled out of the station-wagon and floundered through the mud and débris. To be able to stand on one's feet, albeit ankle-deep in flood water, and take great gulps of rain-sodden air, was wonderful. Luckily Typhoon Tessie was taking a pause before she went on to wreak more havoc, and the rest was easy. In spite of Jake's injury, we made a hundred yards up The Peak in record time. Here we were safe from the landslide and Howard stopped. He seemed to know exactly where he was.

'You'll find a driveway,' he said, pointing, 'and a big white house. It's not far. Some Canadians rent it. Their name's

Murdoch. They'll look after you.'

'I know them,' Jake said. He was leaning heavily on me and breathing hard.

'Teng says they've taken Monica out to my junk. It's in Plaimm's Bay. If you can get through, tell the Marine Police. If the lines are down, God knows. Murdoch will do what he can. He's a good chap.'

'Plaimm's Bay. Okay, Howard.'

'I'm coming with you,' I said to Howard. To Jake I added: 'Listen. If you have any problems, get on to Government House – John Milment. He'll see they take their fingers out.'

As he stumbled up the road Jake turned and shouted something, something about Ruth and the junk, but the wind whipped his words away, and I couldn't wait. Howard was already splashing down the road. I caught him up as he came to the landslide and together we ploughed through the mud and rocks and earth. The flashlight was a big help, but all the same I was thankful to reach the far side.

'Where's Teng?'

Howard didn't reply. He was running for the car – Jake's car – which was sitting at an angle, its nose buried in the bank. There was no sign of Teng and, suddenly distrustful, I repeated my question urgently. For answer Howard flung open the car door and Teng lurched towards me. I seized him. A split second later I realized he was dead. He had been shot through the head.

'How – how did it – ' I began.

'Pull him out,' Howard said, gasping for breath. 'Quick. We must hurry. I think Monica'll be safe till I get there, but . . .'

I didn't argue. Between us we got Teng out of the car and threw his body to the side of the road. Howard took the wheel, ignoring the blood and God knows what else there was on the seat. I don't believe he noticed. Personally I was glad I didn't have to drive. I ran round the car and got in beside him. He was already reversing away from the bank.

'I had to kill him,' he said. 'He wouldn't go back. But I couldn't leave you and Dasser and – and Cheung, could I? I've known Cheung a long time. In a way, we were friends.'

We said no more. Howard, concentrating hard, drove like the devil. And I needed to think; there were a lot of things

I wanted to ask, but they could wait.

We were in the urban area now and the road was less littered, rocks and mud and branches replaced by garbage and the odd neon sign. But there was flooding where the drains couldn't cope, and a certain amount of traffic. Swerving round a corner on the wrong side, we met a taxi head on. Howard didn't brake. He accelerated. Up on the pavement, scraping the side of a house, winging the cab, we were through. I took several deep breaths.

'You have a gun, Howard?'

'Yes. It's in my pocket.'

'You found it in the car?'

'No. It's mine. I got it from my bedroom when they let me fetch the bandages.'

I swore to myself. I couldn't ask Howard to give me his own gun. Yet I didn't trust his judgement. If Monica were threatened he could go off half-cock. I had been a fool not to take Teng's gun, but at the time I hadn't thought of it.

For more than a mile we didn't speak again. Howard was driving as fast as he dared, but it was raining hard and we had turned south, away from the lights of Kowloon and the red shadow of the Mountains of Nine Dragons across the harbour. We were on a minor road and the going was rough. A sudden bluster of wind shook us. I thought I could smell the sea.

The car braked sharply. 'This'll do. There's some shelter,' Howard said. 'We'll leave the car here and go down to the beach and signal to the junk. Someone will be on the look-out.'

'Sure. The *taipan*'s expecting us and Cheung and Teng — and probably Jake. We're not exactly going to take him by surprise, are we?'

'What do you suggest? Have you got a better plan?'

I had thought hard about the problem, but I had had neither the time nor the ingenuity to solve it. We should have to play it as it came. However, a little guile wouldn't hurt. I rummaged in the glove compartment for some string.

'How many on the junk? Do you know, Howard?'

'No, but we can ask the chap they send to collect us.'

'Fine. Then I'll deal with him and you can take us out to the junk.' I tried to sound optimistic, which was more than

I felt. Unless Jake could bring about a miracle I could see myself feeding the fishes before the night was out. 'Let's go.'

The path to the beach was steep and the torrential rain had turned it into a mud slide. We sat on our bottoms and slid, breaking the descent with our legs and hands as best we could. It was a wild, spine-jarring ride, hideously uncomfortable and probably dangerous, though it was too dark to see the hazards. Unable to check myself I landed in a heap on top of Howard, who had gone arse over tip the last few yards and was winded. While he gasped and wheezed and fought for air, I disentangled myself and sat up. There wasn't a bit of me that wasn't bruised or lacerated or, if there were, that bit hurt too. And it was no consolation that Howard, who was older and in not such good shape, had taken an even worse beating.

I was relieved when he stopped choking and produced the flashlight. It was a large rubber-covered object and had survived intact. Howard, I suspected, had protected it at cost to himself.

'I – I don't know if there's any particular recognition sign.' He was still gasping. 'But I doubt it'll matter in this weather. They'll come.'

'If they see us at all.'

Sheltering my eyes against the driving rain I peered into a black, soggy, salt-tasting blanket. The darkness was impenetrable. But I could hear the slam of the waves on the rocks and it was too easy to picture the mountainous seas.

'There they are!' Howard shouted. 'They've seen us.'

'Where?' I was disbelieving. The response from the junk had been too quick. 'Are you sure?'

And then I saw the little winking light. It wasn't where I had expected in the middle of the blanket, but somewhere up at the top. The junk wasn't in the cove. It was way out in the open sea.

'We'll never make it,' I said positively.

'The boat will be here in ten – fifteen minutes.' Howard over-ruled me. 'Even in rough weather, this bay's very sheltered. I – I know it well.'

. . . and used it often, I thought; but I said nothing.

We waited under the cliff in impatient misery until we heard the throb of an engine. I told Howard what I wanted

188

him to do. Then we went down to the beach. By now my eyes had adjusted to the dark and I could see the outline of the boat and a figure in an oilskin bringing her in.

Howard shouted a greeting in Cantonese and the figure responded. He wanted to know how many of us there were. Howard said there were two, Cheung had been delayed but he'd be along soon. Howard was holding me by the arm and I was trying to look abject, which wasn't difficult. Howard pushed me forward and I stumbled, making it obvious that my hands were tied behind me. In fact, I had a loop of string round one index finger and it needed only a quick jerk to get free. The unsuspecting Chinese began to help me into the boat.

'My niece – Monica Cayton – she's on the junk?'

'Yes, of course,' he tittered.

'And the *taipan*'s aboard and Yo Chan, I know.' Howard's casualness was admirable. 'But who else?'

'There's Fook-wei – and the other prisoner, the American girl.' He tittered again. 'Why do you – ?'

He never finished his question. He had told us all we needed, and more. I remembered Jake shouting something about Ruth when we left him on The Peak, something only half heard. And now Ruth too was a prisoner. I hoped to God that she and Monica were both unhurt. That titter had turned my stomach.

I hit him across the windpipe with the ridge of my hand and he fell back, nearly knocking Howard into the sea. I knew he was dead – I had felt the bone break – but I had no compunction. I pulled him into the bottom of the boat beside me.

'Come on!' I said to Howard. 'If we take too long they may get suspicious.'

It's never easy to undress a body, and it wasn't made easier by the circumstances. The trip out to the junk was no joy. Howard had to fight to keep the boat head-on to the waves; one broadside would have sunk us. We climbed a peak to descend into a trough to climb another peak. It was a roller-coaster on a wet, windy night with someone throwing buckets of salt water over us at intervals. But there was no pretty, screaming girl to hold, only a dead Chinese to slide into the heaving sea after I had deprived him of his oilskins. At least there wasn't time to be afraid.

And I was thankful for my efforts when we reached the junk and a searchlight was directed on us. The hood of the jacket, pulled well over my face, and the general shapelessness of the oilskins made a wonderful disguise. I kept my head down and did my best to help Howard lash the boat so that it didn't smash itself to matchsticks against the junk. Then I followed him up the rope ladder, scraping my knuckles and barking my shins as it slithered from side to side.

The ladder went up and up and I didn't realize the junk was riding a wave until we were going down again. I clung on desperately, praying I wouldn't fall, praying I wouldn't be sick. Howard was already safely aboard. The searchlight went out; it had been intended to help us secure the boat. Then the junk was climbing and I was climbing with it. Willing hands heaved me on to the deck.

The young Chinese – presumably Fook-wei – never knew what hit him. He fell backwards against the side just as the junk gave a lurch. Before I could get hold of him he had over-balanced and was gone. We didn't hear him strike the water. There was a hubbub of noise around us, the wind howling, the waves slapping against the wood, the masts groaning. We had no need to be quiet.

I got out of the oilskins and, hanging on to anything that offered a support, staggered after Howard to a hatchway. I considered staying there until Yo Chan came up to see what had happened to Fook-wei and the boat, but in the storm, which seemed to be worsening again, this wasn't a practical idea. Besides, Howard wouldn't have agreed. He couldn't wait to get to Monica.

He thundered down the stairs and into the saloon with me on his heels. Here he stopped so abruptly that I ran into him. It wasn't an impressive entrance. And, dazzled by the bright light swinging from a beam, we were both slow to take in the scene before us.

The two girls were there – and Yo Chan. Monica sat in a padded leather chair that was fixed to the floor. Ruth, covered by a grey blanket, lay front downwards on a bunk. She didn't move. Yo Chan, with a cat's smile on his broad face, stood balancing himself against the motion of the junk. He was no longer the downtrodden skipper I had last seen at the Marine Police Headquarters, or the suave Mr Wang of Temple

Gallery, but an honour guard to his *taipan*. He held a machine-pistol in a negligent but effective grasp.

'Monica! Thank God! You're all right. They haven't . . .'

Howard's voice trailed into silence. He stared at Monica in a strange, puzzled way. He couldn't believe what he saw. His every instinct screamed at him not to believe.

'Monica. Monica – my dear.'

'Hallo, Howard. And Keith Sterling. Good heavens, what have you been doing to yourselves? You look dreadful.'

'Monica! I don't understand.'

My reactions were quicker than Howard's but not, I must admit, so very much quicker. I had been prepared to risk my life to save Monica Cayton from the *taipan*. But Monica Cayton was the *taipan*. Bitterness welled. Memories blotted my mind – Peter Krail dead in the street, the treatment I had received at The Toothless Dragon, the love Monica had pretended to promise when what she promised was death by drowning, the people she had used, the yellow roses I had been fool enough to send her . . .

'Howard, where are Cheung and Teng? They're not with you?'

I answered for him, the story we had agreed. 'Teng is dead. Jake Dasser shot him. Cheung will be here when he's made some arrangements. He told us to go ahead.'

'And you came willingly, Keith?' Monica showed no concern for Teng.

'I hoped to save you – from yourself it seems, *taipan*.'

She laughed. 'What about Jake?'

I saw Ruth lift her head, and regretted I had to lie. 'He's badly wounded. Cheung will bring him – if – if he's still alive.'

'We can't wait too long, *taipan*, not even for Cheung,' Yo Chan said.

'No, we'll have to leave soon.' She turned back to me. 'Keith, if it's any consolation, you and your colleagues have become such a threat that Peking has decided to close down this operation.'

She brushed her forehead with the back of her hand. The stitches under their film had disappeared, but there had been no deception about her hair. The ugly bald place was hidden by a bandeau. It seemed to irritate her.

'You'll never get to China in this junk – not in a typhoon.'

'We don't intend to. Peking has set up a rendezvous with a motor gunboat. And the storm – we're only on the edge of the typhoon – has its advantages. No one's going to worry about territorial waters until Tessie has passed.'

'Are you proposing to take us all to China – or is that an indelicate question?'

'I shan't bother with Ruth Cecil. We caught her spying round my house earlier today, but she's of no importance. We shall take you, Keith, and Jake Dasser, if he gets here. Your knowledge could be a big help.'

'I see.'

'Do you, Keith? Do you realize that one of these days – not in your lifetime or mine, perhaps, but sooner or later – the Chinese will control the world? We're working towards it now. We're setting up a high-grade intelligence system throughout the West.'

'You mean you're blackmailing eminent visitors to Hong Kong and saddling them with communist agents that Howard brings across from Red China.'

'Yes. Peking uses its embassies and its business travellers, just like the West, and it gets some help from the overseas Chinese, but that's not enough. We need our illegals too. Unfortunately Chinese can't pass themselves off as Westerners so they can't infiltrate – but they can be planted where they'll do most good. Haven't you heard of agents of influence, Keith?'

'And how many of these agents of influence have you managed to plant?'

'There were fifteen on the list originally.'

'Fifteen! A rugger side. Of course, Peter Krail was keen on rugger. Fifteen to play.'

'I don't know what you're talking about.'

'It doesn't matter. Tell me about the top men who've got these dragons on their backs. I'm filled with curiosity.'

Monica's smile was wide. 'Dear Keith, I'm sure you are, and how you'd love to get the information back to Charles Crowne.'

I made a hopeless gesture. 'Of course.'

She told me. She reeled off a list of shocking names. She was proud of them – justifiably from her point of view. Two or three of them meant nothing to me, but there were enough

I knew to bring down governments and make Watergate seem a minor scandal.

'I'm impressed,' I said, 'very impressed.'

Monica laughed. Yo Chan began to urge her not to wait for Cheung. I interrupted him. I had to delay them. There was always the wild chance that Jake had managed to send help. And now it was vital; I had to pass on to Crowne what I had learnt.

'What about Howard?'

'He'll be coming with us, naturally. I couldn't leave my dear uncle behind.'

Howard sat, ignored and dejected, on the bunk beside Ruth. Like a dog, at the mention of his name he lifted his head. His face was expressionless, his eyes very bright. He stood up. Instinctively I moved towards him, but Yo Chan waved me back with the machine-pistol.

'Uncle? I'm not your uncle,' Howard said. 'God forgive me, I'm your father. And you knew it, Monica. You must have, if you're the *taipan*. It's the only reason you were able to blackmail me, because I promised my sister – your mother – you would never –'

'Of course, dear Howard. I understand. But I've known for years. John Cayton told me on my ninth birthday. He had to explain what incest was. I'd never heard the word before. It's not a pretty word, is it? Not even today, when anything goes.' She shrugged philosophically. 'Ah well, Josh taught me not to mind, to turn it to advantage.'

My brain, jolted by the fact of incest – and it certainly had been jolted – was suddenly very clear. I said: 'Josh Cayton was a communist, a Maoist?'

'Yes, indeed. How clever of you to guess, Keith. He was part Chinese, though no one knew it, and a personal friend of Mao. He hated the West. He was a wonderful man. I worshipped him. Those mealy-mouthed Farthingales couldn't have chosen a better father for me.'

She looked squarely at Howard, and I saw his eyes widen and reflect the years of love and deceit, of commitment and compulsion. I don't think I could have prevented what happened next – I don't know that I would have if I could – for Howard walked calmly up to Monica and shot her between the eyes. She must have died instantly.

And in that instant, as Yo Chan hesitated, I hurled myself across the saloon. The junk rolled and I got him off balance, his gun flying to a corner.

The struggle was brutal but short. Yo Chan, horrified that he had let his *taipan* die, fought like a fiend. He was stronger and heavier than I and once he had his short thick fingers round my throat I knew I hadn't a hope. My ears rang, my chest heaved and the red mist in front of my eyes dissolved into nothingness. I never heard the second shot.

I regained consciousness to find myself on a bunk. Howard was wetting my lips with brandy. Ruth was propped on an elbow, watching. I felt very tired, and I must have dozed again. When I woke the saloon was full of Marine Police. Ruth was still there, and the bodies of Monica and Yo Chan. But Howard had gone – and so had the boat we had lashed to the side of the junk.

Debriefings, enquiries, arrests, postings, sackings, cover-ups – lots of cover-ups. They weren't my business, but post-mortems are always trying. I found this one especially so.

At Christmas, back in London, I received a sheaf of cards from people as diverse as H.E. and Lady Milment, Ruth Cecil and Joan Hackard. Nothing from Howard, but I hope he made it to one of the islands and is still somewhere in the East; after all, he saved my life. And Lord Reddington sent me the Lui Chi-shung as a present. I understand why he didn't want to keep it himself – Crowne told me in confidence. In the gallery at Hua Bai Lord R had signed a confession that he had killed his wife with an overdose of drugs because he couldn't bear to see her suffer more. True or false, it didn't matter; the idea, once planted in Bill Rouge's mind, would have festered for ever, and Lord R would do anything rather than face this. As for me, funnily enough, I don't want the Lui Chi-shung either; it reminds me too much of Monica Cayton and . . . But I don't know what to do with the bloody thing.

TOMORROW'S TREASON

Palma Harcourt

'Palma Harcourt's novels are splendid' *Desmond Bagley*

When scandal broke over British diplomat Jon Troy's head, his powerful American father-in-law was only too eager to hush things up – provided Jon agreed to a divorce and to being hustled out of Washington. Then the two men met again in Norway, where Jon found himself trapped in a network of violence, double dealing . . . and treason.

'A swingeing story set in uppermost American echelons and among diplomats in Norway' *The Times*

'another teasing yet totally satisfying "diplomatic" thriller' *She*

Futura Publications
Fiction/Thriller
0 7088 2497 8

A FAIR EXCHANGE

Palma Harcourt

'Palma Harcourt's novels are splendid' *Desmond Bagley*

Derek Almourn, first secretary of the British Embassy in Washington, is deeply involved in NATO affairs when he marries the beautiful daughter of a Democratic senator; when a terrible 'accident' gets the couple posted to Oslo he begins to suspect his wife of working against him.

'bubbling readable little thriller' *Observer*

'a good story' *Daily Telegraph*

Futura Publications
Fiction/Thriller
0 7088 2498 6

CLIMATE FOR CONSPIRACY

Palma Harcourt

'Palma Harcourt's novels are splendid' *Desmond Bagley*

For Mark Lowrey, the posting of Ambassador to a newly independent republic of Canada was almost too good to be true. But all too soon Lowrey learns that his plum appointment is not quite what it seems – for the Russians are plotting to detach Canada from the Western Alliance, with the ambassador cast in the role of scapegoat.

'With this, her first novel, Palma Harcourt joins the happy ranks, commanded by Helen MacInnes and Mary Stewart, of women who can write a rattling good spy story' *Standard*

'good lively picture of diplomatic life'
Daily Telegraph

Futura Publications
Fiction/Thriller
0 7088 2574 5

DANCE FOR DIPLOMATS

Palma Harcourt

'Palma Harcourt's novels are splendid' *Desmond Bagley*

Catherine Rayle, history don at Oxford, becomes Britain's first-ever woman permanent representative to NATO in Brussels. But her initial instinct to refuse the position was a good one, for Catherine gets drawn into a cloak-and-dagger world involving a defecting Russian ballet dancer; suddenly all are dancing, to a tune they have not called.

'The story unfolds with pace and excitement' *Evening News*

Futura Publications
Fiction/Thriller
0 7088 2573 7

THE LAST OF DAYS

Moris Farhi

'A SENSATIONAL NAIL-BITER . . . MARVELLOUSLY
PLOTTED, SURPRISE FOLLOWING SURPRISE . . . A
PASSIONATE TALE, PASSIONATELY TOLD'
Publishers Weekly

In the wilderness of Jordan, Abu Ismail, the most
charismatic figure in Arab politics, receives the Word
of God: he is AL MAHDI, saviour of Islam and
Mankind. His mission is to precipitate The Last of
Days by unleashing Holy War.

Two men, an Israeli and an Arab, join forces to
prevent a nuclear holocaust. Their odyssey through
the tragic landscapes of the Middle East is one of the
most extraordinary and compelling stories of our
time.

'Entertainment at its most exciting . . . Farhi has two
great gifts. First, he can make the most extraordinary
characters come alive . . . Second, he evokes place
quite masterfully' *Listener*

Transcends the stock limitations of the genre . . . rich
in detail and character. It is a cracking good read. But
it is much more . . . the narrative moves to a nail-
biting climax which is dramatic and satisfying'
Literary Review

Futura Publications
Fiction
0 7088 2493 5

All Futura Books are available at your bookshop or
newsagent, or can be ordered from the following address:
Futura Books, Cash Sales Department,
P.O. Box 11, Falmouth, Cornwall.

Please send cheque or postal order (no currency), and
allow 55p for postage and packing for the first book
plus 22p for the second book and 14p for each additional
book ordered up to a maximum charge of £1.75 in U.K.

Customers in Eire and B.F.P.O. please allow 55p for
the first book, 22p for the second book plus 14p per
copy for the next 7 books, thereafter 8p per book.

Overseas customers please allow £1 for postage and
packing for the first book and 25p per copy for each
additional book.